Forgotten Promises

First Chance Publishing

Cockeysville, Maryland

Copyright 2007 by Denise Skelton

Cover art by BookaDesign

ISBN 978-0-9790877-1-4
ISBN 0-9790877-1-6

First Chance Publishing
76 Cranbrook Rd.
Suite 232
Cockeysville, Maryland 21030
(443) 912-8719

Printed in the United States of America

LCCN # 2007937603

Thank you to Lisa Girolami of Long Beach, CA. Lisa was the winner of my contest to name the new book.

Sometimes it's hard to say who I should thank first, maybe the readers. Whenever I get a letter from someone telling me how much they like one of my books, it makes all the times that I wake with an idea at 4 am worth it. Then there are those I can name: Kathy, who when I asked for help was right there; Kristen, who when I sent her emails and pestered her she just kept on going; my family, who always tell me that they have faith in me; my sister and friend Diana, who is my one-woman cheering section, promotion advisor and very best friend; or my wonderful husband, James, who seldom complains when I burn dinner, and when I tell him some crazy idea I have for my stories he laughs and always says that's a great idea.

This time I think it's Mrs. Alice Dorm, who is an exceptional inspiration. She is one of the smartest, strongest, most loving women I know. When I'm down I think of how courageous she is and the encouragement she has given me and I'm able to dust myself off and move on to the next chapter.

Thank you Mother Dorm. I love you.

Denise

Chapter One

June

Turning into the parking lot, Tyler Green slowed his white 1993 Ford pickup to a crawl. Turning the wheel hard, he maneuvered it into a parking spot across from the apartment building, hoping that the large tree would be enough to at least shade the truck and keep it from reaching a blistering 110 degrees before he returned. The air conditioner wasn't working; it hadn't worked in a year, so any relief, however small, was welcomed.

As he got out of the truck, he reached in the slightly rusted bed to gather three grocery bags. He had only a few hours before he needed to be back to work at the fire station, still, he could relieve the day nurse and stay with Felicia until the evening nurse arrived. While he waited he'd make chicken salad with extra large chunks of chicken and celery…just the way Felicia liked it.

Tyler entered his apartment and made a beeline for the kitchen. The apartment wasn't anything special—it wasn't too big, or too open, or too luxurious. The furniture was used, but still in good condition, and nearly everything matched. The walls were a plain white, but a few pictures—Felicia's doing—gave the entire apartment a more homey look, instead of simply stark.

Well, Tyler thought absentmindedly, *It's nothing to brag about…but it is home.*

"Hi, Tyler. You're home early," Kay, the registered nurse who usually worked the weekday shift, said as she rounded the kitchen island. She reached around him, putting a small bag on the refrigerator door.

"Yeah, I thought I would give you a break. I want to spend some time with Felicia, make her dinner." Kay met his gaze, opened her mouth, then pinched her lips together. "How's she doing today?" Tyler asked as he removed the contents from the shopping bags.

Kay hesitated, knowing that Tyler didn't want to hear what she had to say. She had been helping Felicia for a while now, and while she liked Tyler as much as the next person—sometimes she wished that he was a little more, she didn't know, receptive to Felicia's condition. She knew that as much as the doctors or she or even Felicia told Tyler that Felicia wasn't getting better, he didn't hear it. "She's very weak," Kay said apologetically. "I just gave her an injection. She might sleep most of the evening, and if she doesn't, I don't think she'll be up to eating."

"I'm making chicken salad. I'm sure it'll be plenty. I'll save you some for lunch tomorrow. Felicia really loves my chicken salad," Tyler droned on as if he hadn't heard a word she'd said.

"Tyler."

"I usually make it with—"

"Tyler, listen to me." Kay rested her hand on his arm, stilling his movement. Then taking a deep breath, she said "Felicia's not doing well today, and I don't know…"

"I'm going to check on her," Tyler said quickly, and

then brushing past Kay, he walked down the hall toward the bedroom.

The dark blue curtains in the bedroom were drawn, keeping the late afternoon sun from bathing the 10- by 12-foot room. When Tyler saw Felicia lying motionless on the bed, his heart tightened and he automatically heaved a heavy sigh. Then he immediately scolded himself as he suppressed a gag.

He hated that smell. It's the smell of a place with almost no ventilation. The smell of illness. The smell of death. He hated himself more for the very thoughts that entered his mind before he had a chance to block them. The idea of just driving away and never coming back, never looking back. Wondering…why them? Of all the people in the world, why did he have to watch his wife die slowly? Why was he cursed to watch her hurting daily, while he was left sitting on his hands watching her suffer so? Thinking, why can't this just end? Why can't it be over?

Tyler leaned against the doorframe, watching her frail frame that nearly disappeared on the queen-size bed. She looked so aged and withered for someone only 27 years old. Her once beautiful mocha skin was drawn and ashen, all life gone. Her once glorious mane was gone, leaving only smooth, tight skin behind.

That's what the chemo had done to her. No…the chemo had weakened her, but the cancer was the culprit here. It was gradually eating away at her, and it would continue until there was nothing left. Tyler watched the spasmodic rise and fall of her chest as she struggled to take each breath. She slowly turned her head to meet his gaze.

"Hey," he said, forcing a smile.

Felicia smiled weakly at him. "Hey," she said, reaching for his hand.

Tyler's chest tightened again in the emotional pain that seemed to haunt his every moment, and he tried to breathe evenly as he went to the bed and sat down on the side. "How are you feeling, my love?"

"No pain," she whispered. "Just tired." She took his hand. "I need to talk to you."

"Sure, what do you want to talk about?" he asked, his finger lightly brushing her brow. It was meant to be a loving gesture, but all he could think about was what she once was, and what her cancer had stolen from her. Stolen from both of them.

"Tyler, I need you to promise me something." Her voice was so weak, but in the stillness of the room, he could easily hear her.

"Anything, baby."

"I need you to promise me that when I'm gone—" She grimaced as she sucked in a painful breath. "When I'm gone, you'll start living your life again."

"You're not going anywhere, baby."

"Yes, I am. We both know it Tyler—I'm dying."

"No," Tyler said, shaking his head. Tears stung his eyes, and he tried to hold them in, if only for her.

"Yes," she said, a lone tear streaming from the corner of her eye, marking her cheek. "Tyler, its okay, I'm not afraid anymore. I've accepted it. But I don't want you to sit around mourning me. You should celebrate my life, our life and the good times we had to gather. You can't dwell on my death, baby…it won't do either of us any good."

"Don't talk like that."

"I have to say this, Tyler…I want you to be happy. I want you to find love again, and maybe…maybe have children. Something that I couldn't give you." The pain in her voice, the sheer agony, tore at Tyler's heart. He could hear, too, that she was resigned to her thoughts. To her fate.

"No. I'll never find anyone to love as much as I love you." The honesty in his voice shook him to his core, and he found that he was no longer able to keep the tears that had been threatening to spill from leaking out of his eyes.

"Yes, you will. You just need to open your heart. You've been taking care of me for so long. You put your career on hold, gave up the dream of having a child, all for me."

"It was for us; we needed to get you well."

"Tyler, I'm not going to get well. I'm tired. I'm so very tired, but I can't let go. I can't let go until I know you'll be okay. Until I know that you will find happiness, find love—" She gulped. "I need to know, Tyler…"

"Baby, you're my life. I'll never love anyone like I love you."

"Yes, you will. Tyler, just promise me that you'll be happy."

"I promise," Tyler barely whispered past the lump in his throat. He leaned forward, his lips brushing hers. When he drew back her eyes seemed to sparkle like they once had, and she smiled up at him as if nothing in the whole world was wrong. He tried to take a deep breath, ignoring the smell of the room, and reached for the copy of Catcher in the Rye by J.D. Salinger that sat on the nightstand.

"I love you, Tyler."

Tyler smiled down at her, brushing her brow again. "I love you too, baby." Opening the book, he cleared his throat, "Where were we? Do you remember what page I stopped on?" Tyler looked at her and immediately knew that she was gone. He closed his eyes, dropped his head and sobbed silently. It was like a dam had broken, and the tears came flowing freely. Then with trembling hands he set the book on the nightstand and scrubbed his face, brushing tears from his cheeks.

"I love you, my Felicia. I'll always love you…and I'll never love anyone again."

September

Holly inhaled a sharp breath as his warm tongue traveled from her earlobe to her neck. She shivered as a hot breath blew gently against her neck and his full lips trailed gentle kisses toward her collarbone. "You are so bad, Mr. James."

"You know you like it, Mrs. James."

Officer Holly Lawson James spun around in her chair to face her husband, Edmond. Smiling, she bit her lip in that all-too-knowing provocative way that she knew drove him crazy. He moved away slightly, grinning down at her.

"Yeah, I do." Grabbing his shirt collar, she quickly pulled him toward her before he could move farther away. She kissed him deeply, completely oblivious to the catcalls they received from other police officers in the squad room.

"Damn, baby," Edmond said once he drew back and looked into her jade green eyes. "Do you know what you've done?"

Her gaze traveled down his lean body, clearly toned from time on the job, to the large bulge in the front of his jeans. She grinned. "Mmm, nice."

He groaned. "How am I going to make it from here to the door without everyone noticing?"

"I don't know. I guess you'll just have to walk fast," Holly retorted in a playful manner, smirking seductively.

Edmond groaned again, sitting on the edge of her desk and taking her hand. "So, beautiful, I thought you were going to pick up Abby and head home?"

"I am. I just need to finish up a few things," she said, gesturing toward the stack of folders on her desk. "It shouldn't take more then twenty minutes or so, then I'm out of here." He nodded as he lightly brushed his thumb across the back of her hand. Holly looked up at him, his dark eyes held hers, and in their depths Holly saw such love that she truly was overwhelmed with joy and happiness. She knew without a doubt that she was still madly in love with this man and could never see that changing.

They had had a bumpy road in their relationship early on. Holly had to deal with Edmond's family thinking that she wasn't good enough for him, and she had even been called a few names that she wasn't supposed to hear. A few of his family members had a problem with their racial differences, including Edmond's older sister Karen. Edmond had stood by Holly's side when his family had argued, though, declaring his true and everlasting love for her, and telling his family that they either accepted the woman that he was truly devoted to or he wanted nothing to do with them. It took time, but they were able to get through it, and while at times Holly still felt some hostility from Edmond's sister, at least they were able to coexist.

Edmond brought her hand up and kissed it. "Do

you have any idea how much I love you?"

"Of course I do, baby."

"No, I don't think you do." He looked at the hand he held. "I know that I don't always tell you..."

"Ed."

"But you and Abby are my life. I don't know where I'd be without the two of you."

"Where's this coming from? Are you all right?" She leaned forward and made eye contact, searching for a telltale sign that something was wrong.

He smiled lovingly at her. "I'm fine."

"Ed, I know that you love me and Abby. I know that we're your life, like you're ours. And I also know that I'm so damned lucky to have what we have."

"Have I told you lately that you're the smartest, sexiest, most beautiful woman I've ever known?"

Holly squeezed his hand. "Baby, are you sure you're all right?

He looked at her for a long moment. Then, clearing his throat, he said, "Sure, I'm just feeling a little sentimental all of a sudden." Holly watched him closely. "I'm fine babe, I promise you," he assured her.

She didn't know why, but she suddenly felt uneasy. A knot was in her stomach, and she didn't understand it, but she knew—somehow—. She looked across the room at the other police officers gathering to be briefed on the bust.

"Ed, do you have to go on this bust...I mean... can't the other guys handle it instead?"

"I've been working this case for 13 months; I have to be there." He glanced over his shoulder then turned back to her. "I'd better get over there."

"What time do you think you'll be home?"

"Not sure...probably before ten. We have that tip

on Tyrone Nixon; they say he's holed up in a house down in Eastern Cape. We have extra manpower, so things should go smoothly."

Leaning forward, he kissed the tip of her nose. "I'll see you later, babe. I love you."

She reached up, pulling his head closer to hers, kissing him deeply. "I love you too," she whispered. Then she watched as he crossed the room to the group of officers, all wearing protective vests. He glanced at her, winked, then turned back to his team. Holly sighed and whispered a fast prayer for his safety while finishing up at her desk.

• • •

Jocelyn Prescott stood in the doorway of her kitchen, watching Tyler open the box that held a replacement water filter. Sighing to herself, she shook her head. Such a handsome young man her baby was, she thought. At 6'1" and normally 210 pounds, he had striking good looks and a dazzling smile that could steal the heart of any woman who would lay eyes on him. In the last year and a half, though, his weight had dropped dramatically, his chestnut complexion seemed dull, his sparkling hazel eyes had become lifeless, and his ready smiles were few and far between, even around family. He seemed to be a shell of himself. A shell of the man he once was.

"Tyler, you look tired," she said, moving across the room and sitting at the kitchen table as she watched Tyler reach to the back of the refrigerator, exchanging the water filters.

"Aunt Jos, you should really change this water filter on time."

"I can never remember when I need to change that darn thing."

"The last time I changed it I wrote the date on the side of the filter," Tyler said, pointing to the number scrawled on the side of the white tube.

"Oh, is that what that's for? I had no idea." Jocelyn faked innocence.

Tyler looked at her, giving her a half smile, half smirk. "Aunt Jos you're one of the smartest people I know. You know I'm not going to buy your not knowing when to change the water filter."

She sat back crossing her arms over her ample breast. "Well if I ever want to see my favorite nephew, I usually have to come up with more creative alternatives than just asking. Seeing how he's always so busy and all."

Tyler sighed, sounding guilty and defeated. "I'm sorry, Aunt Jos. I've been real busy studying for my up-coming test."

"So you're going to do it? That's great. I'm so proud of you. I can just see you, my nephew, the fire chief."

"Hold on. I haven't taken the test yet. I don't even know if I'll pass."

"Oh, my baby's a smart man! You're so much smarter than those other men who think they can take it. There's no doubt in my mind that you'll pass that test."

Tyler smiled at his aunt. If there were ever a person who was a wonderful inspiration to him, it would be his Aunt Jocelyn. Jocelyn Prescott was Tyler's mother's sister, and she had raised him from the age of six. When his mother and father were busy drinking and drugging, and leaving him with anyone who had a roof over their head, his Aunt Jos would always find out where his parents had left him, rescue him and bring him home with her. He loved her like she was his mother, and he knew that she cared about him like a son, for which he would be eternally grateful. "Thanks, Aunt Jos."

She sat forward, resting her elbows on the table. "I assume you're still not sleeping? You look tired."

"I'm sleeping okay."

"Are you still sleeping on the sofa?" Tyler hesitated, not wanting to lie, but unwilling to worry his aunt. "Now I know you are. You took too long to answer."

"Aunt Jos, I'm fine."

"If you like, I can come to the apartment and pack up a few of Felicia's things. Maybe give them to charity? I know she would like that."

"No, ma'am, I'll take care of it later."

"Are you sure? I don't mind. I can bring your cousin Yvette. She's lazy as all get out, but she's good for an hour or so."

"No, I'll take care of it. I'll do it." He saw her face, and inwardly sighed. "Soon, I promise."

"Tyler, it's been three months and I know you're still in mourning, but that room has been locked up since the day of the funeral. I just think it might help if you moved a few things out. Take it slow at first."

Tyler looked down, studying the water filter he held. The day after Felicia's burial, Tyler had a housekeeping service come in and had them clean the room from top to bottom, leaving it spotless. Then he had new curtains hung and new bed linen put on the bed. After everyone had left, he removed all of his belongings from the room, and closed the door, never entering the room again. He looked up, meeting his aunt's concerned gaze.

"Okay, Aunt Jos. You can come over next Saturday."

• • •

Holly checked her reflection in her rearview mirror, after applying additional lip-gloss and running her fingers through her shoulder-length wavy red hair, she closed the visor. Her vivid green eyes were bright and alert, not showing any sign of the fatigue she felt nearly all over. Work hadn't been physically hard, but paperwork always left her with a drained feeling. The knot in her stomach that hadn't quite left wasn't helping matters, either. She got out of the car and crossed the yard to the house of her daycare provider, Saundra Henson. It was a cozy size, with an open downstairs that was perfect for her line of work. As she mounted the step, she glanced toward the far side of the yard at three boys in a close huddle. She paused, watching as the tallest of the three poked something on the ground with a stick.

"What do you guys have there?"

"Hi, Aunt Holly!" 6-year-old David Meyers yelled, as he stepped back from the other boys.

"Hi, honey. What are you guys up to?"

"Nothing," the oldest of the three boys said quickly—too quickly for Holly to believe him. She watched them as they stood ramrod still, and it made her think of three prisoners caught in the center of a spotlight in the prison courtyard at midnight, holding shovels and a pick. Holly left the porch, walking to where the boys stood. The oldest, Ian, turned and started walking slowly toward the backyard.

"Freeze, buster," Holly said, stopping next to the pile of ash and what remained of smoldering paper.

"Okay, where are the matches?" she asked, looking at each boy as she stomped the remaining flames. Ian was 9 years old and was quite tall for his age. He seemed like a smart kid, but he was a little more street smart than Holly thought a 9-year-old should be. Holly couldn't help but wonder what sort of a man he would grow up to be. Then there was Frank. At eight, Frank weighed around 115 pounds and had a round face and bright blue eyes, and seemed to be a good kid as far as she could tell. Saundra confirmed her thoughts by stating that Frank never got into mischief unless Ian was around. Then there was David. He was Holly's best friend Dee's cousin. David's mother, Terry, and Holly had been mortal enemies for the last three years. The two had grown from calling each other names to living life as if the other didn't exist, which suited Holly just fine. How Terry managed to find the same childcare provider that Holly used had completely baffled her. But David was a good kid; it wasn't his fault that his mother happened to be Satan's firstborn.

"Matches," Holly demanded, holding out her hand. She looked at each boy again. David, who was steadily gnawing his thumb nail as if it were his last meal, and Frank both hunched their shoulders.

"We don't have any matches…honest," Ian offered. He looked at her with his head slightly tilted, his blue eyes bright and sincerity in his voice. Holly was sure that it had worked on many adults.

She stepped in front of Ian, her hand still held out. "Lighter." He looked up at her, biting his lower lip. Then after a minute he sighed dramatically and dug into his pocket, producing a yellow lighter, and placed it into Holly's hand. "March," she demanded, pointing toward the house. Each boy's shoulders sagged, but they headed toward the house. Holly followed, keeping an eye on them.

"Hey, Saundra," Holly said as she entered the house.

"Hey— Oh, boy," Saundra said as she spotted the boys lined up in front of the sofa. She walked to Holly and gave her 22-month-old Abby.

"Hi, baby." Holly smiled, taking the baby and giving her several kisses in rapid succession. "How's Mommy's angel today?"

"So what happened?" Saundra asked Holly as she glared at the boys.

"Why don't I just let them tell you?"

Holly waited until the boys finished telling Saundra what they were up to. After Saundra sent them to the family room to wait for the impending doom when their parents picked them up, she turned to Holly.

Holly bounced Abby, who squealed and laughed, her pudgy hands grasping her mother's blouse. Holly bounced her again, and Abby grinned at her mother with her light reddish brown spiral curls framing her small round face. The bright green eyes that she inherited from her mother seemed to shine brighter against her fawn complexion.

"How was she today?" Holly asked.

"She's going to be a handful, that one," Saundra said, sliding the yellow tote bag containing Abby's items over Holly's shoulder. Abby looked at the daycare provider, her eyes bright, then she shyly laid her head on her mother's shoulder. "That little stinker figured out how to take the safety lock off the cabinet and took the cinnamon crackers outside to David and the other boys, and the four of them ate every last cracker."

"Abby!" Holly said to her daughter as the toddler

buried her head farther into her mother's shoulder. "I'm sorry," Holly said to the other woman, but she couldn't suppress a grin.

"Don't worry about it. You might want to change the child locks on the cabinets, though, before she gets into trouble."

"Thanks," Holly said, turning toward the door. "Sorry," she said again as she stepped onto the porch. Saundra waved her hand and smiled. Holly moved to her car, placed Abby into her car seat and strapped her in. She looked up at her daughter, who was intently studying the way her mother was fastening the harness of the seat.

"Don't even think about it, little girl," Holly said, laughing at the look on her daughter's face.

Turning the car into the narrow driveway, Holly waved at the woman and two men standing on the front porch. Her sister-in-law Karen walked slowly down the steps, meeting Holly at the car.

"Hi. What are you doing here?" Holly asked as she got out of the car and made her way around to the passenger side back door. She leaned into the car and took the baby from the car seat. She closed the car door, balancing Abby on her hip.

"Holly, I've been trying to call you."

"Sorry about that, it's been a piss-poor afternoon. I tried to use my phone, and it's not working, the piece of crap. Then, after picking up Abby, I went to the supermarket and dropped a half-gallon of milk…" Holly paused. Seeing the look on Karen's face, she felt dread well up inside of her. "What? What's the matter?"

"Holly, you need to go to the hospital," Karen said, taking Abby.

"To the hospital? For what?"

Karen let out a sob. "It's Edmond."

The drive to the hospital went by in a complete blur. Holly didn't remember which road she took or how many cars she swerved around, but she knew that she had left squealing tires and blaring horns in her wake. She only remembered seeing the hospital looming in front of her, like a giant beast waiting to devour her. There were several marked and unmarked police cars in the lot. She pulled her car into the fire lane, driving on the curb, inches away from the building. She didn't care if she got ticketed or even towed—nothing like that mattered right now. She jumped out of the car and took off running toward the emergency room. There was only one thing on her mind: Edmond.

She noticed their captain, Craig Galloway, standing across the corridor surrounded by several other police officers. She crossed the space briskly.

"Holly," Galloway said, turning to her.

"Captain, how's Edmond?"

"Holly, lets have a seat." Placing his hand on her arm, he tried to usher her to a row of chairs across the room.

"I want to see him before they take him to surgery," Holly said, quickly brushing his hand away. "I need to assure him that everything's going to be all right. Let him know that I'll be here waiting when he wakes up." Galloway hesitated. "Which room is he in?" Holly demanded.

"Holly…he's gone…I'm sorry."

"No," she said, shaking her head and taking a step back, tears welling in her eyes. "No, he's not—Ed wouldn't leave me! I have to go. I have to talk to him…" She continued moving away as he advanced. It felt as if the stark walls were closing in on her, like she fell into a dream and it turned into a nightmare. She had to struggle to breathe. "You don't know what you're saying—" she moaned.

"I'm sorry," Galloway said, stepping close, preparing to take Holly in his arms.

"No," she whispered, pushing at the wall of his chest. Then turning, she ran in the direction of the treatment room, calling her husband's name.

Chapter Two

"Detective Lawson," Holly announced, trying to balance the phone on her shoulder.

"Hey, you got a few minutes?" Holly's best friend Deanna Harrison asked quickly.

"Not really," Holly answered honestly. Across the room stood a partition that separated three rows of four desks from the captain's office. She watched the top of Captain Colman McGuiness' head move from one end of his office to the other. At 5'5" he looked about as wide as he was tall. His blue eyes were a striking contrast against his almost white, blond hair and his red complexion that looked like a painful and permanent sunburn. He looked to be around 40, though Holly didn't know for sure—and didn't care, to be frank. He never smiled or joked, never met the other officers after work. He was always serious, always on point, and no one ever wanted to be near him. No fraternizing with the officers, no sharing personal information, none of that for him. Holly watched as his head moved across the space in the office.

"I need a favor?"

"I hope it doesn't have anything to do with work.

The last time, McGuiness chewed me a new one and threatened to have me suspended."

Dee laughed. "It's that bad?

"Yeah. Girl, he's out to get me. I'm sure of it." Holly rose slightly from her chair, trying to peek over the partition. "Hence, you get busted again, you're on your own." Dee and Holly were friends since childhood, and Dee owned a private investigating firm. They handled mostly divorce and insurance-fraud cases, and Dee was always getting into tight situations.

Situations like hiding in storage lockers or shinnying up someone's tree to get photos of her clients' cheating spouses. On occasion, she would get caught and taken down to the local police station, where, if she wasn't able to talk her way out of her predicament, she would, as a last resort, call on her best friend.

"Don't sweat it, my peeking in windows days are over," Dee said cheerfully—a little too cheerfully, Holly thought.

"Over, huh?" Holly asked. She knew Dee, and she knew better then to believe that if the opportunity presented itself, Dee wouldn't let the chance to close a case slip by her.

"Really," Dee said sincerely. "I haven't gotten in trouble since that thing over in Elmwood."

"What thing in Elmwood?"

Dee paused. "Um, nothing."

"Mm-hm," Holly said again.

"Well anyway," Dee quickly moved on. "The reason I'm calling is because—" Holly only half listened to Dee, as she watched the top of McGuiness' head as he paced the 12-foot space. He stopped, facing someone standing in the doorway, and then Holly saw his head shaking from side to side. When he threw his hands in the air she knew what was coming.

"Shit," she murmured, her teeth worrying her lower lip.

"Lawson!" he yelled, the sound reminding her of a blow horn. "My office! Now!"

"Gotta go," Holly said quickly, cutting Dee off and hanging up the phone. Glancing over her shoulder, she contemplated her odds of sneaking out of the squad room without McGuiness spotting her. Her desk was on the right side of the rows, the third desk in a row of four. She judged the distance, trying to calculate her chance of escape.

She didn't like the odds.

Eighteen feet of open space, nothing to duck behind, no desk, no chairs, nothing. "Shit," she mumbled. Then pushing her chair back and standing, she squared her shoulders, straightened the jacket of her gray suit, and marched into McGuiness' office. He turned, meeting her gaze, and she smiled sweetly at him.

"Morning, sir. Can I get you a cup of coffee?"

"Morning, my ass," McGuiness bellowed, his nostrils flared slightly. His normally red skin took on a color that she hadn't thought possible. "Lawson, what the hell is wrong with you?"

"Sir?" She raised her brows, trying to achieve a look of innocence.

"Don't 'sir' me Lawson. What the hell is this shit I hear about you threatening a suspect?" He seemed to turn redder as he spoke, if that were at all possible.

"Um…sir, with all due respect, I didn't threaten anybody."

"Telling Rivers that you knew quick and easy ways to break a man's arm and that the human hand has 27 extremely fragile bones?"

Holly's brows rose higher, this time trying to achieve a naïve look. "That wasn't a threat."

"You tell me then, what was it?" He sat on the edge of the desk, folding his arms as he glared at her.

"I was trying to intimidate him, like he intimidated Mrs. Atkins...Kind of like you're trying to do to me right now," Holly said, grinning as she watched more color rush to McGuiness face. Holly knew that he didn't like her; she wanted to believe that it was because he felt inadequate as a man...but she knew the real reason was because of the incident that occurred when they first met.

They were at a diner the officers frequented—it was just your average diner, nothing fancy about it. It was clean, had decent food, and better prices. Holly had met her partner, Mitch Daley, and a few of the other officers there for breakfast before the shift started. While they waited for their meals to arrive, they overheard a customer a few tables over giving the waitress, Svetlana, a hard time. Holly knew Svetlana was not the sort to argue with anyone, so Holly decided to take it into her own hands and see what the problem was. "No, there's no problem," Svetlana said, shoving her pad in her apron and picking up the plate from the table.

"Yes, there is," the customer said, glaring at his waitress. "My eggs are not over easy, my toast is burnt, and I have yet to get a refill on my coffee."

"Mister, if you look around, you'll see that the place is pretty packed. And it seems as if they are shorthanded today. Why not give Svetlana a break?"

He turned around and gave Holly an even nastier glare. "Why not mind your own damned business?" After a succession of ooh's from the other officers within ear shot, Holly proceeded to tell Svetlana how she should excuse Mr. Eggs-over-easy-burnt-toast. That he was frustrated because at 40 he was probably still living with his mama, and was used to her making his breakfast just right. And that he was surely pissed off that he couldn't find a woman who measured up to mama or that he was possibly more pissed off because he didn't measure up to any man. As she said the last part she held her thumb and index fingers apart about an inch. Then turning to him she added, "Am I right, Mr. Eggs-over-easy-burnt-toast?" The look on his face—the one of shock, and maybe even a little embarrassment— stayed with her throughout the rest of the morning, and she felt fairly good about herself for standing up for the poor waitress.

Later that morning Holly arrived at the station. Captain Craig Galloway was due to retire in a month, and everyone gathered in the room where they held roll call. That's when she had found out that Mr. Eggs-over-easy-burnt-toast was, in fact, Steven McGuiness, the new captain. She later heard through the grapevine that Captain McGuiness lived with his 72-year-old mother. She only hoped for McGuiness' sake that she was way off the mark about his measuring up to other men.

Holly stood in the office doorway patiently waiting as McGuiness ranted and raved about proper procedures, and policies against officers threatening civilians. *Damn, wonder if his skin is as hot as it looks. Don't think I've ever seen a face quite that red before.* She knew she shouldn't poke a sleeping bear with a stick, but damned if she couldn't help herself. On its own accord her grin broadened, bringing on a whole new stream of reprimands.

Finally, with no more provoking grins from Holly,

McGuiness' rant finally diminished. "And if I ever hear of you bullying a suspect again, your ass will be in a sling so fast, you won't know what hit you."

"Yes, sir," Holly answered, hanging on to her straight face for all she was worth. She couldn't help wanting to giggle; as his anger faded, McGuiness' face was slowly changing from a reddish-orange shade of vermillion back to its usual brick red, but it was doing so in streaks. This made him sort of resemble an embarrassed zebra.

As she quickly made her way out of McGuiness' office, the snorts and laughter from her co-workers had her smirking. Sometimes she couldn't help feeling a little bad for her boss, but on the other hand, he didn't make any effort to earn respect or friendship from the rest of the department. He just yelled at and berated everyone on the squad, regardless of whether they were actually doing a poor job or not.

Sinking down in her squeaky chair back in her dingy cubicle, brightened only by pictures of her daughter, she turned her mind from her boss's tantrums to the domestic abuse case she was working on. For the rest of the afternoon, she was caught up in making a case against a card-carrying member of the scum of the earth—a repeat offender whose long-suffering wife had finally summoned the courage to press charges after the man had methodically and purposefully broken his 5-year-old daughter's arm in three places. What made Holly's job easier was that the sorry asshole did this in front of several horrified witnesses.

The wheels of the system worked slowly, and sometimes not at all, but if putting in long hours could keep this man from hurting his wife and child again—

and a slick lawyer from getting him off with a lighter sentence—she'd keep going until she dropped.

Pulling her car in front of the childcare provider's home, Holly brushed her waist-length hair from her face, and absentmindedly she swept it up quickly and tied it into a knot on the back of her head. She wore very little makeup—a little mascara and clear lip-gloss was all she'd bothered with—so she didn't even look at her refection in the mirror.

Getting out of the car, she walked across the yard and was met by five-year-old Keith Wilkerson as he raced across the yard.

"Hi, Aunt Holly."

"Hey," Holly said, looking up at the bigger boys on the other side of the yard. She looked down at Keith. "What are you up to?"

"Playing ball… Well, I want to play ball, but David keeps saying I'm too small, but I'm not."

"Honey, they don't want you to get hurt."

"I won't get hurt; I'm a big boy," he said, dropping his head and tugging his left ear. He looked back up at Holly. "Aunt Holly, can you tell them I'm big enough to play?"

She looked at the much bigger boys across the yard, asking, "Where's Abby?"

"She's in the house doing her homework." Holly watched as Keith's 12-year-old brother David was tackled by a boy who looked like he could easily outweigh him by 15 pounds. She cringed inside.

"Do you think you can go and let her know I'm here?"

Keith looked over his shoulder at the other boys

then back at Holly. "Sure," he said as he raced up the steps and into the house.

Holly followed him inside. "Hey," Holly said to the childcare provider.

"Hey," Saundra said, looking at Holly's gray slacks and black pullover top. In the last five years, she didn't think she'd seen Holly in any other colors besides blue, black or gray, and she wondered if the younger woman had any other colors in her closet.

"How were things today?"

"Good, no mishaps." Holly nodded, hearing 7-year-old Abigail loudly enter the room.

"I'm not giving it to you!" Abby said adamantly to a girl who was at least three years older and a full foot taller.

"What's going on?" Saundra asked the two girls

"Abby won't give me my eraser."

"Abby," Holly said. Her voice held a slight warning.

"She took Keith's favorite pencil and she said she left it in school and I'm not going to give her eraser back to her until she gives Keith's pencil back," Abby declared placing her hands on her small hips. Holly suppressed a grin of pride, turning from her daughter.

"Give it back!" the other girl demanded, placing her hands on her hips also.

"I said no," Abby said with her little head swinging from side to side, her small chin set stubbornly.

Saundra sighed, "Okay, Abby, will you give it to me?" Abby shook her head briskly.

"Abby," Holly said slowly, "Give Ms. Saundra the eraser."

"But, Mommy?" Abby said, her eyes pleading, "She took Keith's pencil, the one I gave him for his birthday, and it was his favorite." Holly sighed, looking down at Keith. He looked at Abby, who he considered, in his words "his best friend in the whole world," with admiration. Then biting his lip he glanced up at Holly, his eyes large, as if he thought he should say something but didn't know what.

"Okay, I'll tell you what," Holly said. "Why don't you give me the eraser? Then when Macy gives Keith the pencil back I'll give her the eraser."

Abby thought for a moment, glaring at the other child before nodding in satisfaction.

"But?" Macy said in protest.

"Tomorrow when you bring the pencil home, you can give it to Keith," Holly said, putting the eraser in her pocket. "You'll get your eraser and everyone will be happy."

Once in the car Holly glanced in the rearview mirror at Abby's 7-year-old face. She still held the slight baby look—with round, full cheeks and wide eyes— but even at such a young age, you could tell that she was going to be a gorgeous woman. Her mother's Irish and her father's African American heritage had combined to create a beautiful child.

"So how was your day?" Abby eventually asked the question that she had been asking her mother every day for the last year, sounding much older than her seven years.

"It was good," Holly answered, smiling. "How about yours?"

"Fine," Abby answered, then paused before saying, "Next month is the parent-child lunch."

"Is it that time already?" Holly asked. "Do you

know what day it is? I'll take that day off."

"My friends all have their daddies coming," Abby said, waiting a heartbeat before she added, "Even Ashley's daddy is coming."

"Even Ashley's dad, huh?" Holly said glancing in the mirror.

"Her daddy got caught by her mommy in the shower with his secretary and his—"

"Okay, Abby."

"Ashley's mommy said if she saw him again she would kill him and cut—"

"Abby, I get the picture."

"But he's still going to the lunch." Holly looked in the rearview mirror at her daughter again, knowing that there was some reason for this story.

"O-kay," Holly said slowly.

"I was wondering if I could ask Uncle Ben if he could go with me."

Holly considered what her daughter had asked as she slowed down to make a right onto the main street, then merged into the left lane. She pulled onto the beltway, heading north.

It had been five years since Edmond had been killed. Abby was a baby and her daddy's little girl. At first, she cried often and frequently asked for her father. Holly knew that she missed her father, but after a while, she seemed to adapt. Her best friend Dee and Dee's husband, Ben, were Abby's godparents and they spent quality time with her. She didn't want Abby to be disappointed if Ben was busy. "Abby, Uncle Ben might not be available"

"Mommy, I'm not a baby; I'm old enough to understand that. I just want to ask. If he says he can't come, I won't be mad. I promise. I just want to have a dad there, too." Abby hesitated, and when Holly said nothing, she added, "Please, Mommy."

Holly sighed. "Okay, Abby, we'll ask him."

Chapter Three

To Holly's relief and amazement, Ben chose to reschedule his business trip to Europe to spend time with Abby, whom he referred to as his "favorite goddaughter." This always made Abby giggle and remind him that she was his only goddaughter. Ben Harrison ran Harrison International, a multi-million dollar corporation, but unlike many successful men, he always put family ahead of profit.

The parent-child lunch at Abby's school was an event held two Saturdays a year, once for moms and their kids, and once for dads. By 8 that morning, Abby had already picked out and rejected four different dresses. She was thrilled to have her Uncle Ben accompany her to the lunch so she could show off to her friends. "Mommy," Abby sighed, sounding amazingly adult, "I don't have a single thing to wear."

"Relax, baby," Holly said from where she leaned against the doorframe, sipping her first cup of coffee of the day. "You've got beautiful clothes. We'll find you something."

"But, Mommy, Uncle Ben will be here in a few hours and I have to be ready!"

Knowing that she'd have no peace until her child

was dressed and prettied up, Holly sighed and went to help Abby with her fashion crisis.

Ben, always punctual, was there to pick her up by 11:30 a.m. The second the doorbell rang, Abby raced toward the door. She wore a white floral dress with a red satin ribbon and patent-leather Mary Janes. Her soft curls bounced as she ran. "Uncle Ben!" she yelled.

Holly followed more slowly and smiled at her best friend's husband. "Take this child off my hands, please?" she begged. Grinning back, his vivid green eyes twinkling, Ben swung Abby into his arms.

"You driving your momma crazy?" he asked, swinging the little girl around in a circle.

"Uncle Ben." Abby laughed happily, giving him a big hug before he set her down.

He held her arms up looking at her outfit. "Wow, you look absolutely beautiful."

"I had to look my best today, since I knew you'd be all dressed up," Abby said, tugging on his suit jacket that was probably hand-tailored and cost a fortune.

"Go get your purse, honey," Holly said, knowing how much her daughter wanted to have everything just perfect down to her matching miniature purse. When Abby trotted out of the room, Holly gave Ben a quick hug.

"Thanks for rearranging your schedule like this. You know how hard these father-daughter things can be on her."

"Hey, I get to have lunch with a beautiful girl, and Dee won't even shoot me when I get home. What's not to like?" He smiled, and Holly was reminded again how lucky her friend was to have married this wonderful man.

"I'm ready!" Abby shouted.

Ben held out his arm formally. "My lady?"

Abby set her hand on his arm like a little princess, holding her head high, but squealed loudly when he opened the door. "A limo!"

Ben winked at Holly, and she waved as the two walked to the waiting car, where a uniformed chauffer stood at the open door. Holly bit her lip as she felt her eyes mist with tears. The love and kindness that Dee and Ben dished out on a regular basis never failed to surprise her.

• • •

"Tyler, I wish you would reconsider. You could easily get a position as a chief in L.A. It might take some time, but I know that it will happen. I have an apartment already so we don't have to worry about that. You can give them your notice, settle everything here, and then meet me in L.A."

"Erica, that's not going to work."

"But, Tyler, you won't even consider this! You haven't given it any thought. We've been in a relationship for almost a year now. Is it so easy for you to see me leave?"

"No, it's not easy, but what do you want me to do? I have my career here and I just signed the contract for my new house. I can't just up and move now."

"Don't even get me started on that." She held her hand up to silence him. "You go and sign a contract on that…that monstrosity without even discussing it with me."

"You know that I've been looking for a house."

"It was supposed to be us looking for a house. Us, not just you," she yelled.

"Erica, we never talked about getting a place together. Not one time have you said anything about wanting to move in together. For the last three months you've been focused on your move to L.A., and I understand that. You're planning to move. But you get upset when I make plans for my future?" Tyler sighed, his frustration evident. How could he tell her that he was relieved—that a weight had lifted from him?

He loved Erica. He really did. He just wasn't in love with her. Sometimes he felt like a heel, but it couldn't be changed. He couldn't be changed. Since Felicia's death he hadn't let another woman get close to that part of him. The part of him that wanted to spend the rest of his life with someone. Someone that he could love with all his heart. "I'm confused, Erica. What do you want from me?"

"Damn it, Tyler, you could at least ask me not to leave. At least pretend that you don't want me to go."

Tyler stepped in front of her, and placing his finger under her chin, he tilted her face up to meet his. "Erica, I don't want you to go, but it would be selfish of me to ask you not to do this. It's an opportunity of a lifetime, and I care about you too much to ask you to sacrifice that." Erica's eyes were filled with hurt, but also resolve.

"I know," her forehead touched his shoulder, and Tyler knew that the yelling was over. Inside, a small piece of him cried for the love and affection that he had once shared with another.

• • •

In a 12- by 10-foot room, sitting in the corner, Janet Summers pulled her sweater up around her shoulders. It was cold in here most of the time, nothing like her chic apartment or her cozy room in her parent's luxurious home—the beautiful home she grew up in. Everything said and done, it was a far better place than where she'd been residing for the last seven years.

She had been moved here three months ago, and before that she resided at Dwight Correctional Center, as a guest of the state of Illinois, complements of a district attorney, her extremely incompetent attorney, and that no-good whore who ruined her life.

But even with all that had happened in the last seven years, Janet was happy; she was in love with the perfect man. His name was Ben, Benjamin Harrison. He was handsome, the most handsome man she'd ever known. He was sweet and sexy and wealthy, and best of all he loved her. Everything in their relationship was perfect, until she came along.

That good-for-nothing whore Deanna Meyers. She saw how happy Janet and Ben were, and she wanted it, so she set out to steal Janet's love, and to ruin her life. She succeeded, too. That bitch managed to steal Ben away from her, and Janet had no alternative but to get rid of her. Of all the criminals in the world, Janet had to hire one who was a moron. That idiot Jake and Dee got together and ruined her plans. If they hadn't, he wouldn't be dead, and she wouldn't be in this godforsaken place. Then that witch turned everyone against Janet. That whore even managed to turn Janet's own parents against her—imagine! And in the end Janet cried as her mother and father stood by and let them take her to that awful place.

But that all changed when Ben started coming to see her. He only came to see her a few times and he had to sneak into her cell, but he did it. She remembered the first time Ben had come to see her. Her cellmate, Doris, had spent the day in the infirmary.

Janet woke with a start. The ward was pitch black, and she figured there must have been a power outage. Then she heard a rustling sound and was able to see movement from the corner of the cell. She remembered that her heart slammed so hard in her chest she thought for sure that she would have a heart attack. She cowered in the corner, afraid. She was just able to make out a silhouette across the room. When the rustling moved closer she was able to make out the outline of the person who stood before her. All she could hear was her raspy breathing and the blood rushing to her ears. This was it. All the things she feared would happen to her in such a horrible place were about to come to pass. As the figure moved closer she peered close. She was only able to focus on the eyes of the dark figure that stood before her. She knew those eyes, those beautiful green eyes. "Ben?" she'd whispered. He didn't answer her.

He moved close to the bunk, guiding her on her back and lying over her. When she called his name again, he whispered yes in her ear. He reeked of beer, and she didn't remember Ben ever drinking beer. He seemed so different, but she knew he was still the same. They made slow, passionate love, and time seemed to shift backward to a moment when he was still hers, when she wasn't in such an awful place. When she was happy.

After that night, Ben had come to see her a few more times. He never made love to her again—Janet guessed that he didn't like to see her that way, and wanted to wait until she was free from her hell. They would sit and talk all through the night. When Doris came back from the infirmary, Janet told her about their visit. Ben even visited her a few times while Doris was asleep, but when Doris stirred, waking groggily and asking Janet who she was talking to, Doris always pretended that she didn't see him. Janet knew that Doris was trying to be a friend; if she acknowledged that she saw Ben, then someone might find out about his visits. Then a month after Ben started coming to visit, her attorney came to see her. She had told Janet that they were going to do some sort of evaluation and that they were going to see about moving her into a maximum security hospital. Janet asked if Ben had something to do with the move and said that he visited her in her cell and that he told her that he would help her.

Once they started the evaluation, Janet realized they thought that she was ill, that she was crazy. They didn't say crazy, but she knew what they meant. She knew what they thought. She didn't care, let them think she was crazy. She knew the truth. She was going to get out of that hellhole soon, and Ben was going to help her.

Chapter Four

"Hey, cuz," Tyler's cousin Rashard said, answering the door. He left the door open, allowing Tyler access as he walked down the hall toward the kitchen.

"What's up?" Tyler greeted, closing the door and following Rashard down the hall toward the kitchen. Jos was standing at the sink, her hands submerged in a large bowl of green beans, and Tyler's cousin Yvette was sitting at the table reading the morning paper.

"Morning," Tyler said, greeting his aunt and cousin Yvette.

"Well good morning," Jos greeted. Yvette looked up from her seat at the table, then looked back down at the newspaper she held.

"So, did Erica get off okay?" Jos asked Tyler.

"Yes, ma'am," Tyler answered. After waiting a few moments he said, "She asked me to move to L.A. with her." Jos peeked at him from the corner of her eye but remained silent.

"Yeah?" He nodded. After what seemed like a lifetime she said, "Well?"

"No. I'm not going, Aunt Jos. I'm not moving to Los Angeles." Seeing the look of relief on her face and cousin Rashard's, he nearly laughed. "I knew it was killing you to find out.

"Well, if you knew that, why didn't you just tell me?" Aunt Jos exclaimed, a smile on her face.

Tyler grinned, hunching his shoulders. "I wanted to see how long it would take before you asked." She shook her head, turning back to her task.

"Whatcha doing?" Tyler asked Jos.

"I'm snapping green beans. I'm making a big pot to take over to church for the dinner this evening. I'm taking some cornbread, too."

Tyler looked at his cousin Yvette. "Hey, Vett, why don't you help Aunt Jos out."

She looked at him again. "I'm busy."

"Busy wasting time," Rashard said shoveling a fork full of hashbrowns in his mouth.

"And just what are you doing that you can't help snap them beans?" Yvette asked sneering at Rashard.

"I'm eating breakfast if you can't tell."

"Well you need to hurry up so you can help your mama snap them beans." Tyler and Rashard looked at one another then at Yvette. Yvette was 41 years old and perpetually unemployed. She and Rashard both lived with his aunt. Rashard was 32 and a manager at the local auto parts center. He said that he was living with his mother because he wanted to save money to buy his own house, but Tyler thought that Rashard was worried about leaving his mother, since Yvette had a tendency to move whatever loser she was sleeping with at the time into his aunt's home without notice.

Tyler shook his head as he spoke. "And you can't help because?"

"I'm searching for a job," she said, hiding behind the paper.

Tyler looked at the paper she held high, blocking her view of him. He felt his anger toward her bubble, but forced it down to a calm simmer. "Ah, and I suppose they have lots of jobs listed in the entertainment section."

"I've been searching the paper for hours. I'm taking a break."

"You say Erica got off okay," Jos said, drawing Tyler's attention away from Yvette.

He shook his head again before looking at Jos. "Yes ma'am, she left last night.

"How did she take you not going with her?"

"She was a little hurt, but she understands."

"Is that so?" Jos said as she continued to snap her beans.

"Humph, you're sure she ain't dumpin' your ass?" Yvette asked.

Tyler glared at Yvette and then glanced back at his aunt. "Tyler, I'm sorry to hear that."

"Aunt Jos, who you fooling, you didn't even like Erica," Yvette said snapping the newspaper as she turned a page and then snapping the paper again much to Tyler's annoyance.

"It's not that I didn't like her. It's just that she's so…fake."

"No, she's not," Tyler quickly protested.

"Yeah…right," Yvette said quickly. "She's all natural, everything from the color of her eyes and hair, even her $10,000 teeth.

"No," Jos said thoughtfully, "She doesn't seem genuine. When she talks to you, it feels as if it's all an act."

"That's her television persona. She's really shy and she hides behind the person Erica Tolbert, newscaster, is."

"If you say so," Yvette said, still not willing to let go of the topic at hand. "But why does she need fake boobs?"

"She did that for her career."

"She's a news anchor; people are going to mostly see her from the neck up. Unless," Yvette said, a grin slowly spreading across her face, "She's planning on using them to help her get ahead...if you know what I mean."

Tyler glared at her. "You mean like you would do?"

"All right!" Jos said quickly.

"For one, I wouldn't need fake tits," Yvette said tightly, "Secondly—"

"Yvette," Jos warned.

"I personally think they are great," Rashard said, wiggling his brows at Tyler.

"You would," Yvette said in disgust. "Don't you have somewhere to be?"

"Nope, I don't have to be at work till later. I'm closing. So I have all morning to spend with my sweet and loving cousin," he said, grinning at Yvette. She grunted, rolling her eyes at him.

"Did you have the settlement on the house?" Jos asked Tyler.

"No, ma'am, not till next week."

"Well, let me know when you move in. I have a lot of things stored in the attic that you might like for it."

"What house?" Rashard asked.

Yvette put the paper down and leaned on the table.

"Tyler is buying a house," Jos said proudly

Rashard grinned broadly at Tyler. "For real?"

"Yeah," Tyler said, grinning back.

"Congratulations, cuz." Rashard leaned forward, slapping Tyler on the back.

"Well, it's about damn time."

"Yvette," Jos cut in.

"Well, it's true." Yvett grinned and folded her arms. "So, you're finally spending some of that money you have stashed. It should be against the law for people to have that much money and not use it."

"What are you talking about?" Tyler looked at his cousin. Tyler had grown up with Yvette. When Tyler moved in with Jos permanently, Yvette had already been living with his aunt for three years. Tyler was six, and Yvette was nine. Yvette was an unhappy child who always seemed mean and spiteful. Back then, Tyler didn't understand any of it; he just knew that he didn't like his cousin very much. She would hide his toys or break them. She would pick on him and rally the other children in the neighborhood to do the same. Tyler would silently absorb what she dished out.

Oh, he would cry, but he wouldn't let Yvette see him cry. He'd go to his room, sit in the back of the closet and cry until his tears were used up. Then he would be ready to face the world again. He never complained or told his aunt Jos. When he was younger, he didn't know why he didn't tell on Yvette. He just felt he shouldn't. As he got older, he realized that he didn't tell because he didn't want to be discarded for being a problem. Maybe that was why his parents had thrown him away. As a child, he could never understand why Yvette was so very hostile, but as an adult, he knew it was because she suffered from the same ailment that he did: The ailment of having parents that didn't want you. Tyler valued his family above everything, and that was something he had learned from his Aunt Jos. She would always tell him, "Your friends, they don't have to love you, but your family will always love you." And Tyler loved his family dearly, but he had to admit that he had no love in his heart for Yvette. At 41, Yvette was still mean and spiteful, and she was also greedy and hateful.

"All that money you got from Felicia's insurance and you don't do anything with it."

"All what money?" Rashard questioned. Tyler looked at his aunt. She hunched her shoulders, indicating that she had no clue as to what Yvette was talking about.

"If you didn't want to spend it, that's your business but you don't need to be hoarding it like some old miser."

"What money are you talking about?" Tyler questioned again.

"The money you got from Felicia's insurance policy, the $210,000."

"Wow!" Rashard said looking at Tyler. "You got 200 grand stashed?"

"He's got a lot more than that," Yvette said, folding her arms. "And I bet he never spent any of it. Well, at least not until he gave your mama $15,000 to get this kitchen redone."

"Yvette, you been snooping again?" Jos asked angrily.

Yvette sucked her teeth dramatically, rolling her eyes again. "No, Aunt Jos, I ain't been snooping. I heard you and Tyler talking about it last year right before you got the work done. I don't know what the big secret is. So he's loaded and he gave you a few bucks to get this dump fixed up. What's the biggie?"

"Yvette, how did you know about the insurance

money I received? No one knew. Aunt Jos didn't even know how much it was." Yvette looked at him challengingly, but remained silent—something rarely done. "Well?" Tyler demanded.

Yvette stared at Tyler for a moment, then sucking her teeth again she said. "A'right. When we moved Felicia's things from the apartment a few years ago, there was this letter from the insurance company telling you about the money. I don't know what you were saving it for."

"Yvette, for all you know I could have given that money to charity."

"I know you didn't, I saw your bank statement one day. It said you had a whole hell of a lot more than $210,000 in the bank. Being a fire chief must pay well. That and you living in that cheap ratty-ass apartment."

Tyler felt his left eye twitch as the anger he pushed back earlier came rising through his body. He clenched his jaw tight before asking, "How the hell did you see my bank statement? I don't even have any mail coming here."

"Oh, it was in that old gym bag you're always toting around," Yvette said as if it were something everyone did. Tyler looked at her like he could have killed her. He opened and closed his hands clenching his fists to control himself. "Well," Yvette went on, "if you didn't want people to see your stuff, you need to put it away."

"It was zipped. Inside my bag," Tyler said tightly.

"Whatever," she said, waving her hand.

"No whatever; that was an invasion of my privacy, Yvette."

"Yeah, whatever," she said again, picking up her paper.

"Dag mama, I don't know how you put up with

her," Rashard said, shaking his head. He glanced over at Tyler. "You all right man?" Using his fingers, Tyler massaged his temples. He closed his eyes, taking a deep breath. "Tyler?"

"Yeah, I'm okay. I'm just picturing Yvette as a man, and me kicking the shit out of her."

• • •

Janet shuffled into the recreation room. She pulled her pale pink sweater closed, folding her arms tightly across her chest. Her mother had brought her some clothes, nothing like she would have chosen herself, and certainly nothing that she would want Ben to see her in, but it was better than the things she was forced to wear at Dwight.

Looking around the room, she couldn't for the life of her see how anyone could stand being in such a horrendous place. The staff kept most of the people doped up, and they looked as if they were just surviving—not really living. They were either moping around or sat in their chairs looking as if their minds were not in the same universe as their bodies, let alone the same building. Look at them, she thought, several of them had lifeless facial expressions; most of them looked dazed and confused. She grunted. "Fools."

She looked at a man who sat across the room. Lloyd was his name, Lloyd Bates. His too-long hair was limp and hung around his shoulders, and his sunken eyes stared lifelessly.

Janet glared at him, but only for a moment. She tried not to pay too much attention to the people here. As far as she was concerned, they were beneath her. But she didn't want to have an altercation with this man in particular. She had heard whispers from the staff; she'd heard them say that he was unjustly fired from his job and that the people he worked for had had him blackballed in his field. Before he was able to find another job, he and his wife had lost their home and everything they had worked for.

At that point he'd lost it, going into his former job and killing his employer and three co-workers. After that he went home, killed his pregnant wife and attempted to commit suicide by shooting himself in the head, the poor bastard. It was said that he didn't talk to anyone. They weren't sure if he could still speak, but he was subject to sudden outbursts of violence. The most recent had resulted in injuries to two of the orderlies.

Janet sat at a table on the far side of the room feeling lost and alone. Ben hadn't been to see her in a while. She knew he wanted to visit her, she could feel it, but she knew that everyone was working against them. Before she'd left Dwight, Ben had told her that he would help her get out of there. That he couldn't stand seeing her there. She closed her eyes, resting her head on the back of the chair. She missed him so. Maybe that was it. He was working on getting her out of here. She watched as Melissa M., one of the nurses, walked into the break room. Melissa had an innocence about her, and Janet didn't understand how someone like her would choose to work in such a place.

She watched as the young woman walked around greeting the residents and passing out sugar-free cookies and apple juice. When Melissa reached Lloyd, she set the cookies and juice down and patted his hand gently. Lloyd glanced up, but his face still held a blank look, his eyes fluttering slightly. He looked at the cookies, his lip trembled, and then he resumed his blank stare.

Janet looked around the room, then biting her

lip she pulled a tattered photo from the pocket of her sweater. In her hand she held a photo of a raven-haired man with striking green eyes.

Her Benji. She slowly rocked back and forth, whispering sweet endearments to him; she believed that her love would carry her words across the miles. From her lips to his ears.

Chapter Five

Heading into her bedroom, Holly removed her shoulder holster. She checked her weapon before laying it on the dresser and retrieving a lock box that was on the top shelf—low enough that she could get it quickly if she needed to, but high enough to keep her daughter from finding it, God forbid.

She put the weapon in the box, locked it, and placed it back where it needed to be. Her hand accidentally brushed another box. A box wrapped in a deep blue fabric. She took the box from the closet on an impulse and set it where the lockbox had been on her dresser.

She carefully opened it, as if afraid that if she touched it too much, it would fall apart. Her smile was bittersweet as she removed two ticket stubs. Our first date, Holly reminisced silently, as she set them to the side with great care. She continued to remove things—Edmond's badge and a card that he had made for her after a particularly bad fight they had had.

The lace around the edges was yellowing and starting to peel, and the color had faded, but she cherished it like nothing else. Carefully opening it, she slowly read Edmond's scrawling writing.

Holly, you mean so much to me—
Your love makes me a better man; makes me
more than I can be.
You are my sweetheart, day and night.
I hope that we will never again fight.

Tears burned the back of her throat and stung her eyes. She laughed and held the card to her heart. She had to take a few deep breaths to calm herself enough to set the card on the dresser. She left the room, still recovering, and headed toward Abby's room.

She smiled—simply seeing her daughter's room put her at ease. It was messy, but almost in an organized way. Holly picked up a glue stick from Abby's pencil box and took another look around before situating herself on the edge of the bed.

Abby was growing up so very fast. The few dolls that were in the room were hardly played with, and Holly knew that her daughter would much rather play outside, or with Keith when he was over.

When Abby was alone, she would rather read than play with toys—but even then, she had chosen books that weren't as feminine, or childish. She much preferred Goosebumps or The Boxcar Children to anything else.

Holly took one last long look around the room before getting up and heading back to her bedroom. She glued the lace back in place on the card Edmond had made, returned the contents to the box and put the box back on the top shelf of the closet. After returning the glue stick to Abby's room, she headed toward the stairs. She paused when she saw a face peer into the window: Terry.

Holly and Terry had been bitter enemies for quite

a while—they had known each other nearly as long as Holly had known Dee. Even when they were young the two never got along.

Terry was the sort of child who wanted what everyone else had, and usually got just that. As a teen, Terry always wanted the boyfriends her cousin had, and she normally got most of them; it had always pissed Holly off that someone could be so very bitter.

God forbid anyone should ever piss her off, too— There would be hell to pay, and Terry could never see the line that shouldn't be crossed. Several years ago, Terry and Holly had a bitter, all-out screaming match, and the revenge that Terry took was to punch holes into all the condoms she could find in Holly's dresser. The end result was the conception of Abby.

Ever since then, Holly had hated Terry with a bitter passion.

After Edmond had died, Terry had simply showed up at Holly's door, giving her condolences and offering to help. After that it seemed to Holly that Terry was always there; she would often show up at random, helping clean, cook, take care of Abby, or just be a presence in the house so that Holly wouldn't be quite so alone.

It had taken Holly a long time to let go of the deepseated hatred she felt against Terry. Whenever she would show up unannounced, Holly would snap at nearly anything Terry would say, and overall be extremely rude and off-putting. Terry would never say a word about it, and instead would laugh and take it all in stride.

One day Holly was in one of her rare sentimental moods, and had asked Terry why she would come to help her, when Holly treated her so awfully. Terry just hunched her shoulders, saying, "You're like family and that's what families do."

They still had their arguments, although it had been more than a year since the last one. When they did argue it was never pretty. To Holly, Terry was like that uncle who when you saw him coming, you whispered "damn" to yourself. You knew that his visit would always be eventful, but in the end it was also entertaining.

Moving along the wall so as not to be seen, Holly quickly yanked the door open. Terry jumped and squealed, "Girl, you scared the heck out of me."

Holly laughed. "What the hell are you doing peeking in the window?"

"I knocked, but you didn't answer, I saw your car and knew you were home." Terry paused. "Anyway, guess what I have?"

Holly looked at the eager grin on Terry's face. Five years earlier Holly would have said something like "crabs." Holly bit her lip, suppressed a laugh, and then said, "I have no idea."

"Tickets to Disney on Ice's Finding Nemo."

"Really? That's great. Abby would love to go, but I waited too long and I couldn't get the tickets."

"I have two extras," Terry sang.

"How'd you get extra tickets?"

"David has to work, and little David doesn't want to go. So if you want to go, the tickets are yours."

"Abby would love that. Thanks."

"No problem," Terry said, waving her hand.

"Here," Holly went to the table next to the door where her purse sat, "Let me pay you for them."

"No, don't worry about it. If Abby can keep Keith from whining for the three hours we're together, it will be well worth the cost of admission."

• • •

Tyler pulled his Expedition into the driveway. Turning the truck off, he looked up at the house.

It needed work. A lot of work. It definitely needed a new paint job. He leaned forward, looking up at the second floor before taking in the whole house. Maybe some new windows before winter arrived and definitely some new steps. He didn't want to think about the work that he needed to do on the inside, either. He smiled broadly. Even with all the work he had in front of him, it was okay, because it was his house. He nodded and then whispered to himself, "I'm home."

He got out of the truck, taking the box from the back seat and going onto the front porch. He and Rashard, along with a few of Tyler's friends had moved his things from the apartment earlier that day. With the heavy stuff all moved in, he just needed to move a few of the small boxes that had been left behind, clean the apartment and turn in the key. He walked onto the porch and used his key to open the door. The house had three bedrooms more than he needed, but he'd fallen in love with the old place when the real estate agent had shown it to him. Not to mention that he made a steal when he got it. Sure, it needed some work, but once he was finished he would nearly double his equity.

As he walked through the house he thought back to the last time he saw Yvette.

Pissed beyond belief that Tyler was getting a house, she'd been running her mouth off more than usual. Yelling at Rashard for helping Tyler move, complaining that Tyler never helped them out when they needed it…even going so as far to say he owed her for looking out for him when they were growing up together. Talking about all the times she'd been there for him—hah. She must have been thinking about all the times she'd tormented him and tried to make his life a living hell.

It seemed like every time he was around her lately, he felt his patience getting shorter and shorter. Yvette had always been spiteful, but since she'd opened the subject of his money, she'd become downright hostile and vindictive.

Rashard, always the more easygoing of the two, had told her to shut up, but Yvette had been unstoppable, knowing just which of Tyler's buttons to push. When she couldn't get him angry by hollering about how greedy he was, she slyly started implying that he'd given Felicia a little push at the end, just to hurry things along. Confused at first, he'd just stared at her, watching her eyes narrow and her smile twist meanly.

"That's right, Tyler. I bet that's what happened. Poor ol' Felicia's dying anyway…why not help her out and get that money a little sooner?"

When he realized that she was trying to imply that he'd killed Felicia—the woman who'd taken half of his soul with her when she'd died—he'd lunged for Yvette without thinking. Rashard had grabbed his arm and tried to talk him down, but Yvette had continued on.

"See? Look at that temper you got on you. You coulda done it. Hell, for 200 grand, I coulda done it."

Breathing heavily and more mad at his cousin than he'd been in his entire life, Tyler didn't say a word and didn't struggle to break out of Rashard's hold on him. He just shot Yvette such a killing look that she'd turned pale and run back into his aunt's house.

"You know her man," Rashard said quietly. "Always wantin' what she ain't got and sniping on anybody that got more than she does. Don't pay her any attention."

Still not trusting himself to speak, Tyler turned and

walked slowly to the moving truck. He'd put up with a lot from Yvette over the years, but he'd be damned if he was ever going to talk to that malicious bitch again.

• • •

The trip to the United Center was incredible; the kids were very cooperative. They didn't argue once and rode quietly, almost whispering to each other when they talked. The seats they had were in the center, close enough to the stage that the kids didn't complain that they couldn't see, but also close enough to one of the many exits so that Holly could easily take Abby on her many bathroom excursions.

Holly had insisted on paying for popcorn and cotton candy for the kids, and she purchased drinks for Terry and herself. It was the least she could do after Terry had given her the tickets. After the show, they were going to go out to dinner, but Terry suggested they might want to wait and see how the kids made it through the first part of the evening before making plans for dinner. Before exiting the center, Holly stopped and bought Abby and Keith balloons with Nemo on them. Terry tied Keith's balloon to his wrist, but as they walked to the car he untied it and it flew away. That was when the evening took a turn for the worse.

For the last ten minutes Keith had been whining, working on both women's nerves. "I had lunch with Dee last Wednesday," Terry said, looking out the window as they drove, trying unsuccessfully to ignore her son. "She told me that you were thinking about starting to date."

"Yeah, we talked about it."

"I think it would be good for both you and Abby."

Holly remained silent, not wanting to venture into this sort of discussion. Terry went on, "Before me and David got married, I think little David missed out on a lot of things that Keith has. You know, having both his mother and father together and us doing things as a family. It might be nice if Abby had a step-dad."

"Dating with a child would be difficult," Holly said

"No, not really."

"I'd have to get a babysitter and—"

"Not a problem. You can just drop Abby off at our house. If I have something to do, I can take her with me."

"What if the guy that I like turns out to be some nut?"

"You'll check him out before the first date, I'm sure of it. And you wouldn't have Abby around someone that you didn't feel good about." Terry paused. "So... how about I fix you up?"

"Let me think about this... No."

"Come on Reds, I have good taste in men." Holly looked over at her frowning. "Hey, I've grown; I would look for substance now." Holly chuckled. "Okay, substance...and a great butt. All right, we can do this. How about if I pick the date, and Dee approves him?" Terry said grinning.

Holly shook her head. "I don't know. I'll see." As the seconds passed, Keith's whining seemed to be picking up momentum. "You want to stop at Martellito's?" Holly asked, glancing over at Terry.

Terry grunted, "You wanna take that," she gestured toward the back seat to the whimpering child, "In Martellito's?"

"McDonalds." Holly nodded.

During the ride back to Terry's house Abby and

Keith picked up where they had left off with their balloon dispute.

"Abby, can I have the balloon?" Keith asked Abby, for what seemed like the hundredth time.

"No."

"Please!" Keith begged, dragging out the word.

"Keith, shush!" Terry said angrily.

"Please!" Keith begged again.

"No!" Abby said firmly.

"Just give it to him for god sakes," Holly said, meeting Abby's gaze in the rearview mirror.

"No, I want it. It's mine," Abby said, holding the balloon away from Keith as best she could in the confines of the vehicle.

"I'll get you another one. A bigger one."

"But I want this one," Abby said, her chin set.

"I want it!" Keith cried even louder.

Terry laid her head back against the headrest, closed her eyes and groaned, "Please make it stop."

Gripping the steering wheel with her left hand, Holly reached in the back seat and snatched the balloon from the fighting children, pulling it across the seat. Terry batted at the balloon as it bobbed between the two adults. Then putting down the window, Holly shoved the balloon out, and quickly raised the window. Silence fell in the car. "Now, if I hear another sound, you two will be next," she said to the rearview mirror.

Terry grinned. "Damn, that was way cool."

Chapter Six

The sound of the back screen door slamming shut echoed in the kitchen. The loud bang was followed by the sound of running footsteps. Abby ran through the kitchen, not acknowledging her mother or Dee. "Hey, little girl?" Dee called. A moment later, they heard Abby's footsteps in the living room.

"Abby!" Holly called. They waited as the child appeared in the kitchen doorway. "What's the hurry?" Abby hunched her shoulders. "Did something happen?"

"No, Momma." Dee looked at Holly and bit her lip. They all knew that whenever Abby called her mother Momma instead of Mommy, whatever the child did couldn't possibly be good.

"All right, spill it. What did you do?" Holly demanded. Abby leaned on the table, looking at her mother. "Abby, what did you do?"

Abby bit her finger, her green eyes large. Dee pulled her goddaughter's finger from her mouth, holding her hand. "Um," she said "Well, somebody stole Panda, Mr. Jack's dog."

Holly nodded. "I heard about that." Abby bit her lip. "Go on," Holly urged.

"Mr. Ranks had this dog, and he looked just like Panda." Abby shook her head. "I was going to look at him. I wanted to see if it was Panda."

"Abby you didn't."

"I didn't mean it. He just ran out of the yard. And then Mr. Ranks came out and said that I was trying to steal his brother's dog."

Holly sighed. I couldn't have had a normal little girl who likes to color and play with baby dolls. No, I had to have Nancy Drew and Bart Simpson rolled into one. "What happened next?"

Abby shook her head again, her eyes large and fearful. "He said that he was going to call the police." She put her finger in her mouth, "And then I ran home." The phone rang, and Holly rose from the table to answer it.

"Hi, Lamon," she said without even waiting to hear who was on the other end.

"Do yo know what dat kid did?" he demanded, his Jamaican accent thick.

"I heard, Lamon. I'm real sorry about—"

"She try to steal mi brother dog."

"Now, Lamon, you know that's not true."

"Den why she let him out?"

"She didn't let him out deliberately, it was a mistake. You know how kids are. She was just curious."

"She's a thif I tell you, a thif." Holly looked down at her daughter and sighed.

"Lamon, we're on our way. We'll find the dog, and Abby will apologize to you, and everything will be okay."

"She's a thif—" Holly heard him still saying before she hung up.

• • •

It took two hours before they'd found that stupid dog, and Holly was pissed. They'd looked all around the neighborhood and the surrounding areas. Dee had called Terry, who came right over, bringing her 12-year-old son David to help in the search. They were joined by several neighbors, who offered their help to find the poor pooch.

Holly had asked Lamon to check his yard to be sure that the dog was missing, and he had assured her that the dog was definitely gone. Two hours into the search, Terry had called her to let her know that the dog had safely returned. That he was under the Ranks' back porch fast asleep, and that he had probably been there the whole time. It took everything in Holly not to call Lamon Ranks an idiot when she took Abby back to his house and told Abby to say that she was sorry for opening the gate. After Abby said she was sorry, Holly took her hand, leading her away without a word to her neighbor. She'd thanked everyone who'd helped them and went home, praying for an uneventful evening.

• • •

Tyler walked from the side of the house and opened the back of his truck. He reached inside, rear-ranging the groceries in the blue plastic shopping bags so he could carry them all without making a second trip, when he heard raised voices.

"He has to do what I say."

"No he doesn't. Tell them, Keith; you don't have to do nothing."

"If he doesn't, then he can't play, and you can't either."

"I don't want to play with you anyway, because you're stupid. Who ever heard of a game called 'Bubblegum'?"

Tyler leaned to the left of the truck and saw a little girl about 8 with shoulder-length brown hair, highlighted golden from the sun. He'd met her the day after he'd moved in. Her mother, Valerie Logan, had stopped by and introduced herself. She was on the neighborhood welcoming committee. He couldn't quite remember the little girl's name, but he thought it was Payton, or Paige, something along those lines. He watched as she reached out, pointing at someone in front of her.

"My daddy showed me how to play," Payton/Paige said.

"If you had a daddy, you would know that," said another girl who looked to be the same age and had a creamy mocha complexion and glasses too large for her tiny round face.

Tyler walked from behind the truck to the end of the drive. "Hey now, that wasn't very nice." The three little girls and one boy standing at the end of the driveway literally jumped when he spoke to them. When he realized they hadn't seen him coming he softened his voice. "Why would you say something like that?

"Because," Payton/Paige said looking up at him. "She doesn't have a daddy."

"Do too."

"Na-ah, if your daddy is in heaven, that means he's not alive anymore, and that means you don't have one." The girl that stood next to Paige stated.

"Hey, you girls are friends—you shouldn't fight," Tyler tried.

"She's not my friend. Abby, I'm not your friend anymore."

"So, I'm not your friend, either. And Keith ain't neither, are you Keith?" Abby said, putting her hands on her tiny hips. The little boy who Tyler knew now was Keith looked up at all the girls who were several inches taller then he was. Reluctantly he hunched his shoulders. Abby quickly punched him in the arm.

"Ouch!" he yelled, grabbing his arm.

"Chicken," Abby said, glaring at him.

"Paige, right?" Tyler asked. She looked at him nodding. He smiled to himself, pleased that he had gotten her name correct. "Paige, do you remember me?"

"Yes, you're the new neighbor; you live in Mrs. Nancy's old house. She said, pointing toward his house."

"That's right. I met you and your mom the other day. I don't really know your mom, but I'm sure she would be very disappointed to hear you say mean things like that to your friend."

Paige looked at Abby. Tyler looked down at Abby. She was a cute little girl, with a gentle spray of light freckles across her nose and early signs of stubbornness already showing in her delicate features. Her sandy brown hair was pulled into a ponytail, and the light April breeze blew wisps of hair around her face. "And I'm sure your mom wouldn't like you saying mean things to your friend, either. Sometimes, when I have a disagreement with my friends, we spend time away from each other and think about what happened. Then the next day when we come together we see things differently and everything is all right."

"Paige!" Valerie Logan called as she approached dressed in a white spring dress that accented her slightly too-orange tan and bright blond hair. "Well, hello, Mr. Green," Valerie gushed, embellishing her southern accent slightly. "Is everything all right?"

"Everything's fine, Mrs. Logan. The kids just had a misunderstanding."

"Valerie. Call me Valerie."

"Valerie."

"Abby, Mr. Green is your new neighbor. He's a fire-man." Abby looked up at Tyler then at his house.

As Valerie flirted, Tyler thought about his grocer-ies sitting in the driveway, including his melting ice cream. "It was really nice seeing you again, Valerie, but I need to get those groceries in the fridge," he pointed to the bags by his vehicle.

She looked at the blue bags, and then giggled like a schoolgirl. "Oh, yes, you go; maybe we can get together one evening. I can tell you about the neighborhood as-sociation. We have a fundraiser every year to beautify the open space."

"That would be great. Just let me get settled in."

"Yes. Absolutely."

When Paige turned to walk away with her mother, she turned and scrunched up her nose at Abby. Abby quickly stuck out her tongue, then turned to Keith.

"Come on, scaredy cat," Abby said, grabbing Keith's hand.

"I'm not ascared," Keith said quickly.

"See you later, kids," Tyler said as the kids cut across the lawn, heading toward the neighboring house.

• • •

Hilary Summers stopped in the doorway and watched her daughter intently. The staff insisted that it was not possible to visit the residents' rooms, but the Summers knew people in high places. Too bad those people didn't want to acknowledge them when they needed them the most.

When Janet got into trouble five years ago, all of their so-called friends treated them as if they were pariahs. They didn't seem to understand that Janet just wasn't herself after her breakup with Ben Harrison. Janet had loved him so and couldn't come to grips with the reality that he hadn't loved her as she had thought. Hilary knew there was no chance for Janet and Ben.

Hilary knew it the last time she'd seen him. It was at the yearly charity ball. Janet had insisted that things were going well between her and Ben, that they were taking a breather, giving each other some space. Ben had brought a date to the ball, and when Hilary saw the way Ben had looked at his companion, she knew his and Janet's relationship was over. She tried to tactfully tell Janet what she'd seen, but Janet wouldn't hear any of it. She'd kept insisting that Ben was only trying to make her jealous. She said that he'd proposed marriage to her, and that she refused. And that she would go to him, accept his proposal and everything would be right again. Hilary assumed it was Janet's pride speaking. No woman wants to believe the man that she loved didn't love her back. And no one could have possibly known how fragile Janet's mental state was.

It took years before they rose to their previous status in the community after that fiasco. Never mind that Janet wasn't, and probably never would, be the same again. Janet sat in the corner looking out the window, her blond hair hanging limp, and her bright blue eyes void of the vibrant young woman she once was. Hilary forced a smile before entering the room. "So, what do you think of this room? It could use some work. Your father and I'll make arrangements to see if we can have it painted. I'm thinking a very light pistachio. What do you think?"

"I don't know, Mother. Blue is Ben's favorite color. I think blue would be nice."

Hilary looked at her daughter, a disturbed look on her face. "Janet, honey, what Ben likes doesn't matter. That's why you're here; so that you can see that the only person that matters is you. Nothing else matters…just you, and getting you better."

Janet looked at her mother for a long moment. Ben told me that no one would understand. He told me that they wanted to keep us apart. He told me not to tell them that he came to see me. "Yes, Mother, you're right." Janet turned back to the window as she spoke. "I think a light pistachio will be pretty." She half-listened as her mother talked about her buying new blankets and throw rugs for the room, along with other useless things. Her mind wouldn't keep still, and didn't care about the difference between the two shades of paint her mother had in mind.

Two nights ago, Ben finally came to see her. She was so thrilled to see him. To see his beautiful green eyes looking at her with such love. She'd thought that he had turned his back on her, too. When Ben visited her, he had told her that this would happen, that everyone was trying to keep him away, that they wouldn't allow him to see her. He said that he would be back; that he would help her devise a plan. Help her figure a way to escape and come to him. It was only a matter of time, and then they would be together.

And no one could keep them apart.

Chapter Seven

Tyler walked in his backyard and stopped next to the two sawhorses that were supporting an old door. With a putty knife he tested the stain remover he had spread on the door an hour earlier. The old paint and stain seemed to be coming off easier than he thought they would, and after two hours and two more coats of paint remover, he almost had the door stripped down to the natural wood. He heard a cough and saw movement from the corner of his eye. Looking to his right he saw two sets of bright eyes peering at him over the four-foot fence that separated his house from his neighbors.

"Hey, guys."

"Hi," Keith spoke.

"Keith, right?" Keith's head bobbed up and down. "Hi, Keith, how are you doing?

"Fine.

"I'm Tyler. And you're Abby, right?"

"We're not supposed to tell strangers our names," Abby said, thrusting her chin high. "My mommy says so."

"Your mommy's right, you shouldn't tell strangers your names. Shouldn't talk to them, either." Tyler turned back to the door.

"What are you doing?" Keith asked.

"I'm refinishing this old door. Found it in the basement and thought it was very nice. What do you think?"

"It ain't so nice," Keith commented.

Tyler looked down at the door, then over at the kids. "Hmm, I guess it doesn't look like much now, but when I finish, it will look great."

"Oh," Keith said with a look on his face that said the door business made no sense to him. Tyler laughed and then went back to work.

"Can we help?" Keith asked.

"I don't know. The fumes from this paint stripper are pretty strong." He looked over at them and then at his flowerbed along the house. "I could use some help working in my garden."

Abby and Keith looked at each other a moment, then Abby leaned close to whisper something in Keith's ear. Keith looked at her and nodded. Abby turned to Tyler. "'Kay."

Twenty minutes later, both Abby and Keith were knee deep in soil. They dug up the soft topsoil and laid in the bulbs that Tyler lined up for them. He didn't mention that he'd just planted a few days ago the row of bulbs that the kids were presently digging up. Another twenty minutes later Tyler heard someone calling the children.

"That's my mommy," Keith said, looking down at his dirty clothes, and then he looked up fearfully.

"Your mom said not to get dirty," Abby reminded him. Stepping close and using her soil-covered hands, she tried to brush the dirt from Keith's blue and green striped shirt. "Is she going to be mad!" Abby said, slowly shaking her head.

Tears pooled in Keith's eyes as his bottom lip trembled.

Tyler looked down at a horrified Keith, and then in the direction of the voice that was calling the children. "You know, maybe I should go and talk to your mom, explain what happened." Abby and Keith looked at each other and back at Tyler. "Just let me put the top back on…" Before he had a chance to finish his sentence, Abby and Keith turned and fled from the backyard in the direction of Keith's mother.

Measuring a cup of laundry detergent, Holly poured the liquid in the washer and slammed the door shut. Thank goodness it was Friday; if she had to rewrite another report because McGuiness thought she misspelled or forgot something, she would have ripped him a new one. Hearing a commotion coming from the front of the house, she turned off the light in the laundry room and went to investigate.

"I told you that you had a doctor's appointment, Keith," Terry was saying. "I knew you couldn't stay clean, that's why I brought a change of clothes with me." Tears began to pool in Keith's eyes again. "Oh, for crying out loud, don't start that bawling. Go get washed up and changed." Terry gave him a clean pair of jeans and a fresh shirt, and then pushed him toward the staircase.

"Abby, give Keith a clean towel and wash cloth from the linen closet."

"Okay, Mommy," Abby said, running up the stairs, followed by a tearful Keith.

Terry groaned. "I don't know if I'm going to survive this crybaby stage he's going through."

"It's just a phase. He'll be all right."

"I don't know if I'll be all right. I've been hoping your little spitfire can toughen him up, but whatever she has doesn't seem to be sticking to him." Holly laughed. "So how are you doing, Reds?" Terry asked, flopping down on the sofa.

"Great."

"Have you met your new neighbor yet?"

"I saw the moving truck last week, but haven't had the time to go over and welcome them into the neighborhood yet."

"Well I saw that vulture Valerie Logan heading that way with her talons extended. From the ravenous look on her face and the 'come and screw me' pumps she wore, I'd say that there's a single man living there."

"I don't know. If there is, I haven't seen him," Holly said, picking up the crayons that Abby and Keith had left spread across the coffee table and putting them in the box. "I've been putting in a lot of hours the last couple of weeks. I've been out of touch."

Terry eyed her speculatively. "Maybe you should put on your own 'come and screw me' pumps, get prettied up and go check out your neighbor for yourself. Hell, throw in a chocolate cake. No man could resist one of your chocolate cakes. Neighbor guy's gotta look good—Valerie might be kind of a whore, but she's got great taste in men."

Holly shook her head and dropped the crayons in a basket of coloring books. "You're really stuck on this whole dating thing, aren't you?" She stepped around the room, cleaning up toys. She was bone-tired and knew that if she sat down in the easy chair across from Terry, she'd never get up. Terry rose from her spot on the sofa and walked around the room helping Holly pick up the toys.

"I wasn't kidding about that," Terry replied. "It's been long enough. You need to get out and meet somebody, even if you don't intend to get serious. Damn, girl, don't you even feel the need to scratch an itch once in a while?"

Holly sighed and rolled her eyes. "I haven't had time to scratch anything lately. Besides, not all of us have sex stuck on the brain like you. Besides, just imagine if I hooked up with the neighbor and things went sour. I'd still have to see him all the time."

Abby's voice trailed down the stairs. "Quit crying, Keith! I did not get soap in your eyes, you big baby." Keith's wail was steadily turning into a shriek. The doorbell rang, adding to the commotion.

Terry gestured to the front of the house, dropping the armful of toys into a basket marked toys. "You get that—I'll handle the soap issue," she said loudly over the noise. "We'll finish this later."

Putting both of her hands to her head and rubbing her aching temples, Holly went for the door.

• • •

Mechanically, Tyler buttoned his grayish brown suit coat while someone else handed him a handkerchief. Looking at the white cloth, he wondered what he was supposed to do with it.

"Just put it in your upper breast pocket, Tyler," a soft familiar voice whispered to him. "Tyler, we have to go or we're going to be late for Felicia's funeral."

"Funeral? What funeral?" Tyler struggled to remember but a thick fog seemed to fill his memories.

Tyler's eyes fluttered open. He glanced at the nightstand, checking the time. The clock read 5:35 a.m. He sighed, scrubbing his hand across his face. It had been a while since he'd had that dream. At first, it was almost daily, then weekly, eventually diminishing to monthly. Now he had the dream maybe a few times a year. It didn't hurt as much as it once did and he wasn't filled with the same grief that he'd once felt, but it still hurt. Unable to fall back asleep he ran a mental check of the things he wanted to do today. It was Saturday, and it was his day off.

The past month in the new house had gone by quickly. Tyler loved his new home and things were coming together nicely. He'd painted the living room ecru. Then he had the hardwood floor sanded and finished. Once he found a sofa and coffee table that he liked he would unpack everything in that room and it would be finished. He had considered hiring a contractor to redo his kitchen, but a few of the guys at the station had convinced him they would help him with whatever he'd wanted to do, and that if they couldn't do it, they knew someone who could.

After taking a quick shower and getting dressed Tyler made his way down to the kitchen and made breakfast of ham, scrambled eggs and toast. Sitting at the kitchen counter he sorted through yesterday's mail as he ate. He glanced at the newsletter for the neighborhood association, throwing it aside. He didn't want to read or hear anything about the neighborhood association. He sighed, it wasn't the association that annoyed him, it was the women in the community that were driving him crazy. He'd wanted to be a part of a community where they helped one another, where he could attend the meetings, get to know people and be a good neighbor.

The day that he moved in was long and busy. At the end of the day he was beat and he only wanted to finish unloading his truck, take a shower and sack out. By the time the back of his Expedition was emptied and he had the last box sitting on the dining room floor, the doorbell was ringing. When he opened the door two women were standing there grinning at him with covered dishes in their hands.

A brunette just less than five feet said, "Hello, neighbor. We thought you might be a little too busy to fix yourself something to eat because of all the work you're doing moving in. So I made some chili with cornbread muffins."

"And I made tuna casserole," said the other.

"Well, thank you so much, ladies." Tyler smiled, taking the dishes from the women. "I've been so busy, guess I lost track of time." Tyler stepped to the side, allowing them access to the house. "I'm sorry, please come in. If it's okay, I can get your names and addresses and I'll return the dishes." Tyler turned and headed toward the kitchen with the women on his heels.

He looked around the kitchen trying to find an empty spot to set the plates. "Please excuse the mess. We've just been bringing the boxes in and setting them anywhere."

"Oh, we understand. Besides the kitchen always seems to be neglected until last. By the way, I'm Loretta Palma."

"And I'm Sally Demek." She stepped in front of Loretta and held her hand out toward Tyler.

He smiled and nodded. "Tyler Green." Then glancing around the kitchen he grabbed some paper and a pencil from the counter. "If you ladies don't mind jotting down your names and addresses for me."

"Not a problem." Loretta quickly took the pen and paper before Sally reached for it.

"I really appreciate you stopping by— "

"Would you happen to know where your plates are?" Sally asked him.

Tyler looked around the kitchen at all of the boxes. "Um, not really."

"Don't worry about it," Loretta said, producing a bag out of what seemed like nowhere. "I happened to bring some paper plates. I also brought utensils and napkins. You sit down, and we'll take care of this."

Loretta and Sally busied themselves dishing up the food for Tyler, each telling him about themselves and the neighborhood. Sally lived around the corner with her three sons. She'd said that she was newly divorced and that she worked as a legal assistant. Loretta had moved from the neighborhood a few years ago but still had strong ties to the community. She'd said that her friend Valerie had called her and told her about the new neighbor, and that she wanted to welcome him to the neighborhood. Loretta also said that she was married to a pharmaceutical sales manager who traveled a lot. And then she gave Tyler a seductive once-over that made him feel very sorry for the man she was married to. An hour later, Tyler sat at the kitchen table with a full stomach and a headache. Before they left, Sally had told him not to worry about trying to remember what dishes go to whom, that she would come over in a few days to collect them and see if he needed anything else. And Loretta had mentioned that she lives only 15 minutes away, and that she could come whenever he called …In case he ever needed anything.

And the parade went on from there. It seemed that everywhere he'd turned there were single women practically throwing themselves at him. He liked the attention he received from the women, by all means. What man wouldn't like to have beautiful, available women pursuing him? It was just becoming entirely too taxing.

But he would rather be the one doing the pursuing. When he and Felicia had met, her father had just been assigned to Great Lakes Naval Training Center. They were both high school seniors, and it was halfway through the school year. When Tyler first laid eyes on Felicia, he thought, She's going to be my girl, but Felicia wouldn't give him the time of day. After weeks of asking her out, she finally agreed to go to the movies with him.

Later that evening she'd told him that he seemed like an all-right guy, but that his head was too big and that he acted like he could get any girl he wanted. And his arrogance totally annoyed her, so that would be their first and last date. From that day on Tyler was in love. They had the same friends and would hang out together, but Felicia treated Tyler like just another friend.

During his second year of college, Tyler worked as a pizza delivery person, and as luck would have it, Felicia's house was one of his first stops. They'd exchanged numbers "just to catch up" he had told her. Then a couple weeks later he'd asked her out, and she'd asked him what took him so long. After their first real date, they were inseparable.

Maybe in another month his novelty status would fade and the procession would stop. Seeing movement at his back door Tyler jumped, then groaned when he saw that it was Sally Demek smiling and waving at him through the window.

Chapter Eight

"For you have been my helper; and I will rejoice under the cover of your wings." As the congregation of Sacred Heart Cathedral spoke Psalm 63:1-8, Abby's mind wandered. She looked around at all of the families. Most were mommies and daddies with their children. Abby looked up at her mother, who looked down at her. Using the back of her finger, Holly lovingly stroked her daughter's cheek. Abby smiled up at her mommy and leaned against her, and Holly slipped her arm around her baby, pulling her close.

After the service, Holly went to say hello to Father Moore. While her mother chatted with Father Moore, Abby waited patiently and looked around at the other members of the congregation. Abby had heard her mother say that she liked coming to this church because of the diversity of the membership. Abby had asked her mom what that meant, and her mommy had said that the church had members who were wealthy and poor, Republican and Democrat, and people from different ethnic backgrounds. She liked that they all came to gather to worship. Abby just liked it because her friends came here.

She had never really paid much attention, but now, noticing all the mommies and daddies and kids, she felt like she and her mom stuck out in the crowd—it seemed like she was the only one without a daddy with her. Even though she knew it wasn't true, she felt like everyone was staring at her, feeling bad for the poor little girl whose daddy had died.

Abby watched Paige with her mommy and daddy. Even though Paige's parents were divorced, her dad always came to church on Sunday and he would sit with Paige and her mommy. Paige was her friend and Abby was glad that Paige's daddy could come to church with her, but sometimes she secretly wished that it was her daddy coming to church instead of Paige's.

Abby sat in her room, picking at her Hello Kitty comforter. She was supposed to be doing her math worksheet, but she was too upset to concentrate. After church she had gone over to Paige's house. Paige had told Abby that she was going to spend the next weekend with her daddy, and that her daddy was going to take her to the park and the movies. Paige told Abby that her daddy was nice and that sometimes he would allow her to bring one of her friends along for the weekend. Abby was really excited at the idea of going to Paige's dad's house until Paige told Hanna Cohen that Abby's daddy didn't count as a real dad since he was in heaven. Abby was so angry that she socked Paige in the arm and came home.

Paige was wrong. Abby knew that her daddy did count, even though he was in heaven and she couldn't remember him. But it would be nice to have a daddy who could take her to the park like Paige's dad did, or help her with her math homework, or go to school stuff with her. He wouldn't even have to have a limo like Uncle Ben.

Turning to another page in her spiral-bound notebook, she chewed on the end of her pencil for a second, and then started making a list, "My New Daddy." She thought for another minute or two, and then wrote:

1. Has to be really nice. That was important. Her friend at school, Becky, was always complaining about her step-dad yelling at her all the time and that he was always mad.

2. Has to be cute. Abby didn't really think it would matter to her mommy what her new daddy looked like, and since all boys were pretty much yucky she really didn't care either. But she couldn't really picture her mommy with somebody ugly. Her mommy was too pretty and she needed a cute husband.

The last thing on her list was easy to think of, but was going to be the hardest one to find:

3. He has to be a hero. Abby knew her mom was a hero, since it was her job to keep people safe and catch the bad guys. Plus, her daddy was a policeman, and that made him a hero, too. It made sense that her mom would marry another policeman. The problem was how she could get to the police station to a policeman. She couldn't ride her bike; it was too far away. Besides, if her mommy found out she went off the block, she would be grounded until she was old, maybe even 12. Abby shook her head. She couldn't get a policeman; that would be too hard to do. Abby tried to think of other heroes, maybe one of her teachers. No, none of her teachers seemed quite right, and she wasn't sure how she could get an astronaut's address or phone number.

She heard banging in the backyard and went to her window. Peering out, she saw Mr. Tyler bringing his garbage cans in the yard.

Firemen were heroes, too. There was one who came to her school last week and he talked about how you had to have a plan in case your house caught on fire. When he was done, kids in her class got to ask him questions, and he told them about how firemen didn't just put out fires—they went to car accidents and did first aid and all kinds of stuff.

The fireman who came to her school wouldn't work, because he was kind of old and she didn't know his name, but Mr. Tyler would work. He was really nice, really cute and he liked kids. With the perfect new daddy in mind, Abby raced to her bed and quickly finished her homework. After shoving her books into her book bag she ran downstairs. "Mommy! Can I go outside and play?"

Her mom was in the kitchen, making dinner. "I don't care, baby, but only for fifteen minutes. Burritos are almost ready. Stay close."

With her stomach growling and her mouth watering, Abby ran out the front door and didn't quit running until she got to Tyler's front door. Feeling nervous, she told herself that it was for her mommy's own good. Her mommy never went out with guys, and Abby knew that the only way to get a new dad was to bring one home with her. He'd fall in love with her mommy, they'd get married, and Abby would have a new daddy. Maybe even a new brother or sister, like most of the other kids at school had.

When Tyler answered the door, he was kind of grumpy looking, but he smiled when he realized it was Abby. "Hi, Abby. How are you?"

"Good," she said. She stopped for a minute, still nervous, but then started talking quickly. "We had a fireman visit our school last week, and I was wondering if you could come over to my house and do an inspection thingy and meet my mom and help us do a fire escape plan and maybe have dinner or something, because my mom's really nice and you'll totally like her…"

"Whoa," Tyler laughed. "Slow down. You want me to do a fire inspection on your house?"

Abby thought to herself, No, I want you to marry my mommy and take me to the park sometimes, but she figured that would sound kind of weird. "Yeah, could you? My mom's making burritos right now. You could have some with us!"

"Well, I don't want to interrupt your dinner. Why don't we do this another time?"

"Could you come over later?" Abby asked.

"Does your mom know about this?"

That stumped her for a second, but then she grinned. "I'm sure she knows about fire safety, but with the smoke detectors all being broken—" It was a little lie, but it was for a good cause, and once he got to her house and met her mommy he'd be so happy that he'd forget all about smoke detectors.

"Abby, this evening isn't a good time. How about tomorrow? I can stop by around 7 p.m."

Abby smiled to herself on her way home. Her mom had told her all about how important fire safety was when they bought new fire extinguishers and smoke detectors last year and made a fire escape plan. She just hoped her mom liked Mr. Tyler and didn't mention that.

Chapter Nine

When Holly opened the front door, Dee rushed to her, pulling her into a tight embrace. "Hey," Holly said, returning the hug. "What's going on? You act as if I haven't seen you in ages."

"Nothing. I'm just happy to see you," Dee said, pulling back and looking at her friend. She grinned broadly and pulled Holly into another embrace.

"Whoa, something's going on, I can tell."

"I asked Terry to come over; I want to wait until she gets here before I tell you."

"Oh, lord, what did you do?"

"Nothing." Holly looked at her as if she didn't believe her. "I'm serious, I didn't do anything." Dee practically bounced up and down with excitement. "Okay, I can't wait. Guess who's going to have twins?"

"No!"

"Yes!"

"I'm going to be an aunt?"

"Sure are," Dee said, almost screaming.

"Ooh, a baby," Abby said from the top of the stairs, then charged down and into Dee's outstretched arms nearly bowling her over.

"Not just one baby, but two," Dee said, delighted.

"Honey, I'm so happy for you. How far along are you?" Holly asked.

"I don't want to say anything else until Terry gets here. I just couldn't wait to tell you."

Holly smiled. "My baby's having a baby," she said, faking a sob. Dee laughed.

"Can I help take care of them?" Abby asked.

"As the older god-sister, it's your duty to help take care of them and to look out for them."

Abby grinned, nodding, then she quickly said, "If my mommy had a baby, then I could help you both take care of them." Abby smiled up at her mother.

"Whoa, hold on there, sister," Holly said, her palms held up. She turned to Dee, "See what happens, you come around talking that baby stuff, and messing up my game. You know you can't talk about babies around here without this one," she jerked her head in Abby's direction, "Thinking about little brothers and sisters."

Dee laughed at that. "Sorry."

"Little girl, the only babies that we're having around here are the ones that the mommies and daddies will be taking home when we're done playing with them. Got it?"

Abby sighed, "Yes, Mommy."

"Good girl. Now go upstairs and finish your homework. I'm sure Terry will bring Keith to hang out with you." As Abby raced upstairs to do her homework Holly and Dee went into the kitchen to wait for Terry.

Holly shook her head. "I just can't believe it. You can barely take care of yourself and now you're going to have twins," she joked.

Dee elbowed her in the ribs. "Watch it," she said,

"Or when I'm nine months along and big as a house, I'll sit on you and flatten you like a pancake."

Holly eyed her friend. "Now that's something I just can't picture. You with a giant beach ball under your shirt and waddling around like a drunken duck. We'll have to get you a beeper for when you back up and a 'Wide Load' sign to tack onto your backside."

Dee tried to glare, but the happy grin splitting her face spoiled it. "A 'Wide Load' sign…" The two of them started giggling, and pretty soon were laughing so hard they barely heard the doorbell.

"You stay there," Holly said, holding her hand up. "Sit comfortably while you still can…I'll get it."

"Hey, Reds," Terry greeted as Holly answered the front door.

"Hi, Aunt Holly!" Keith said running past Holly and up the stairs.

Holly laughed at Keith's eagerness to hang out with Abby. "Hey, we're in the kitchen." Holly turned and headed for the back of the house.

"Let me use the bathroom first," Terry said. Holly nodded, continuing toward the kitchen as Terry went upstairs. After using the bathroom, Terry went down the hall to check on Abby and Keith. The door was ajar, and she reached for the doorknob then paused listening.

"I don't think Mr. Tyler is going to get married to anybody. He's really smart."

"Shut up. You're such a baby. He has to get married, because if he won't get married then he can't be my daddy. Understand?"

Keith paused. "I guess so."

"And that's why Mr. Tyler is coming over later. So

he can meet my mommy, fall in love and they can get married. Get it?"

"Yep," Keith said giving a quick nod.

"No, you don't," Abby said, punching him in the arm.

"Ow!"

"What are you guys up to?" Terry asked as she stepped into the room. Abby looked up at her, surprised. "What are you guys doing?" Terry asked, walking to the bed, standing over the children.

"Nothing," Abby said quickly. "Just talking."

"Talking about what?" Terry folded her arms.

"Um…" Abby uttered, biting her lip. "We were talking about Aunt Dee's baby."

Terry frowned. "What baby?"

"Aunt Dee's baby." Abby nodded eagerly. "Aunt Dee told me and Mommy that she's going to have a baby."

"When did Dee say she was having a baby?"

"When she came over," Abby said innocently.

"Ain't this a bitch," Terry shook her head in disbelief. "Everybody knows it before I do." Terry marched out of the room headed for the kitchen.

"So, I hear you have a bun in the oven?" Terry said when she walked into the kitchen.

"Aw, man, how did you find out?" Dee asked, disappointed that she wasn't the one to tell Terry her good news.

Terry nodded her head in Holly's direction. "Holly's demon child."

"Abby!"

"Sorry, Momma!"

"And why am I the last to know?" Terry asked, her hands on her hips.

"Terry, you're not the last to know, I haven't told mom yet."

"Uh, okay…" Terry said, pleased that she rated above her aunt. "So, when is the little tyke due?"

"Late November, so I guess you already know that I'm having twins."

Terry's brows rose. "For real?"

Dee grinned, showing her cousin her dimples. "Yup, twins. I'm going to have a mid-wife in the birthing room. I want the room to be decorated with soothing candles and have calming music to put everyone at ease. And…I would like you two to be there with me."

"Cool," Terry said.

"Uh…" Holly said slowly. "I can't do that."

"Come on, Hol."

Holly shook her head. "Dee, you know I can't get with that blood and pain thing."

Terry laughed. "I think it's hilarious that you can't deal with blood but you're a cop. You've seen dead bodies before. And knowing you, I'm sure you've shot someone before."

Holly smirked. "Yeah, so?"

"How can you shoot someone and not get freaked out about that?"

"Because I'm the one who shot them," Holly said in a tone that declared, I can't believe you'd ask me that. "At work I can detach myself, and it's not the same. It's a combination of the blood and the pain and knowing the victim. It makes me queasy and freaks me out."

"But you've had a baby," Dee said.

"Yeah, but I didn't have to watch."

"When I had David, I was so doped up that they could have done anything to me and I would not have remembered."

"I had an epidural," Holly said. "I wanted to go natural…that was, until the pain really started to set in, then an hour into the labor I was calling Ed every son of a bitch I could think of and begging for drugs."

Dee laughed. "Well, I for one want to remember the entire experience. I'm going natural."

Terry and Holly looked at one another then burst out laughing. "She's so cute," Terry said.

"Is she ever." Holly agreed. "All that will change when the first real pain hits her. All of that 'I want all of my family to be around me, let's hold hands, play soothing music and burn candles' shit will fly right out the window."

"The pain will be so bad we'll have to pry her ass off the ceiling," Terry said, still laughing

"Are you guys trying to talk me out of this?" Dee asked, a doubtful look on her face.

"Nooo," Holly said, and then snickered. "We just want to prepare you."

"The birth is the easy part," Terry said. "Wait till they press down on your stomach to get the placenta out."

"No," Holly said, quickly throwing her hand up. "Wait till her milk dries up." Terry cringed, her hands flying to her breast.

"Oh, god, I don't know about this," Dee said. Terry and Holly both laughed again.

"You'll be fine," Terry said waving her hand. "Just don't talk about people." She quickly added, "That's why Keith's head is so big."

Holly grinned, then said, "And why one of Abby's ears is lower then the other." Dee looked momentarily horrified. Holly burst out laughing. "Man, you're easy." Dee sucked her teeth and pushed Holly's shoulder.

"Hmm, speaking of ugly people," Terry said, peeking at Holly, "I hear you have a date."

Holly looked up after she realized that Terry was speaking to her. "Where'd you hear that?"

"From your daughter."

"No, you couldn't have. You must be mistaken." Holly shook her head.

"Nope, I heard it with my own ears," Terry said in a singsong voice. Holly frowned at Terry, waving her hand. "I don't know all the details," Terry continued, "But I hear he should be stopping by anytime now, your little angel arranged it all by herself."

"Oh, boy," Dee said.

"No..." Holly said. Terry grinned nodding slowly. "Abigail Katelyn James!" Holly yelled quickly.

"Yes, Momma?"

"Oh, dear lord," Holly moaned, laying her forehead against the cool table.

"Ooh," Dee whispered as Terry giggled.

After a moment, Holly sat up straight, her face red. "Abby! Get your butt in here!"

Abby walked into the kitchen, her green eyes large and innocent. She had changed from the blue jeans and pink sweater that she had on to a navy blue dress, complete with ankle socks and dress shoes. "Yes, Momma?"

Holly looked at what her daughter wore. She barely got her in a dress for church on Sunday, and when she did, Abby wanted to wear pants underneath. Oh, this is bad. Real bad. "Don't you 'yes momma' me. What did you do?" she asked, struggling to hold her anger in check.

"I know," Terry said, smiling at the child. Abby looked at her scrunching her nose up.

"Abby, I'm waiting for an answer?" Holly demanded.

"Um?" Abby hedged.

"You have a date, with the nice man next door," Terry chimed in.

"What?" Holly yelled as the doorbell rang.

"And that, my dear, would be your date," Terry said, grinning and gesturing in the direction of the living room.

Holly stood glaring at her daughter. "Girl," she said through clenched teeth. Abby faked a cringe, taking a step behind Dee's chair, and peeked up at her mother.

When Holly opened the door, she felt as if time shifted. She looked up at the man standing in front of her. Her heart raced and her palms became wet. For the first time in her life she was actually at a loss for words and the only thought that came to mind was Wow. "Mrs. James?"

She blinked, uh? Oh yeah, that's me. "Yes."

"My name is Tyler Green. I just moved into the Stinebeck house next door." Holly stood staring at him. "I'm sorry to disturb you, is this a bad time?" Holly shook her head. "I wanted to stop by and introduce myself." Holly nodded. He paused. "And, well I've already met your daughter." Daughter? Holly thought to herself. Oh yeah. "At the local schools we have fire safety week. Yesterday Abby said that they had theirs and also mentioned that you didn't have working smoke detectors or an escape plan."

Holly frowned finally realizing what he had said. "What?"

"I'm here to—"

"No, there has been some misunderstanding."

"Abby mentioned that you didn't have a fire escape plan. She said that they had a drill in school and that you were unable to attend and were unable to implement a plan here at home."

Holly felt her left eye twitch, *little girl you are so going to get it.* "Mr?"

"Tyler, Tyler Green."

"I'm sorry, Mr. Green, there has been a terrible misunderstanding."

Tyler glanced over Holly's shoulder. "Good evening, Abigail." Abby smiled shyly, nibbling the index finger of her right hand.

Holly looked over her shoulder, seeing Abby, Dee and Terry standing behind her. Dee and Terry were grinning, while Abby looked sheepishly at her mother. "Oh, yeah, good job, kid," Terry said in a heavy breath. Dee elbowed Terry, still grinning at Holly.

Holly rolled her eyes at the trio and turned back to the door. "Mr. Green, like I was saying, I'm a police detective and I know the importance of safety."

"Yes, ma'am, I understand."

"And I don't need any help," Holly continued.

"Yes, I'm sure you probably have everything in order, but now that I'm here I could just go through the house, check everything out, see your escape route, and maybe give you some pointers. It shouldn't take long."

Holly looked at the tall stranger. She sighed. "I guess it couldn't hurt." She stepped aside, allowing him entrance into the house.

Chapter Ten

Glancing around the neat and comfortable home, Tyler walked from room to room inspecting the smoke detectors. Everything was bright and airy, with a crisp spring scent. He felt Abby and the three women following him closely. He went through the inspection, conducting himself in a professional manner when he felt anything but professional. In fact, he felt nervous, which threw him slightly off balance. He focused on what he was doing while he tried to examine and figure out what was causing his nervousness. It wasn't the inspection; he'd done so many of these he could do them in his sleep. And he'd never felt uneasy about being in a stranger's house. He found himself glancing at Abby's mother often. Her vibrant red hair hung loose around her shoulders and down her back. She had large green eyes under beautiful long lashes. When her eyes met his, she bit her sensuous full lip and looked away. Tyler's pulse jumped quickly, as he turned away, too, and continued his task.

Fifteen minutes later, Tyler finished the inspection and followed Holly to the living room with Abby and a grinning Dee and Terry in tow. "Well, two of the detectors need batteries."

"Umm. Yeah. I've been meaning to change those," Holly hedged.

"And it might be a good idea to have a fire escape ladder in Abby's room. If there's ever a fire, she can get out of the window quickly."

"Ha!" Holly laughed quickly, and then caught herself, clamping her lips tight.

"Mrs. James, a lot of parents have installed them in their homes. It's a safe and effective way for their children to escape fire."

Holly wrinkled her nose as she shook her head. "My kid would not be able to overcome the temptation to climb out of the window instead of using the front door."

He looked at Abby, her eyes shined like diamonds at the idea.

"Oh, no, that's not a good idea," Dee said shaking her head.

"Bad idea," Terry agreed, shaking her head, too.

"Aw, man," Abby whispered, her smile quickly turning into a pout.

"O-kay," Tyler said slowly, "What about installing a fire extinguisher in her room. Holly let out a half snort, half laugh, while Terry and Dee continued shaking their heads.

"I never get to have any fun," Abby whined before turning and leaving the living the room.

Tyler grinned, showing perfectly even white teeth and extraordinary deep dimples. The room fell silent as the three women watched mesmerized. Holly stood rooted in place as she got a good look at him. His short-cropped hair was an even mass of black curls, his skin looked like smooth milk chocolate, and his strong jaw was dusted with a light five-o'clock shadow. And his thick, perfectly shaped brows arched over the darkest, most soulful eyes Holly could ever remember seeing. Instantly Holly felt an overwhelming surge of guilt.

Tyler shifted the papers he held and reached for Holly's hand. "Mrs. James, it was nice to meet you. Other than changing the batteries in the detectors, you seem to have things in order. Do you have any questions?"

Dee nudged Terry, knowing it would set her cousin in motion. "She'd like to know if you're married. Seeing anyone? Straight?"

"Ohh, too much," Dee whispered.

Terry dropped her voice lower, but not low enough so that Holly and Tyler couldn't hear her. "I'm just asking; she won't do it." Holly cringed visibly, crimson slowly creeping into her cheeks.

Tyler laughed. "No, I'm not married, no girlfriend, and I'm definitely straight," he said, his eyes never leaving Holly's face. Holly's mouth went dry; she felt things she hadn't felt in a while. Her breasts tingled, her nipples beaded and felt extremely sensitive against her lacy bra. She brought her arms up covering her breast, hoping Tyler hadn't noticed.

Dee gave Terry another gentle nudge. "Well, shit," Terry said abruptly. "Why don't you ask her out for heaven sakes."

Terry's words brought Holly out of her momentary trance. "Mr. Green, it was nice to meet you. Welcome to the neighborhood. I know you'll love it, there are a lot of great people that live here." Holly spoke as she ushered him out the door. "Thanks for stopping by. I'll get those things you mentioned taken care of."

He smiled, nodding. "Nice meeting you, too. If you ever need any help, just give a shout. Ladies," he said to Terry and Dee as he headed out the front door.

"Girl, are you crazy? Don't let him go. Ask him out," Terry said.

"I'm not ready for this yet."

"The other day you were," Dee said.

"I don't know, not him."

Terry placed her hands on her hips saying, "What's wrong with him? He looks like he just escaped from a Chippendales review."

"There's nothing wrong with him. I don't know," Holly said. "It's just not right." She turned and left the living room.

• • •

"Everyone up and hit the showers. Now!" screamed a female nurse's aide.

Moaning was heard up and down the long hallway, which held thirty women in fifteen double-occupancy rooms. Some women were able to share a room with a halfway decent human being, but some had to room with someone whose mind was almost gone. Janet was lucky; she didn't have a roommate...yet.

Janet looked up at the ceiling and whispered to herself, "Another day at the loony bin. I hate getting in the shower with other women, but rules are rules."

Janet got up, automatically made her bed and mechanically went to the dresser, which faced the beds, and got clean clothes for the day. She placed her items on the taut spread and went into the bathroom. Beth, one of the girls in the next room, reached into the cracked tiled area with black mold growing thicker each day in between the tiles and turned on the shower while Janet pulled down a towel from the open shelves. There was no bathroom door. Privacy was left behind in another world. It was 7 a.m. and another day of the supposedly insane began. Two showerheads hung on opposite walls, which gave them some privacy; at least they didn't have to look at each other while they showered. They had fifteen minutes to shower and dress before the aide came by their rooms to inspect them, as well as their beds, before they could go to the dining room for breakfast. This was just as bad as prison except there were no rusted bars to look through.

In the room across the hall, Janet noticed one of the patients in a catatonic state was being washed in bed by a nurse tech. The patient would stare in one direction for days. No matter what position you put her in she would remain fixed. Janet noticed the patient was helped into a wheel chair and wheeled into the shower by another nurse tech. The tech's voice was so soft one could barely hear her. The patient supposedly killed her husband and two children of six and eight because a voice told her to. Janet turned her attention to finishing dressing. A tap on the open door warned them to get to the dining room.

Once they entered the dining room the patients were required to walk up to a four-sided cart that held their individual trays. Each side had numbers to designate the rooms and an A or B for their bed areas. "A" meant door person and "B" meant window person, but since Janet didn't have a roommate she usually went to the A side, which was the side she reached first once she entered the dining room. They had to obtain their own trays and find a place to sit. Most patients sat in approximately the same area or seat each day, marking their territory.

After getting her tray and sitting in her usual seat, Janet picked at her food, barely putting anything in her mouth as depression weighed heavily on her shoulders. She did not belong here. She was not insane; she was just caught up in some stupid political agenda. She and a hundred-some other inmates from prisons were sent to mental institutions for the criminally insane across the United States to lessen the census and open the doors for new criminals. That was what her roommate Doris from Dwight had told her. At first, she was glad to get out of that rat hole, but as time went on she realized things weren't any better in a mental institution.

Across from her sat one of the new inmates. If it weren't for the breasts Janet would have thought she was a man. She had a large nose nestled above firm, slender lips that rarely sputtered out anything worth listening to. A shaved head reflected the overhead lights of the dining room, while piercing slate blue eyes glared at anyone who dared look in her direction. The tattoo of a skull clenching a black rose on her left upper arm, and a four-inch scar on her left cheek reminded Janet this individual was not someone to upset. Large hands grasped a fork, which jabbed at eggs and sausage she then greedily shoved in her mouth.

"What are you looking at girl?"

Janet's trance was broken by the harsh words. She didn't have an answer, so she remained quiet.

"I said what the hell are you looking at?"

"Ah, nothing, I-I was just daydreaming," stuttered Janet, now looking at her plate of scrambled eggs and waffles.

"I don't think so, girl. Just keep your eyes off me because you are not my type."

"I wasn't looking at you, I was just thinking," Janet said nervously while she grabbed her fork and began slowly putting food in her mouth.

Janet practically felt the hatred from the blue eyes that glared aggressively at her.

The allotted time for breakfast was forty-five minutes. Five minutes before the breakfast hour was up Janet picked up her half-eaten tray and carried it to the cart where she had gotten it. Walking through the small hallway that led into the patient lounge she felt someone bump into her. She tried to turn around but a strong arm was now around her neck tightly, making her gasp for air. Her left arm was stretched behind her back, causing the top of her shoulder to sear painfully.

"I told you to stop staring at me, bitch. Now you're gonna pay."

Janet felt her body slammed into a wall several times. A flash of white rushed over her field of vision and she felt herself slowly sliding to the floor. Her head throbbed, then everything faded.

A cool rag on the side of her head dripped water into her ear, and she heard a masculine voice softly humming an old tune. She couldn't open her eyes no matter how hard she tried. The voice soothed her. Was it Ben? She felt hands caressing her face while the humming continued. She knew that song but couldn't remember the name or the words. A warm muscular body lay beside her, and the humming louder now.

Finally, her eyes were opening and her room came into focus. What happened, and how did she get here? She glanced around. She was alone. She attempted to get up when a searing pain crossed the left side of her temple. Nausea escalated, but she didn't think she could make it to the bathroom. Inhaling and letting the air out slowly she managed to control the feeling. Gingerly her left hand reached up to her head and she felt a soft egg shape that made her nausea return instantly. With her right hand, she reached for the call bell and she nervously pressed the red button.

"Yes, can I help you?"

"I need something for nausea and for the pain in my head. I—" Janet paused then said, "I fell."

"Someone will be right there, Janet."

Janet was terrified; she didn't understand what had happened. She remembered being attacked in the hall by that lunatic. But how did she end up in her room. She closed her eyes, willing the room to stop spinning. Yeah, she was terrified, but moreover she was pissed. How dare that bitch put her hands on her? She would pay for this little incident. Oh, yeah, she would pay. And this episode could work to Janet's advantage. Yes, this could definitely help her escape this hell. Janet glanced across the hall toward the bathroom, but decided she better remain lying down before the pain made her fall off the bed. It wasn't easy for her to move her body as the pain seared in spasms. By the time a nurse entered the room she had dozed off again.

After receiving something for her pain, Janet was able to get up with minimal assistance. An aide helped her walk to the lounge where all the other patients were gathered. This time each day the patients would congregate. Some would be seen by a medical doctor, a psychiatrist, or their social worker. All would be overseen by the nurses on shift.

Janet sat quietly watching the other patients in

the patient lounge. Some sat and stared at nothing, no blinking noted. Another patient sat in a wheel chair, drooling all over herself and moaning constantly. A group of four women had gathered at a round table whispering and pointing their fingers at each other. Over in the smoke room, enclosed with safety glass on two sides, sat several other women who chainsmoked. It was hard to distinguish their features through the heavily smoke-filled area they were in.

A petite blond woman used both fists to pound on the smoking-room door, calling out, "Let me in, I need to smoke. Open this damn door."

One of the nurses quickly walked to her side and gently escorted her to a seat. Janet overheard the nurse say, "Mrs. Ingram, you know you do not have any smoking privileges. You will need to talk to your psychiatrist to give you permission to smoke. Dr. Morgan should be in to see you and the rest of his patients in the next few hours. Come to the table and I'll get you a deck of cards to play some solitaire."

The woman who'd attacked Janet sat staring at the wall. Janet looked her way studying her. Then she quickly turned away. She could swear that she'd seen the woman's tattoo move. Taking a breath Janet looked around the room.

She closed her eyes, dozing off, as the pain pill started taking full affect.

"Ahhhhhh…grrrrrrr." A loud scream and stomping behind her jolted her awake. She turned her head just in time to see one of the female patients running down the hallway naked. Several nurses on the floor ran after the patient, coming from all directions.

"Joe, we're going to need the restraints. Maggie,

get a hold of one of her lower limbs and Bob, help Maggie by holding down the other lower extremity. Sara, June...grab her upper extremities while I give the 5-mg Haldol injection," Bonnie Fallston, one of the head nurses instructed.

A pair of arms that flailed in the air were grabbed and subdued while a pair of feet ended at one of the nurses' shoulders and the other foot smacked into another nurse's hands. Strategically, the nurse pinned the woman to the floor, and immediately Bonnie gave the agitated patient an injection. The staff held the patient down for at least two minutes to make sure the medication was taking effect.

As the patient began to relax she became limp. Sara and June assisted her to a standing position and escorted her to the seclusion room, where she was placed on a cot.

Policy was that the patient in a combative state was to remain restraint free for thirty minutes after receiving a chemical restraint. During those thirty minutes if the patient would become more combative, then four-point leather restraints were to be applied and more medication was to be administered.

Janet looked across the hall to the seclusion room then over at the woman who'd attacked her. Janet grunted. Woman my ass. She's no woman; no real woman would look like that, or carry herself in that manner. The barbarian. She put her hands on me. She hurt me, and no one hurts Janet Summers. She'll pay for that. She'll pay dearly.

Immediately, all the patients resumed their previous activity. They were talking to each other, or themselves, staring into space, or watching an old "I Love

Lucy Show" on the television. Janet didn't try to join any of the groups; she preferred to be by herself. "Was Ben here this afternoon?" She hadn't seen him, but she was pretty out of it so he could have been. She nodded, pulling her sweater closed. "How would I have gotten on the bed if someone hadn't put me there? Surely if someone on the staff had found her, they would have been there when she awakened or at the least would have said something about finding her on the floor. Yes, it was Ben. He'd come to see me and found me there and took me to my room. He could only stay a little while, and that was who she felt lying next to her. He was here, and I know he will be back."

Chapter Eleven

Parking her car in front of the house, Terry got out and walked up the sidewalk toward the Lawson house. Abby was sitting on the front steps alone. "Hey, kid, where's your sidekick?" Abby sighed heavily. "Trouble in paradise?"

Abby looked up at her frowning. "Uh?"

"Nothing." Terry chuckled shaking her head. "So what's up? Are you and Keith fighting again?" Terry paused. "You didn't tell him that he wasn't your best friend again, did you? Because the last time you did, he cried until we got home."

Abby sighed. "No, he's still my best friend."

"Great." Terry watched the child for a moment, then leaning closer Terry whispered. "You can tell me what's wrong, I swear I won't tell anyone, and I might be able to help."

Abby looked up at her, then back down at her light blue tennis shoes. "Do you ever miss your daddy?" Terry was taken aback for a moment. She had expected Abby to say something about arguing with one of the neighborhood kids or her mother not letting her get her way. The last thing she would have thought of was her asking about her father.

"Well, yeah, sometimes I do. It's been a long time since I lost my dad though, but I still think about him."

Abby sighed again. "How old were you when your daddy went to heaven?"

"I was close to the age you are now."

"Do you think Mr. Tyler would be a good daddy?"

"Uh. I don't know. I don't really know Tyler. He seems like a nice enough guy."

"Do you think my mommy likes him?"

"I guess she likes him. But I don't really know."

"Do you think she would marry him?"

"She doesn't know him well enough. Where are all these questions coming from?"

Abby brought her right hand up to her mouth biting the nail of her thumb before she looked up at Terry. "I was thinking that maybe Mommy could marry Mr. Tyler, then she could have a husband and be happy… and I could have a daddy."

"Abby, just because you think your mom should marry someone doesn't mean she will."

"But the other mommies think he will be a great husband and daddy."

"Who told you that?"

"Paige said that she heard her mommy tell Ms. Chan that. You said you think Mommy likes him?"

"Hey. Sometimes grownups don't always do things the way kids do them. Kids are great, you like someone, bam end of story. With us grownups, it's a little more complicated; it takes us time to decide if we like someone, and then more time before we decide we love them. If it's meant for your mom and Tyler to be together, they will."

Terry stood, preparing to go into the house. "Do you think my daddy would be sad if I got a new daddy?" Abby asked shyly.

Terry looked down at Abby's sad face, then sitting back down she smiled, wrapping her arms around the child. "No, baby, I don't think your daddy would be sad."

"Hey, Reds, what's up?" Terry said coming in the front door.

"Nothing. Just waiting for your cousin and her husband, they were supposed to be here an hour ago. Ben is supposed to be putting together the swing set that I told you about."

Terry looked at her and chuckled. "You're gonna let 'Mr. Handy' put something together?"

Holly remembered when she and Edmond had gotten married. They had purchased an Ikea entertainment center, and Ben and his brother Kyle came over to help Ed put it together. Holly and Dee sat on the sofa and watched the men, trying to contain their laughter. It was almost like watching a colorized version of the Three Stooges. Someone was either getting hit or dropping something. And all three men had different ideas of how the thing should go together, saying that the directions were not correct. When the entertainment center was complete it looked like it was leaning to the left a little more than it should have been. "Yeah, they bought the thing for Abby, so it's kind of hard for me to tell him, 'I know you bought the swing set and all, but since you're all thumbs, I don't think it's a good idea to let you put it together. I'd be better off letting Abby do it herself.' "

Terry chuckled, "Yeah, you can. I'd tell him in a heartbeat."

Holly shook her head. "I'm sure you would. Hey, come outside and help me drag the swing set box out of the garage."

"Nope," Terry said quickly.

"Why not? Your kid is gonna spend almost as much time on it as Abby will."

Keith walked into the kitchen immediately after Holly finished her statement. "Aunt Holly, Abby won't play with me."

Holly looked down at him. "Go down in the family room and get the coloring book and crayons. If you act like she's not there, she'll get mad at you, but then she'll want to color with you."

"But I don't want to color," he whined, "I wanna ride the bikes and she won't."

"Keith," Terry said, "Holly just told you that if you go and color, Abby will change her mind and want to color with you. Then you can ask her to ride the bikes."

"But," he whined a little louder.

"Keith, go in the other room!" Terry demanded. When he opened his mouth to speak she pointed saying, "Go!"

Holly stood and walked toward the back door. "The more time that he spends on the swing set, the less time he'll spend bugging us," Holly said in a singsong voice.

"You know, you're right," Terry said, standing. "Let's get that baby moved."

Twenty minutes later, Holly and Terry had only managed to move the box 10 feet. "Push." Holly strained to shove the box.

"What do you think I'm doing? This thing weighs a ton." After moving the box another five feet, the women decided the box was just too heavy and wasn't worth the trouble of killing themselves to get the kids out of their hair. They agreed it would be best to let Ben move the box since it was his bright idea to buy the swing set in the first place. They went to the back porch and sat on the steps. When they heard banging coming from next door, Terry stood and looked over the fence.

"Ooh," she said, waiving at Holly. "You gotta see this." Holly stood to peer over the fence. "Wow," Terry breathed. In the next yard a shirtless Tyler strolled across the yard. A sheen of perspiration glistened on his back. He wore jeans, work boots, and a tool belt hanging low on his hips. Reaching into the tool belt he took out a few nails and the hammer. Then holding a section of siding he nailed it in place. The muscles in his back rippled with each stroke. "Ohh," Terry said, "I'd let him nail something to my house anytime."

Holly tilted her head as she watched. Her eyes slowly traveled the full length of his body. "Oh, yeah. You and me both."

"Having fun?" A male voice whispered in Holly's ear. Holly jumped, turning around. "I can't believe you two are over here gawking at that poor guy," Ben said, laughing and shaking his head.

"We're not gawking," Holly said defensively, her cheeks flushed. "You guys are late," she added quickly.

"The babies were hungry," Ben said, patting his wife's belly.

"You sure it wasn't the mama that was hungry?" Terry asked.

After three hours of watching Ben put the swing set together, and laughing as he banged his thumb or dropped something on his foot, Terry decided that her entertainment for the day had come to an end, and it was time to go home. Taking a very disgruntled Keith with her, she had to promise him that they would come over in a few days so that he could play with Abby to finally get him out the door. Holly walked with Terry into the house and returned with three glasses of iced tea. After giving Ben a drink she sat with Dee, chatting and watching Ben. Holly heard banging and glanced to her right.

"So how's Tyler doing?" Dee asked.

"I don't know, I guess he's all right."

"From the way you've been checking him out, I'd say you thought he was more than all right."

"Don't you go getting any ideas."

"I'm not, I'm just making an observation"

"Well, don't."

"But you are attracted to him."

"So. Doesn't mean anything. Half of the single women in the neighborhood are attracted to him."

"Yeah, but I've seen him checking you out, too."

Chapter Twelve

"What are we waiting for, Mommy?" Keith asked his mother from the back seat. Terry glanced over her shoulder at him.

"Nothing, just thinking." They'd been sitting in the car in front of Holly's house for the last ten minutes. Terry bit her lip in thought as the conversation that she'd had with Abby replayed in her mind. Tyler seemed like an all-right guy from what she could tell. She'd only seen him a few times, but he was friendly and looked like a hard working guy. And no matter what he was doing, he always took time to talk to the kids. Holly usually acted as if she didn't notice him, but Terry saw Holly checking him out a few times. When she said something Holly quickly dismissed it or changed the subject. Maybe she needed a little nudge. Maybe they both did. She could do this, she was good at making things go her way, and maybe she could do something to get Holly a husband and a step-dad for Abby.

After another five minutes, Keith said, "Mommy, can I go and play with Abby while you think?" Terry glanced back at him again then starting the car, she prepared to pull away from the curb as one of the neighborhood women walked down the street and onto Tyler's porch. This is not going to be easy, with the sharks circling the prey, and Red's resistance. "Shit," she whispered.

"What's wrong, Mommy?"

"Nothing. Just sit tight." If she was nothing else, she was resourceful. Terry waited until the other women walked around the side of the house calling Tyler's name. She waited as the mailwoman put the mail in Tyler's box then moved down to the next house. She turned to Keith, "How would you like to stop for an ice cream cone on the way home?"

"Before dinner?"

Crap! "Yeah…before dinner." He nodded, his eyes large, giving her a big smile. Terry glanced over her shoulder at Holly's house again. "We're going to play a game. It's called…pretend you're asleep. I need you to close your eyes and keep them closed until I tell you to open them." Terry bit her lip. "If you can do that, you win and you get an ice cream cone." Keith nodded eagerly. "Are you ready?"

"Yes," he said with a quick nod.

"Play sleep." He folded his arms and closed his eyes tightly. Terry chuckled, shaking her head and got out of the car. She quickly walked to Holly's mailbox and removed the mail. She looked left then right and walked to Tyler's box and switched the mail. She got in the car, turned to her son and said, "You can wake up now."

Keith opened his eyes excited. "Did I win the ice cream?"

"You sure did."

"Mommy, I like the sleep game."

"I'm sure you do," she whispered as she pulled the car away from the curb.

"What the hell is this for?" Holly and Dee heard Ben say from across the yard.

Dee shook her head. "Poor baby. He can make millions in a year, but can't put together a child's toy. He put the cribs together for the babies last week."

"How'd that go?"

Dee hunched her shoulders. "He said when you paid over $3,000 for a crib, who would think that you would have to have an engineer's license to put it together?"

"He's not doing so bad," Holly was saying when one of the legs that held up the teeter-totter fell off.

Dee shook her head. "Don't worry, I'll come over tomorrow, and we'll fix it."

Another 45 minutes later Ben proudly announced., "There. It's all done."

Holly and Dee walked across the yard. "Looks good," Holly said, looking at the pile of screws, and odds and ends lying next to the swing set. "Uh, what's all this?"

"Oh, that's just extra stuff," he said, waving his hand dismissively.

She bit her lip suppressing a laugh, "O-kay."

"Ready to go, sweetheart. We have to meet Lisa at 6 and I need to go home and shower first."

"Sure, honey, if you can go start the car, I'll be right out." Ben kissed Holly's cheek. "Thanks," she said patting his arm. When Ben went into the house, Dee turned to Holly. "Don't let the kids use that." She gestured toward the swing set. "We'll fix it tomorrow."

"Right," Holly said, watching her friend enter the house. Then she turned back to the swing set.

"Your friend's not very handy, is he?" Tyler asked from over the fence.

Holly glanced at him, and then looked away quickly. "No, he's not." Tyler walked to the end of his yard and over to Holly's, opening the gate and walking to the swing set. "We can probably have this finished within a half-hour, I'm sure," he said, bending and picking up some of the spare parts. Within an hour Tyler and Holly had the swing set completed, and Holly had found out a few things about her neighbor. She learned that he had also lost a spouse and that they had really wanted children but couldn't have any.

"There you go," Tyler said, stepping back and taking in the swing set.

Holly looked down at the pile of parts. It wasn't nearly as large as it was before, but it still concerned her. "What's all that?"

"That's just extra stuff."

"Extra stuff? Yeah. Okay."

He laughed. "No, really. Some of it is extra parts." He paused, and then said, "And some of it is handymen extra parts."

"Which is?"

He scratched his head. "Those are parts that we handymen can't figure out what to do with." She looked appalled. "Don't worry; the swing set is absolutely safe. I guarantee it."

She examined the swing for a moment then nodded in satisfaction. "Thanks. It's getting late, how about you have dinner with us. We're having leftovers, it's not much, just spaghetti and meat sauce, with garlic bread, but you're welcome to join us."

He nodded. "Thanks, I'd like that. Let me go home and shower. What time should I arrive?"

"Seven should be good."

He smiled. "See you then."

After taking a quick shower and sliding on a white tee and jeans, Holly went into the kitchen and pulled the meat sauce that she'd prepared the night before from the refrigerator. She put it in a pot and turned the flame down low. Then she poured the pasta into a pot of boiling water.

What the hell was she thinking asking Tyler over for dinner? She'd watched all the women in the neighborhood practically fall at his feet. Was he going to think the reason for her invitation was the same as the other women he'd met since moving in to his new house? Would he think that she was trying to snag herself a husband like the other poor souls he'd encountered? No, he didn't think that, she was sure of it. Of course he'd think her invitation was to show her gratitude for his help with finishing the swing set. Then why was she so worried? She thought about Tyler's warm smile and his deep brown eyes and immediately felt a pang of guilt.

She leaned against the counter. *Why should I feel guilty? I haven't done anything.* But she did feel guilty. She felt guilty for allowing Abby to spend time around Tyler, even if it was just as a neighbor. She felt guilty for thinking Tyler was attractive and the surge of desire that rose in her whenever he was around. Five minutes later Abby came bursting in through the back door, running through the kitchen. "Abby, it's almost time for dinner. Go upstairs and wash up. And change your top," she said as she took a loaf of Italian bread out of the cabinet, sliced it in half and put butter and seasoning on it before popping it in the oven.

Holly set the table using their better china. Then stepping back she shook her head and started to remove the plates when the knock on the back door stopped her. "Shit." She placed the plate back on the table and went to the door.

Tyler stood on the porch wearing a yellow polo shirt and dark blue slacks. He smiled up at her and her heart fluttered. He held a brown paper bag toward her. "I know red wine goes well with pasta," he said as Holly took the bottle out of the bag. "But since Abby can't have wine, I thought cranberry apple juice would be good, too."

Holly grinned. "That's very nice of you." She stepped to the side. "Come on in." He followed her inside the house and when he brushed by her, Holly got a whiff of his sweet scent.

"Smells delicious."

"Thanks. Have a seat."

He pulled the chair from the table and sat down. "Do you need any help?"

"No, everything's taken care of." She stepped to the stove, picking up a spoon and stirring the pasta. Her heart was beating faster than normal and her hand shook slightly. She gripped the spoon tighter, willing her hand to stop trembling. "I'm just waiting for the spaghetti to boil. Excuse me," she said leaving the kitchen. "Abby," Holly called up the steps.

"Yes, Mommy," Abby answered coming to the top of the steps.

"We'll be having dinner soon."

"Okay." Abby turned, disappearing from the top of the stairs. Holly sat on the third step from the bottom, leaning forward and resting her face in her hands.

"Are you okay?" Holly heard Tyler ask. She looked up to see him standing next to the stairs looking at her with concern. "Is everything okay?"

"Oh, yeah. I just needed to sit down for a moment; it's been a long day."

He nodded. "You just sit there, I'll take care of the—"

"Hi, Mr. Tyler," Abby said bouncing down the steps.

"Hi, Abby. Your Mom's been working real hard today, and she needs a break. What do you say to you helping me in the kitchen while she takes it easy?"

"Sure." Abby raced down the remaining steps and squeezed past her mother.

"I can do that," Holly said, grabbing the railing and getting to her feet. Tyler took her by the shoulders, and turned her toward the living room.

"Nope. Abby and I have got this. Go put your feet up until it's ready."

Shaking her head, she started to argue. "Not polite to disagree with a guest," Tyler interrupted. "Go."

"Not polite to boss your hostess around either," Holly answered tartly, but sank down on the couch anyway. It felt good to sit after the day she'd had. She closed her eyes for what felt like just a moment, listening to her daughter's light giggle and her handsome neighbor's deeper voice. When she heard that deep voice say her name, she opened them quickly.

"Must've been quite a day." Tyler smiled. "You just dozed off for a few minutes."

Embarrassed, Holly jumped to her feet. "I'm so sorry. You came here for dinner, not to wait on me hand and foot."

"I've had days like that, and everybody needs somebody to step in sometimes. Come on, Abby's already at the table."

Tyler had enhanced the basic leftover pasta sauce with some garlic and a few unidentified but tasty spices. The bread was in a basket, covered with a napkin to keep it warm, and Abby bragged delightedly that she'd added a little olive oil to the noodles to keep them from sticking. "Tyler said that's how his aunt taught him!"

Holly felt a little pang in her heart. There was no mistaking her daughter's attachment to Tyler. With the candlelight glinting off her best dishes and conversation flowing easily, it was almost like the three of them were a little family. And she mentally kicked herself for enjoying the feeling as much as Abby appeared to.

"So, have the neighborhood vultures quit circling yet?" she asked when Abby finished a story about her friend forgetting her lines in a school play. She tried to keep her tone light and friendly, but she couldn't quite help the pang of jealousy she felt at the thought of some of those beautiful women parading by Tyler every day.

Tyler grinned wryly. "I've got more casseroles in my freezer than I know what to do with. I don't know why women always think a single man needs to be fed." He met her gaze instantly. "Not that that's why I think you invited me tonight!"

Ironically, Holly felt better after his stumble. He was really just as awkward with the situation as she was. "No way," she said cheerfully. "Just a thank-you for a job well done on the swing set. It was a really nice, neighborly thing to do."

From there, Abby took over the conversation again, chattering about how jealous Paige was of the play equipment and how she was going to talk her mom into buying her a better set, and Holly felt satisfied that she'd hit the right tone of friend-to-friend with her comment to Tyler, rather than single-woman-to-tasty-catch.

The rest of the dinner went by smoothly, and she was surprised and a little disappointed when Tyler glanced at his watch and got to his feet. "Nine o'clock already. I'd better get going—got a long day ahead of me tomorrow. Thanks for inviting me over. I had a great time."

"You can come back tomorrow, Mr. Tyler," Abby said quickly.

Tyler's eyes met Holly's for a second before he leaned down. "Sorry, Squirt, I've got stuff going on. But we'll do this again soon, and I'll cook at my house next time."

He smiled at them both and left, leaving Holly feeling a little empty inside. *I am not going to turn into one of the vultures,* she thought to herself, and tried to squash back the guilt that crept in over how good she felt after spending the evening with Tyler.

Holly watched as another one of the endless stream of women walked toward Tyler's front door. She hadn't talked to him since that day she'd invited him over for dinner, except for the few times his mail ended up in her mailbox. He'd only been living there a little more than two months and he seemed to know more people then she did after living here for seven years. She'd spoken to Valerie Logan last week, and Valerie had said that Tyler had offered to help with planting a tree in the open space. And that for the community festival, he was going to see if his fire station would participate in the parade. He was even going to help coach the community youth baseball team. She didn't understand how that had happened, when he didn't even have a kid. She watched Abby and Paige run from the side of the house across the street to the Chan house. Then the woman that visited Tyler came out of his house and walked down the street. Holly didn't know much about her. She did know that her name was Rita Devaul, and that she was one of many single mothers in the neighborhood. She leaned forward peering out the window to get a better look at Tyler's porch. She didn't know why the hell she even cared. It didn't matter to her that they all took turns racing to his house when they saw his truck in the driveway. "Who cares if every female in the state visits him? I sure don't," she said, dropping the curtin and walking toward the back of the house.

Chapter Thirteen

Terry slowed her car in front of Holly's house and watched as Valerie Logan marched purposefully down the street carrying a box. She walked onto Tyler's porch and squatted down, placing the box at the front door. She moved a few things in the box before she rose and left the porch heading back to her house. Terry watched the other woman as she entered her house. Then, waiting what she considered a reasonable amount of time, she left her car, cut across Holly's yard and sneaked onto the porch. Squatting down she saw that the box held something covered by a bright yellow napkin. On top was an envelope with a daisy lying on it. Terry opened the card, which read, "Every man deserves a home-cooked meal after a hard day's work." Terry snorted and moved the napkin, seeing a covered pot of beef stew with red potatoes and a slice of chocolate cake.

"What'cha doing?"

Terry shrieked and tumbled backwards, falling on her bottom. She looked up at Abby. "Girl, you scared me half to death." Terry grabbed Abby's arm, pulling her down and out of plain view. "Stay down. We don't want anybody to see us."

"Why?" Abby asked.

"'Cause," Terry said, taking the top from the stew and dipping her finger in it. She tasted it, and then whispered, "That bitch."

Abby frowned. "Is it nasty?"

"No, it's great." Terry bit her lip as she contemplated what she wanted to do, and then looked at the confused expression on Abby's face. "I need you to do something for me. I need you to run home and look in your momma's spice rack. Bring me the bottles of cream of tartar and red chili powder. On the way back grab a small stick." Abby watched her for a moment. "Well, what are you waiting for? Go ahead." Abby rose to move. Terry pulled her down again. "Hey, don't let anyone see you."

A few minutes later Abby returned with the spices and a stick. Terry took the tops off of the spices and sprinkled some into the pot, then thinking about it she poured the rest of both bottles in and stirred the stew with the stick. "That should do it." She peeked over at Abby. "You like chocolate cake?" Abby nodded. "Yeah, me too." She took the cake from the box and covered the pot with the napkin. Then she took Abby's arm and crept from the porch, dodging around the side of the house to Holly's backyard.

• • •

Tyler walked into the house carrying the box that he'd found on the stoop. He took the box to the kitchen and set it on the table, then walked into the living room and turned on the stereo, pushing play on the CD player. In The Sky Today by Ken Navarro pumped from the speakers. He walked to the front window and saw Holly's car turn into her driveway. He leaned against the window frame and watched as Holly and Abby got out of the car. Abby grabbed a bag that was on the back seat and ran to the house. Holly walked to the mailbox, removed the mail and stood at the end of the drive as she searched the letters. She wore steel gray slacks and a light gray sleeveless blouse. Her hair was pulled back and tied in a loose knot at the back of her head, with soft wisps framing her face. Man, she's beautiful. He'd spoken to her a few times since she'd had him over for dinner. Mostly when the mail carrier mixed up the mail and they had to exchange it. She didn't say much; just asked him how he was doing or about work. It was as if she were afraid that he would pounce at a moments notice, but he didn't think that was the case. He'd almost bet that Abby got her fiery personality from her mother.

Holly intrigued him. From what little time he'd spent with her he could tell she was intelligent and funny. And she was absolutely beautiful, from her flawless, creamy skin to her flaming red hair and her vibrant green eyes. He watched as she made her way back up the drive to her house. Then turning from the window he went upstairs to change out of his uniform.

As Tyler ascended the stairs the phone was on its third ring. He walked briskly to the living room to pick up the cordless phone and answered on the fourth ring. "Hello?"

"Hi, Tyler," Valerie said. "I was beginning to think you had to work late."

"No, I just got in."

"I hope your day wasn't too stressful?"

"No, it was fine. Thanks for asking. And thanks for dropping off the stew, I really appreciate it."

"It was my pleasure. Have you tried it yet? It's a

family recipe, and if I must say so, its one of the best pots I've made yet." Valerie continued to talk as Tyler walked to the kitchen and retrieved a spoon. He took the top from the pot and dipped the spoon inside taking a heaping spoonful of the stew into his mouth. He coughed then cursed under his breath. "Tyler? Are you all right?"

"I'm fine," he managed to say as he walked quickly to the sink. Taking a glass from the cabinet he filled it with water and drank it down.

"Have you tried the stew?"

"Uh, yeah. It's, um…amazing."

"Thank you," Valerie said, pleased by his compliment. "I'll let you go so you can have your dinner. Now you make sure you save room for dessert."

"Oh, I'll definitely have room for dessert," Tyler assured her. After hanging up Tyler looked at the pot sitting on his table. "Damn, if this is her best, I'd hate to see her worst." He took the pot to the sink and emptied the stew down the garbage disposal and washed the pot, placing it in the dish rack.

Tyler's stomach growled loudly as he looked out the window over his kitchen sink. His cooking options seemed pretty limited since almost everything was frozen and he couldn't bring himself to eat another casserole. Pizza was sounding better all the time, but the only one that delivered to the neighborhood was Dizzy's and he didn't like theirs. But going out meant eating in a restaurant by himself, and that idea didn't appeal either. Before he could talk himself out of it, he grabbed his keys and headed for the door.

He was still shaking his head at his own stupid impulses when Holly answered the door. She was wearing a comfy-looking pair of sweats with her hair tied up in a messy topknot, and she looked absolutely gorgeous.

She smoothed her hair back self-consciously. "What brings you this way, Tyler?"

"Just wondered if you and Abby had eaten yet." He saw Abby peeking interestedly around the corner behind her mom, and he waved, smiling. She quickly disappeared. "I was going to have some stew, but, uh, it didn't turn out." He heard a muffled giggle from down the hallway, and wondered what Abby found so funny about that. "Anyway, I was wondering if you guys liked pizza."

"Well, I'm not really dressed to go out—," Holly began.

"You look great. Seriously." Tyler waved a hand at his own casual jeans and sweater. "Besides, Pizza Hut doesn't require anything formal."

Holly gave him one of her heart-stopping smiles. "Abby, come on," she yelled over her shoulder. "I know you're back there. Get your shoes on."

The three of them piled into his car and headed for the restaurant, with Abby chattering excitedly in the back seat the entire trip. *That solves the problem of having to think of something to say,* Tyler thought to himself. By the time they pulled into the parking lot, the initial awkwardness had passed, and they were all laughing at a corny joke Abby had heard at school that day.

The only uncomfortable moment of the evening came when Tyler made a trip to the restroom and passed Valerie standing in the take-out line on his way back to the table. "Tyler, what are you doing here?" she asked. "Still hungry after all that stew?"

"Oh, um, I'm saving it," he answered, feeling his face flush guiltily, as it always did when he lied. "I had plans with some friends. I'll, uh, I'll see you later," he said, ignoring her disappointment as he turned tail and almost ran to the table where Holly and Abby waited.

"What's your hurry?" Holly asked.

"Just wanted to make sure Abby didn't get the last breadstick," he joked.

Holly glanced over his shoulder to see Valerie standing in line, her face irritated and disappointed. "Ah," she smiled. "I guess Abby and I make a pretty good cover for all those neighborhood women flinging themselves at you." Tyler dropped his gaze as he nervously moved the salt and pepper shakers. "Sorry, I won't tease," she said, noting his embarrassment.

Later, on their way out to the car, Abby grabbed his hand. "Thanks for taking us, Mr. Tyler!"

"No problem, Squirt," he said, tugging her ponytail. Inside, he was wishing her mom would grab his hand as easily as her little girl had.

• • •

"Come on, Reds, let us come with you guys."

"Terry," Holly sighed into the phone. "It's a community picnic."

"We're at your house so much we're practically part of the community. David and I were going to take the boys to Six Flags, but at the last minute he said that he had to work. The boys are so disappointed, and I don't want to take them to the amusement park alone. Please?" Terry continued before Holly had a chance to say anything. "I promise that I won't eat anything."

"Terry, it's not about you eating—"

"I'll do your laundry on Monday," Terry offered.

"Four loads?"

"Two?"

"Three," Holly countered.

"Deal." Once they discussed the time they were going to meet, Terry hung up the phone saying, "That was too easy."

"What was too easy?" Terry's husband David asked as he walked downstairs.

"Nothing."

"Did I hear you making plans to go out?" he asked her.

"Yeah, Holly invited me and the boys to a picnic."

"Um…I thought you would be home all day."

"Well, I sort of wanted to go with Holly, but I can call her—"

"You know, if you have plans, maybe I'll go see what Brian's up to."

"You sure?" He nodded. "Okay," she said giving him a quick kiss.

Before Terry and David were married Terry's selfish ways kept them from being together, and nearly ruined her family. Terry would date David until she met someone who she thought would give her more, then she would dump David and he would wait patiently until she'd take him back. In her quest to find what she thought was a better life she even went as far as to have an affair with Ben, who was Dee's boyfriend at the time. The problem was that when Terry met the man she had thought was Benjamin Harrison he'd actually turned out to be an employee of the Harrison's. Terry was sure that she and Ben would be married, so she'd arranged to have her family meet her at a restaurant where she and Ben were going to announce their engagement. She thought everything was perfect until the real Ben Harrison showed up, and her Ben confessed that he was really Mike Kellam, Ben's driver, and that when he'd met Terry he thought that once she'd gotten to know him and really loved him that it wouldn't matter that he wasn't a millionaire. Terry was furious, and that stunt nearly ruined her relationship with her family. She had hurt her cousin, who she later realized was her best friend, neglected her then only child, David, and almost lost the man she truly loved. When she'd finally realized that David was the man for her, she tried to change her ways, which wasn't always easy, but she tried to be a good wife and mother.

Terry turned toward the stairs yelling, "Hey, guys, get dressed, we're going on a picnic." She walked through the house to the kitchen and picked up a pair of rubber gloves on her way out the back door. Putting the gloves on, she picked up a mayo jar that she'd placed on the lawn a few hours ago. In the jar there were two teaspoons of sugar and dozens if not hundreds of ants. Putting the top on it and quickly brushing the ants from the outside of the jar, she held it up, grinning.

• • •

With the children running ahead of them Holly and Terry walked through the lush green community open space. They greeted different neighbors they passed and quite a few commented on how pretty Holly looked today. When Terry showed up at her house an hour earlier she was carrying a Macy's shopping bag. Looking down at Holly's white blouse and black shorts Terry asked, "Is that what you're wearing?" Then before Holly had a chance to answer, Terry thrust the bag at her and said, "Go change, I'll put everything in the basket."

In the bag were two blouses, one pink and one yellow, and a pair of white shorts. It had been a while since she'd had color in her wardrobe and she felt good. Maybe I should go shopping, she thought as another neighbor greeted them and told her how lovely she looked today. Holly and Terry chatted as they trudged along. Terry carried the picnic basket while Holly toted two blankets and Terry's tote bag containing sunscreen, a mini chess board and a few other things that Terry thought that they might need. "Where do you want to sit?" Terry asked.

Holly stopped walking. "I guess this is a good spot."

Terry looked around until she spotted Tyler. "Hey how about over there?" she said, and headed in his direction before Holly could protest. When they stopped at the spot next to Tyler, Terry said, "This is a perfect spot." She dropped the picnic basket, grinning over her shoulder at Holly.

"Afternoon, ladies. Hi, kids," Tyler greeted.

"Hi," everyone said almost in unison. Holly opened the blanket, preparing to spread it on the ground as the kids scattered, Abby and Keith running in one direction toward the face painting, and David headed in the other direction to join a game of Frisbee.

Terry sat on the blanket next to Tyler asking, "So, Tyler, how's it going?"

Still holding the blanket, Holly frowned down at Terry. Tyler stood quickly, taking the blanket from Holly and spreading it on the ground saying. "I've been good. How about yourself?"

When Tyler finished helping Holly with the blankets, he walked to his own blanket, squatted down and opened his basket and dug around for something. When Holly was sure that he wasn't looking, she reached over grasping Terry's blouse and snatched her from the blanket. Terry tumbled sideways, laughed and then moved to the blanket on the other side of Holly.

"So, Reds, what do we have to eat?"

"I made fried chicken and potato salad. And I even made enough for you," Holly said grinning at Terry.

Terry smiled sweetly. "Aw, you're such a doll. Tyler, have you tasted Holly's cooking? She's a great cook."

"I've tried her spaghetti," Tyler said watching Holly as she tried not to look at him. "It was very good."

"Well, you haven't had good cooking until you've tasted her chicken and potato salad." For fifteen minutes Terry talked nonstop about everything from being a fireman to what Tyler brought for lunch. When he'd said that he'd made chicken salad, she started on how a lot of men didn't wash their hands on a regular basis, and she wanted to know if he did, and if he could cook. Holly reached for the basket, hoping that if she got food in Terry's mouth it might shut her up, at least for a while. She placed the basket on the blanket and opened it. She looked inside and frowned. "What the hell?" The basket was littered with ants.

Leaning forward, Terry peeked inside the basket saying, "Wow, that's a lot of ants."

"We haven't been here for 20 minutes, 30 at the most, how could there be this many ants so quickly?"

"I don't know, maybe there's an anthill?" Terry said.

Holly looked around searching the ground. "I don't see any signs of an anthill." She sighed. "We can't stay here without any food; the kids will make it unbearable for us."

"I have plenty," Tyler volunteered. "I brought extra so that I could share with anyone who might want some. There's more than enough.

Just then Abby and Keith ran to their mothers. "Mommy, I'm hungry," Abby said.

"Honey, we're having a problem with the food, we might have to leave."

"Do we have to?"

"Really," Tyler said again. "I have more than enough, and if I don't use it now, it might go to waste."

"Yeah, he has more than enough," Terry jumped in. "Let me go and throw this stuff away while you guys feed the kids." Terry hopped to her feet and grabbed the basket.

It turned out that Tyler had brought just enough extra food to feed them—and at least take the edge off the kids' hunger. "Jeez, Tyler, were you planning on feeding the National Guard?" Terry joked.

"You never know when hungry troops will show up," he laughed back. "Who wants to get pushed on the swings?" he asked the kids.

Abby and Keith all but tripped over each other in a race for the only available swing on the playground. David took off to rejoin his Frisbee game. "Excuse me, ladies," Tyler said, "I've got some kids to push."

Terry fanned herself lazily with a paper plate, as she and Holly watched him walk away. "Mmm. Tight ass and good with kids." She said it loudly enough that Tyler looked back in surprise. Amused and a little embarrassed, he walked a little faster, trying to pretend that he hadn't heard Terry's comment.

Holly snorted and poked her in the ribs with a sharp elbow. "Mind your own damned business. And keep those eyes to yourself."

On the walk back to Holly's house, Abby and Keith raced far ahead, fighting about who would use the bathroom first when they got there. David walked ahead, putting distance between himself and the women. Holly slowed her pace, letting the distance between them and David increase before she said, "Okay. Now that we're alone, maybe you can tell me what the hell is going on?" Terry immediately stopped walking. "Uh? What do you mean?"

"Don't give me that innocent act. I want to know what's going on. What was with the way you were acting?"

"How was I acting?" Terry asked innocently.

"Okay…why were you flirting with Tyler?"

Terry looked at her and smiled. "Is someone jealous?"

"Hell, no."

"Yeah, you are."

"Look, I just want to know what's going on, I mean if you're trying to get with—"

"What? No. I'm a married woman."

"It's not like it never happened before."

"Well, it's not happening now," Terry said indignantly. "I can't believe that you would think that I would do that."

"I didn't say that I thought you would."

"You didn't say it, but you meant it."

"No," Holly groaned in frustration. "Look, I see all these women chasing after him, and it just pisses me off to think that my own family would do that, too."

"I was not flirting with him; I was just trying to be nice. I'm very happy with my life and my husband, thank you very much." Holly looked at her then glancing around, she nodded.

"Okay. What made you suggest that Tyler take us all out to dinner?"

"There wasn't much chicken salad, and you know the kids are probably still hungry."

"Terry, I can make something at the house."

"It's your day off, and I thought it would be nice."

"Terry."

"And I have a bag in the car that I forgot to give you. It's a dress and it'll look fabulous on you." Terry grinned at her. "So, you like him don't you?" Terry asked.

"No." Holly denied, hiding her grin.

"Yeah, you do. And I'm family. You said I was family. You love me."

"Temporary insanity," Holly said turning and walking away.

"You know you do. Tell the truth, you love me," Terry said keeping pace with Holly. Glancing down Holly grinned and bumped Terry slightly with her shoulder.

Terry felt a squish under her foot as something wet oozed into her sandal and between her toes. "Aw man, I stepped in freaking ice-cream." Holly laughed. "You did that on purpose. Shit. And it's strawberry. I hate strawberry," Terry complained as Holly walked ahead whistling.

Chapter Fourteen

Moments before Tyler showed up to get Holly, Terry and the kids, Terry's cell phone rang. Before Tyler knocked on the door Terry and the boys came out of the house past him. "Oh," Terry smiled up at him. "Thanks for the dinner invite, but I forgot I told my husband we would meet him for dinner after work. Holly and Abby are inside waiting for you, though. Have a good time," she said walking past him. Tyler watched her go from the porch then turned toward the house and knocked on the door.

"Come on in," Holly called. He entered the house. "We'll be down in a minute." Tyler stood in the living room, his hands in his pockets, waiting. He glanced up as Holly descended the stairs. She wore a pink and white floral dress that moved romantically when she walked. Tyler stood staring as she walked toward him. He felt his mouth gape but couldn't manage to close it. When he saw the look of uncertainty on Holly's face and saw her turn to go back upstairs he stepped forward.

"No. I'm sorry I didn't mean to stare. Um, it's just. You're stunning." She bit her lip and blushed, which made her look even more beautiful.

"Thank you," she said, walking the rest of the way

down the stairs. "About Terry wrangling dinner out of you. Sometimes she can be a bit much, but most times she means well."

"No problem."

"Well, dinner's on me."

"No," Tyler said, shaking his head.

"I insist. You bought pizza."

Abby came running into the room, wearing a purple-flowered sundress. "Mom made me put this on," she complained.

"You look great, Abby. Holly, let a man buy two beautiful ladies dinner. And something a little nicer than pizza this time."

"Shall we?" He held out an arm for each of them, and formally escorted the two from the house. Abby stuck her little nose in the air, and pranced regally on her tiptoes, making Tyler and Holly laugh.

"I guess if you're going to dress like a princess, at least you can act like one," Tyler remarked. "What kind of dinner would you like, Princess?"

"Something fancy," she said. "Princesses can't just eat any old food."

"Abby, fancy usually equals expensive…"

"I know just the place," Tyler said firmly.

The Italian restaurant he took them to wasn't the priciest in town, since he didn't want to make Holly uncomfortable, but it did have actual musicians and little candles in red, leaded-glass jars on each table, which thrilled Abby. More than once, Holly had to swat her hand away from the candle on theirs.

"But, Mommy, the jar's so pretty," she whined. "I just wanted to see if it felt bumpy."

Holly could barely concentrate on her daughter's behavior. Her thigh kept bumping Tyler's under the little table, and the warm strength of it was incredibly distracting. She could tell he was feeling the same way—she could feel his eyes on her, even when she wasn't looking at him.

When the waitress came back to the table to drop off Tyler's credit-card slip, she was carrying a small brown box. Smiling, she handed it to Abby and wished them all a good night.

"What's this for?" Abby asked excitedly. Holly looked at Tyler questioningly.

"You'll have to open it in the car and find out."

The second the doors slammed, Abby was tearing into the box. "Mommy, it's one of those pretty glass jars!"

Tyler said quickly, "It's just to keep your jewelry and stuff in—no candles."

"Thank you so much! How'd you get her to bring me one?"

"ESP, I just thought about it really hard—"

"More like you wrote her a note on the charge slip," Holly laughed. "You didn't have to do that."

"That's all right. I figured she'd like one."

Their eyes met, and Tyler paused with his key halfway to the ignition. The second seemed to last forever, and Holly finally broke the connection looking out the window.

"You're going to spoil her. Both of us," she added softly, so he couldn't hear.

At seven o'clock on Monday morning Holly and Abby walked out of the house into the backyard. Holly unlocked the shed and pulled out Abby's bike and safety gear. She waited until Abby had her knee and elbow pads on and her helmet strap fastened before she asked, "Ready?"

Abby grinned up at her mother. "Yep."

"Let's go." Holly jogged alongside the bike, cutting across the open field and down to the community park. She kept a steady pace, making sure that Abby didn't get too far behind her. She ran her normal mile and a half before looping back around and heading home with Abby riding alongside her.

She was going in to work later than usual this morning. After she dropped off Abby at Saundra's she was going to meet her partner Mitch, and they would go over the Rivers case once more to be sure that they had a solid case against him. Even after all of their efforts they couldn't convince some of the witnesses to his daughter's assault to testify in court. She guessed she couldn't completely blame them. After Mrs. Atkins ended up in the hospital with a fractured skull, and the media publicized the connection between the elderly woman and the Rivers case, all of the witnesses had seemed to develop amnesia. She and Mitch thought they had enough to go on without the witnesses, and she wanted to be sure that that pig didn't have a way to escape.

When she returned home from her run they would have just enough time to get cleaned up, grab something quick to eat and be out the door in twenty minutes.

As she ran, her mind drifted to Tyler. She really liked him. He was a great guy, genuine, fun and sexy as all get out. And Abby loved him. But there were a few things that bothered her, like the thing with their mail. She knew that it could be explained as coincidence a few times, but two to three times a week was a lot more than coincidence. She didn't know what was going on but she sure as hell was going to find out. The first thing she needed to do was to corner the mail carrier and question her, then she was going to check Tyler's background more thoroughly.

When she approached the Ranks' house, she smiled to herself. It appeared that Lamon's brother must have determined that having a dog was too much trouble, and Lamon decided to keep the pooch. A few weeks ago, the Ranks' had an invisible fence installed so they could give the dog access to the front yard. For the last month whenever Holly and Abby would jog past the house the dog seemed to be hiding, and when they'd least expect it he'd come running out and scare the heck out of them. Once, Abby fell off her bike scraping her hand. Even though they ran past the yard three to four times a week the dog would seem to come out of nowhere half the time and manage to spook them.

A week ago Holly decided to stop running a block before the Ranks' house. She went around the block to take Abby home. First she put the bike in the garage and then she let Abby in the house. Then after she sent Abby off to shower, she walked back down to the Ranks' house. When she reached the yard, she searched it for the dog. She saw him lying on the right side of the house, half hidden by the shrubs. Holly assumed he was sleeping. She crept closer and squatted next to the dog. "Woof, woof, woof," she roared. The dog yelped and rolled onto his back. "Now, how do you like that, you little bastard?" And then she quickly ran from the yard and hummed as she went home. From that day on, whenever they passed the yard the dog would run to the invisible fence and trot next to them to the end of the yard where he'd sit and watch them as they ran away. This morning as they passed the yard, Lamon was standing on his front porch. Holly waved to him. He looked at her then at the dog and back at her. She gave him a smug smile, never breaking her stride.

"Abby, hurry up, we're going to be late." Sitting on the bed, Abby hugged one of her pillows as she heard her mother call her for the third time. She bit her lip as she looked at the clock. Last night Aunt Terry had come up to her room to say goodnight. She had told Abby to take her time getting dressed in the morning, and to try and wait until the last minute before she went downstairs. Then she said that after they went to the car Abby was to go next door and ask Mr. Tyler if he could help her mommy.

Abby didn't know why Terry wanted her to wait or why she should go ask Mr. Tyler for help; Terry just said it was very important that Abby did everything exactly as she had been told. And it was part of the plan. Abby didn't know what plan Terry meant. They hadn't talked about a plan. But she knew she couldn't keep her mother waiting much longer, or she would be in big trouble. She hugged her pillow tighter, glancing at the clock once more. "Abigail James, you get down here right now!" Holly yelled up the steps. Abby jumped off the bed, dropped her pillow and grabbed her purple backpack before leaving the room.

"Girl, didn't I say we're going to be late?" Holly said, glaring at her daughter.

"Sorry, Momma."

Holly froze and looked down at her, "What were you—?" she paused and then shook her head, waving her hand. "Never mind, I don't even want to know. We have to go." Holly closed the door behind them, locking it. They walked briskly to the car. Holly walked to the driver side, opened the door and got in. She looked at her daughter standing on the sidewalk. "Abby, get in the car," Holly demanded, her patience wearing thin. That was when she noticed Abby looking down at the car with her brows raised and her lips in the shape of an O.

Getting out of the car Holly walked to the passenger side, and then froze when she saw the two flat tires. "Son-of-a-bitch!" she stomped. "Shit, shit, shit." She looked skyward, taking a deep breath. "Okay, I can get a cab, drop you off at school—" She turned in a complete circle, and realized that her daughter was nowhere in sight. "Abby?" She threw her arms up. "Oh great, now I have to run around looking for her." She turned back to the car. "How the hell did I get not one, but two flats?"

"Need a hand?"

Holly turned to see Tyler standing next to Abby. "Looks like you could use some help." He stood with his hands on his hips, wearing a pair of dark blue sweat shorts and a black sleeveless tee. Holly looked down at Abby, who hunched her small shoulders. Holly glanced up meeting his gaze then her eyes instantly traveled down his body from his muscular arms to his powerfully built smooth and oh-so-sexy legs. Whoa baby, she thought and then turned away, quickly facing the car.

"I don't know how this could have happened, and of course there's only one spare. I guess I'll have to call the garage." Holly sighed. "This would have to happen today; I have to get Abby to school and I have an important meeting this morning," Holly said, still looking at the car.

Stepping next to her, Tyler said, "I could drop you

guys off and take your tires over to have them fixed."

"I can't let you do that."

"Hey, it wouldn't be a problem; I have a few hours before I have to be in. It wouldn't take long."

"It would be a big help," Holly said.

"Okay, let me get my keys and I'll drop you guys off and then take care of the car."

Holly called Saundra and let her know that they were running late and that she was dropping Abby off at school, so Saundra knew that she had to pick up Abby at the end of the day. Then Holly called her partner to apologize for being late and to let him know that she would be arriving soon. In twenty minutes, Tyler was pulling in front of Abby's school. Holly had to turn around to check on her unbelievably quiet daughter. If she didn't know better, she'd think they had accidentally driven off leaving the child standing in the driveway.

"Hey, kiddo, you all right?" Abby grinned at her, nodding. Holly frowned at the strange gleam in her daughter's eyes. Then she turned, opened the door and got out of the SUV. She helped Abby out of the vehicle and bent to give her a hug and a kiss.

Once Holly was back inside the vehicle, Abby knocked on the window. Holly put the window down. Standing on her toes Abby peeked over the door in order to see Tyler and grinned broadly at him. "Bye, Mr. Tyler. Have a good day."

"Have a good day, Squirt," Tyler said. They watched as she raced away to meet two other girls. "She's a great kid," Tyler said as he put the SUV in drive and pulled from the curb.

"Yeah, she is."

They drove in silence for a while before Tyler said, "I haven't seen you a in a few days. How have you been?"

"I've been good. Busy. How about yourself?"

"I've been well. I saw you at the kids' game last Saturday." Holly watched the traffic and remained silent. After an awkward moment Tyler said, "Have I done something to offend you?"

Holly squirmed in her seat. "No."

"Your actions say something completely different." He looked over at her then turned back to the road. "If I didn't know better, I'd think you were avoiding me."

"Tell me about your family?" Holly asked, changing the subject.

He smiled at her, raising his eyebrows at her quick shift in the conversation. "Ooookay…Well, my Aunt Josyln raised me—she's a wonderful lady. Then there's my cousin Rashard, he's the manager of an auto supply center and lives with Aunt Jos to help her out. And than there's Yvette."

"Yvette?"

"She's my cousin."

"What does your cousin Yvette do?"

Tyler was silent for a moment. "She's between jobs now. Could be for months, knowing Yvette."

Holly picked up the slight hostility in his tone. "Sounds like you two have some problems"

"That's an understatement."

Holly waited for him to elaborate, and when he didn't she asked, "Is Yvette Jocelyn's daughter?"

"No, like me, Yvette was practically abandoned by her parents, and Aunt Jos took her in, as well.

"Sounds like your aunt is quite a lady."

"She is." Tyler turned his vehicle into the parking

lot of the police station. He put the car in park and turned to Holly. "Holly I—"

"Look, Tyler, you seem like a great guy, and I really like you, but—" She looked around the parking lot, sighing, then looked at him. "Thanks for the ride." She held her hand out for her keys. "I'll have someone come by and pick up my car."

He shook his head. "No, I'll take care of it."

"I don't think—"

"I'll take care of it."

She looked around the parking lot again, then turning back to him, she smiled saying, "Thanks," before getting out of the car.

"It's no problem," he said as she got out of the SUV.

Chapter Fifteen

Holly reached for her cup of two-hour-old coffee and took a sip. She was so engrossed in the file she read that she hardly noticed the cold, bitter taste. She was going over the file for a case McGuiness had just dropped on her desk. It seemed that a mother of three wanted to get the neighborhood thugs off her block, and the thugs were tormenting the family. She had been sitting at her desk for an hour before McGuiness dropped the file on her desk. Up until that time, all she could think about was Tyler. He was a great guy, and Abby did like him a lot. Maybe she should just go with things and see how they progressed. If things didn't work out, it wouldn't be the end of the world. They would move on, no big thing. But what about Abby? If things didn't work out, would he be the sort of man who would shut out Abby, too?

"Lawson! Stop your damned daydreaming and get to work," McGuiness had said, startling Holly when he dropped the file on her desk.

Daley walked in and dropped down in the chair next to Holly's desk. He groaned.

"What's up?"

Daley ran his hands through his hair. "Homicide

just found a body behind the Motel 6 on Algonquin Road." He blew out a heavy breath. "It's Jessica Rivers."

They stood next to the table looking down at the battered and bruised face of 32-year-old Jessica Rivers. The medical examiner went through his findings as Holly and Mitch looked on. *I'm sorry, Jessica. I told you that I could help and I gained your trust, and look where you end up,* Holly thought.

"I'd say the time of death likely occurred between midnight and 4 a.m. She was beat up pretty bad," the ME was saying. "Damage to the liver and spleen caused by blunt force injuries. Gunshot to the right temple indicates that the gun was less than six inches from the victim." The ME paused. "Get this, there are no defensive wounds."

"None?" Holly asked.

"The examination is not complete, but as far as I can tell now, not one."

Jessica had been married to Rivers for seven years. Holly found out from her that during that seven years Rivers had beaten her repeatedly, and that if she tried to fight or block his punches, it only made him more enraged or excited, and he'd beat her longer and more severely. Eventually she'd just stopped fighting, stopped trying to protect herself.

As they walked from the morgue, Rivers walked down the hall flanked by his attorney, a tall, willowy brown-haired woman, and three other men. "Detective Daley. Detective Lawson. What are you doing here?" Rivers asked, obviously faking surprise.

Daley nodded to the attorney as they passed the group. Holly remained silent, keeping her eyes straight ahead as they walked. When Holly and Daley reached the end of the hall they waited near the elevators until they heard the door to the morgue open, then Holly stepped forward and pushed the elevator button. The doors opened with a ding, and Holly reached inside, holding the door open as Mitch called, "We'll hold the elevator for you."

When the group reached the elevator everyone got on, and Holly pushed the buttons for the lobby and the third floor. "Damn shame what happened to Jessica," Holly said, looking up at the numbers.

"Sorry for your loss," Mitch added.

"She was such a sweetheart," Holly said, "I can't possibly imagine anyone wanting to do this to her."

"Before you start, my client has an alibi," Rivers attorney said as Rivers and his group stepped from the elevator.

Holly pressed the open-door button. "Just so we can clear the air, what would that alibi be?"

"I was with Taya and my boys. We were hanging out over at her place." Holly knew his boys. They were each upstanding citizens to hear them tell it. They each had a rap sheet as long as her forearm, listing things from assault to armed robbery. And Taya Hernandez was a know heroin addict. She would do anything, even confess to the Kennedy assassination, for a hit. "We were there all evening, and I spent the night with Taya. Right, baby?" He threw his arm around the young woman's shoulder. She looked at him nervously and then nodded in agreement. "I'm sure you know this: That Jessica, she was a real whore. Maybe one of her many men did what the others wanted to."

Letting go of the elevator doors, Holly watched them slide closed. "You all right kid?" Daley asked

Holly. Holly gave him a quick nod, and as the doors opened, she stepped from the elevator, excused herself and headed to the ladies room. Once in the ladies room she walked to the sink, turned on the faucets and splashed water on her face. She grabbed a few paper towels and wiped her face. Then after wetting the paper towels she wiped the back of her neck. Dropping her head, she took a deep breath. After a few minutes, she threw the paper towels into the garbage can and walked to one of the stalls. She stepped inside and closed the door. Sitting on the toilet alone in the ladies restroom Holly cried for Jessica Rivers.

Chapter Sixteen

Holly walked to the front door and opened it without looking up to see who it was. She knew it had to be Terry. "Hey," she said turning toward the kitchen.

"Hey, thanks for picking Keith up for me."

She stopped and turned back to Terry, "Sure, not a problem. Where's David?"

"He didn't want to ride over with me. I dropped him off at home."

"Oh." Holly nodded. "You could have called; you didn't have to come all the way over here. I would have brought Keith home."

"I wanted to see how you were."

"You saw me yesterday."

"Yeah, I know, but—" Terry shifted her weight from foot to foot. The two of them stood watching each other as if they didn't know quite what to do.

"What's going on?" Holly finally said.

"Holly, can I talk to you about something?" Terry asked.

No, Reds, uh-oh. Not good. "Um, I guess so."

"Can we go into the kitchen?" Holly nodded leading the way to the kitchen. "How do you do it?" Terry finally asked as she sat at the table.

"Do what?"

"All this, raise Abby, have a career—" Terry sighed. "Cope with being alone?" Holly watched her not answering. Terry looked down at her hands and picked at her nails. "David left me," she said quietly. Holly remained silent. "He left me for someone else."

"I can't believe that. I would of anyone else, but not David."

Terry nodded. "She's 23, drop-dead gorgeous, and very, very pregnant."

"What?"

Terry nodded again. "He told me about her, and I've seen her."

"The way you are, you saw this woman and you're not in jail," Holly said. Then she caught herself and tried to rephrase her comment. "I mean I can't believe that you didn't lose it?"

"I would have. I've heard people say that they went into a state of shock when something devastating happened. I always thought it was bullshit, but I actually went into shock, literally. When I saw her standing in my living room I couldn't move; my mind would barely function enough for me to sit down."

"Whoa, slow down, when she was in whose living room."

"In my living room." Terry took a deep breath. "About a week ago, David came home from work. When I heard him come in, I went to the living room to say hi, and there he is, standing with some girl. When I walked in I froze, I don't know, but I immediately had a bad feeling. He asked me where the boys were. I told him that David was out playing ball and that Keith was at the neighbors playing with a friend. Then David says 'Terry we need to talk.' He starts telling me how he didn't want to cause a scene and how he just wanted to tell me what was going on. Like he was telling me that he had to work late or that he needed to have some work done on his car, or some other mundane thing. Me, I'm standing there calm as can be, waiting as he tells me that he's in love with this girl, and that she's having his baby. That's when I notice the pregnant glow and the protruding belly. Somehow I managed to make it to the sofa as he continued to tell me he was coming that following weekend with some friends and taking all of his things and that he would appreciate it if I wasn't there, and that as a consolation prize he was going to let me keep our sons."

"He actually said that?"

"No, what he said was that Shayla or Shale or whatever the hell her name is couldn't handle dealing with two children, and that it would be best if I kept them, and he would pick them up and spend time with them. That was last week and he has yet to come see the boys."

"Damn," Holly said shaking her head. "Abby never said anything about it."

"She doesn't know. I told Keith that his father had to go on a business trip. He keeps asking, and I keep making up excuses. I know that I'm going to have to tell him the truth, but I just don't know what to say." Terry sighed.

"And to top things off David heard everything. He was upstairs. He'd come inside to change his shoes, and I didn't hear him. He knows why his father left. I tried to tell him that sometimes things like that happen, but he says his father hurt me. He was so angry. I guess if I had freaked out things would have been different, but I think he saw me as the victim and that really made him mad."

"This last week I've seen a change in him. He gets so angry whenever Keith mentions their father; he just blows up. And he spends a lot of time alone in his room. He doesn't want to go outside with his friends much. It seems as if he's hiding out or something. If he's not hiding out in his room, he's asking me if I'm okay, or if I need him to do anything for me. I guess he thinks he should take care of me. Funny, huh? Up until the last few years I wasn't there for him like he needed me to be, and now he's taking care of me." The noise she made sounded like she actually choked on a sob. "Anyway," Terry said looking away. She heaved a sigh then turned back to Holly. "I don't really know where to go from here."

"How are you holding up?" Holly asked her.

Terry's lip trembled. "It hurts like hell. I really thought things were going okay. I thought he loved me as much as I loved him." Tears slid down her cheeks. "I know that I probably deserve this, but I just can't stop telling myself that what he did is wrong."

"It is wrong. No matter what happened in the past, when the two of you got back together he basically said he forgave you for the things that happened. You guys started anew. Now for him to do this is not acceptable." Tears streamed down Terry's face and Holly automatically stepped close to her, taking her in her arms. Terry laid her head on Holly's shoulder, allowing the sorrow to overcome her as she cried.

"I think we should shove an apple in his tailpipe," Dee said taking a huge bite from the apple she held.

"We can wedge it in there real tight. Mess up his exhaust."

"No, we could pour sugar in his gas tank," Terry said eagerly.

"No!" Holly said quickly.

"Na," Dee agreed, still eating her apple. "Hol's right. It would take a lot of sugar to do real damage, plus it would take too long to do. We need to hit and run."

"I don't want to hear this," Holly said.

"Hit and run, I like that," Terry said moving to the edge of her seat "What if we break his kneecap."

"What? Oh, hell no!" Holly yelled.

Dee shook her head briskly as she spoke. "We would have to do it so he couldn't tell it was us. That might be a little tricky."

"No, crazy lady! No breaking of the kneecaps will be going on in my presence!" Holly shook her head and her red hair swished from side to side.

"You don't have to go," Dee said, her tone serious. "I wouldn't want to make you an accessory. You being a cop and all." Holly paused, looking at Dee as if she had lost her mind.

"Do you two hear yourselves? What you're talking about is a crime."

"It's a crime the way he treated Terry."

"I agree that what he did was wrong, but you can't just go around shoving apples in people's tailpipes and breaking their kneecaps. Who do you think we are, the mafia?"

"Hey, jilted women mafia," Terry said. "I like that. I could be the godmother. Dee could be Baby Face Harrison and, Holly, you can be Lucky Lawson."

Dee laughed at that. "Yeah, we can take hits from

jilted women, charge them a small fee, and take care of their problems."

"Lord, help us," Holly said, covering her face with her hands. She shook her head then brushed her hair back from her face. When she looked up both Dee and Terry were grinning at her.

"So," Dee said, her voice light, "What do you say, Lucky?"

Holly groaned. "Terry, do you know where David is staying?"

"Yeah, he's staying with Shellac over near Prairie Square."

"Shellac?" Dee asked, frowning, "What the hell kind of name is Shellac?" Terry hunched her shoulders while shaking her head. Holly groaned again as she took a deep breath.

"Is there anything at the house that belongs to him?"

"Yeah, he left a bunch of his clothes, I was thinking about taking them to the dump."

"Okay," Holly nodded. "Let me see if Paige's mother can keep an eye on Abby and Keith for a couple of hours."

"What are we going to do?" Dee asked, excitement gleaming in her eyes.

"Settle down there, sister. We're going to do something that will pacify you two lunatics, make David feel like shit and keep the three of us out of jail…Hopefully."

The ride back from David's new place was noisy. After going to Terry's house and picking up the remainder of David's personal belongings, the trio went to David's new girlfriend's apartment and tossed all of his clothes on the lawn. David and his very pregnant girlfriend came down and watched from the vestibule, and Holly watched as Terry and David got into a heated argument with Terry standing on the front lawn and David standing in the entryway of the apartment building. Holly was grateful that David had the good sense to remain on the stoop or the situation could have escalated. When they were driving from the apartment parking lot, to Holly's horror she saw that either Terry or Dee had used a permanent magic marker and written adulterer on David's car. Neither of the two admitted to the crime, but Terry was the most likely suspect. Dee and Terry talked nonstop about how David was a fool for leaving his family for some girl who obviously seemed to be using him. Holly drove quietly, praying that David didn't get the idea to call the station and try to have her fired. She knew that the chances of him being able to make waves were minimal, but on the off chance that he talked to someone who wanted to score points with McGuiness…well, she just didn't want to go there. After Dee complained for fifteen minutes about how seeking revenge made her hungry, they pulled into a sub-shop parking lot, and Holly waited while Dee and Terry went inside to place their orders.

When they returned to Holly's house, Terry went with Holly to retrieve the kids while Dee went into the kitchen to get a head start on her meal.

"So," Terry said looking at Dee, who was eating a cheese-steak sandwich. "What's going on with the outfit?" She pointed at Dee, moving her finger in a circular motion.

"What?"

"The whole blue sweatshirt, brown corduroy pants thing."

"I was in a hurry."

"Oh, and the orange and white tennies, and pink baseball cap. Now that's hot," she said, giving Dee a thumbs up.

"Bite me," Dee said, wiping her mouth with her napkin but never looking up.

"I think she looks cute," Holly said smiling at Dee.

"You would," Terry groaned.

"She has that pregnant-woman glow going on. When you're pregnant you can wear almost anything and get away with it," Holly said. Terry groaned again and Holly laughed.

Terry glanced at Dee again. "Good lord, what are you having, an elephant?"

"Let her eat," Holly said, offering half of her turkey club to Dee. "This is the only time she'll be able to eat whenever she wants, and whatever she wants without someone saying anything to her." Dee looked at the offered sandwich, paused then took it. "Some people think that it's good for a pregnant woman to eat as much as she wants to.

"That's all she ever does is eat."

Holly snickered then asked, "Is Ben coming to pick you up?" Dee nodded, her mouth full.

"You sure you didn't eat him too?" Terry asked, feigning fear as she took one of Dee's fries.

"Ha, ha, ha. No."

A short while later Ben walked into the kitchen and Dee stood to give him a kiss. He quickly glanced at her outfit, and then laughed.

"What? I was in a hurry. Geez."

Chapter Seventeen

Terry stopped a block before Holly's house and asked the mail carrier if she could leave a card and a rose in Tyler's mailbox. She would have done it herself but things were getting too sticky. It seemed like every time she'd come over while Holly was home, Holly was watching the mailbox like a hawk. She'd asked the mail carrier to do her this small favor and put this little thing in the mailbox, and the other woman just laughed and said, "Uh, no."

Terry ended up giving the woman five bucks, and she was still hot about it. "Ol' heifer," she grumbled as she got out of her car.

Walking onto the front porch, she paused, peeking into Holly's living room window. She watched as Holly picked up Abby's backpack and opened it. As Terry straightened preparing to go to the front door, she froze seeing Holly take a pink rose and a card from the book bag. She watched Holly open the card and read it. Holly looked at the envelope, front and back, and then she read the card again. The card simply said, "You are breathtaking." Terry knew what the card said because she'd given it to Abby. She saw the look on Holly's face. "Shit," Terry whispered, racing from the porch around the side of the house. She looked around the yard and picked up a fistful of pebbles, tossing them one by one at the house. She threw several before one finally hit Abby's bedroom window.

"Mommy said that throwing rocks at the house is bad," Abby said from behind Terry. Terry jumped, wheeling around.

"Girl, come here," she said, pulling the child to the side of the yard. "I told you to put that flower and card on the front porch yesterday." Terry had gone to the childcare providers to pick up Keith and David. She had given Abby the rose and card, saying that it was a special surprise for her mommy and telling Abby to be sure to leave it on the stoop before she went to bed. Terry had made dinner reservations in both Tyler and Holly's name for the following weekend. She'd paid the hostess at the restaurant to call both Tyler and Holly saying that they each had invited the other to dinner at that time. She just hoped it would work and neither of the dumb asses would blow it. All the kid had to do was leave the flower and card to set the romantic tone.

"I couldn't do it." Abby hunched her small shoulders.

"Abby."

Abby heard her mother call from the front of the house. She started to run to her mother when Terry grabbed her around the waist before she could get away. "Hold on." Terry set the child down then sighed heavily. "Okay, what time did you go to bed last night?"

"Eight thirty."

Terry bit her nail. "What to do, what to do?" she said to herself. "Okay, she probably went next door to exchange the mail. Good, so you tell her that you picked the card and flower up when you came home, put it inside your book bag, and forgot to give them to her."

"But I spent the night with Aunt Dee and Uncle Ben."

"What, well why the hell didn't you tell me that?" Terry threw her arms in the air looking at the confused child.

"Abby." Holly yelled again, this time from inside the house.

"Oh, shit." Terry looked at the back door.

"What's wrong?"

"The plan is not going well."

"But I don't know the plan."

"You don't need to know the plan. You just need to know that it's not going well...I don't think your mama would hit me." Terry paused, biting her lip. "Tisk," she shook her head briskly as she spoke. "But I can't take that chance. Gotta go kid."

"Abby!" Holly called again, this time much louder.

"But?" Abby said, looking toward the house, then at Terry's retreating back.

As Terry dodged from the corner of the yard, she looked over her shoulder to see a wide-eyed Abby looking up at her. "Shit," she mumbled and went back to Abby, squatting in front of her. "This is what you do; say 'Mommy, I don't remember.' Playing dumb works wonders. And you being a kid and all...well. Next you need to make your lip tremble, and try to cry before she spanks you, that usually makes us parents feel sorry for you. And for god sakes while you're in the throws of pain, please, please don't mention my name."

Terry ran around the side of the house, sprinting to her car. She nearly made it to the curb when she heard a voice call her name from the direction of the house. She stopped and turned, seeing Dee standing on the second step. "What are you doing here?" Dee asked.

"Damn," Terry whispered under her breath. She heaved a weighty sigh and walked to the steps looking up at Dee. "Hey. What's up? What'cha doing here?"

"I was on my way to get a manicure and I thought that Abby might like to come along."

"Wow." Terry grinned. Great, perfect timing. "A manicure? That sounds absolutely wonderful right now." She glanced up at the house, hoping Holly wouldn't hear them and come out. "I just saw Abby go around back. Why don't you go and wait in the car, I can go get her. I'll come with you guys; we can make an afternoon of it." Terry became more animated the longer she spoke. "Maybe get a pedicure, brow wax, the works. Spend some quality time together. Seven, eight hours should do it. What do you say?" Terry grabbed Dee's arm, gently pulling her down the steps.

"Hey," Dee said removing Terry's hand from her arm. "I wanted to go in and say hi to Holly."

"She's busy right now. I heard talk of a pest, and extermination, something like that. You can talk to her later."

"Let me just go in and say hi. Besides I have to go to the bathroom really bad," Dee said as she walked up the steps.

Terry looked heavenwards. "Lord, if you're listening, please don't make this be the day that I get my just dessert…And if it is, and I die, please make David have the worst case of hemorrhoids that mankind has ever suffered. Amen." She nodded her head quickly before walking up the steps and into the house.

Holly walked into the living room when she heard the front door open.

"Hey," Dee said then frowned at the look on Holly's face. "What's wrong?"

"I don't know," Holly said. "There are some strange things going on. I don't know who or why, but some shit is happening." She walked into the kitchen with Dee and Terry following.

"What kind of stuff?" Dee asked.

Dee and Terry sat at the kitchen table while Holly paced across the kitchen floor. "Okay, listen to this shit. I just found a card and rose in Abby's book bag."

Dee smiled, "Aw, that's so cute."

"The card said, 'You are breathtaking.'"

"Wow," Dee said. "Breathtaking."

"Sounds like she has a secret admirer," Terry said quickly.

"When the hell have you ever heard a 7-year-old say 'breathtaking'?"

"Maybe he's really smart, a genius even," Terry volunteered.

Holly glared at Terry and then said, "And at least two to three times a week I don't get my mail. It ends up in the guy next door's mailbox, and I end up with his."

"That just sounds like a mistake to me," Dee said.

"I spoke to the mail carrier, and she said that she's sure she's not mixing up the mail. But it keeps happening. Then there's the incident with the pizzas."

"What pizza incident?"

"You know how those pizza delivery people are," Terry said, trying to sway Holly.

"Terry was here with Keith. We ordered pizza and the guy didn't come. I called them, and they said that they didn't have our order. So, I placed the order again. An hour later here comes Tyler," as she said his name she shook her head, "With three pizzas, saying he'd gotten a pizza delivery and that the driver said it was for him and that it was paid for. About how he couldn't eat all of that pizza and wanted to give us two of them."

"Hmm, what's wrong with that?"

"Sounds like a charitable guy to me," Terry said.

"Nothing, but you add that to my flat tires and let us not forget the picnic lunch at the community picnic."

"Honey, I don't see what you're getting at."

"Something's going on. I haven't figured out the why yet, but I know…something's going on."

"No," Terry said, "Maybe you're just being paranoid."

"No-o," Holly said shaking her head.

"Dee, don't you think she's being paranoid?"

"I don't know, Terry, one thing, maybe two, but all the things that she mentioned couldn't possibly be coincidences."

Terry instinctively rolled her eyes at her cousin and turned back to Holly. "Reds, I think you're over-reacting."

"He seems like a nice enough guy," Dee said.

"Yeah, he's been doing a lot of things in the community, especially with the kids," Terry said. "He's even taking over coaching the Little League baseball team this summer. He made Abby team captain. You know how she's eating that crap up. It's not too often you meet a guy who's that good with kids. I don't know, I think he might be a catch."

"Ya know, Hol, she might be right. He does like Abby, and we all know how attracted you are to him."

Holly let that last statement go. "I don't know," she said, placing her hand under her chin, "He's a little too attentive toward Abby."

"What do you mean 'too attentive'?" Dee asked.

Terry had a sudden nervous feeling building in the pit of her stomach as she wated Holly.

Holly's brows furrowed in thought. "Why would he seem so preoccupied with her?"

Terry's eyes grew large. "Not preoccupied…Maybe he's trying to win you over?" she said quickly, her apprehension building by the moment. "You know a lot of men think that you need to win the child's heart before you win the mother's."

"That…" Holly clenched her teeth, her cheeks crimson, "Son of a bitch."

"What?" Terry and Dee asked simultaneously.

"I checked him out and he was clean, but that doesn't mean anything. This is just the sort of thing a child molester might do. They try to get close to the children, befriend the neighborhood kids."

Terry's eyes grew large. Oh, hell. "No, he's not a perv. You don't really think he's a perv, do you, Dee?"

"I don't know, Terry, what does a pervert look like? It does seem strange."

Terry brought her hands up, covering her eyes. "Oh, have mercy," she whispered.

"Do your really think something is going on?" Dee asked. They watched as Holly's nose flared and her face morphed into that of someone intent on murder. "Holly, Abby would tell you if anything ever happened to her."

"Yeah," Terry said quickly, feeling like she saw a light at the end of a very long, very dark tunnel.

"I'm going next door and I'm going to have a little

talk with Mr. Green," Holly said calmly.

"That's a good idea," Dee said.

"Nooo," Terry said at the same time.

"She should go talk to him," Dee was saying as Holly left the kitchen.

"The normal, rational Holly should, not the pissed-off, fire-breathing Holly," Terry replied. Then she leaned on the table, her face in her hands. She wracked her brain trying to think of something, anything that would fix the situation. She looked up to see Dee watching her with a strange look on her face. Taking a deep breath, she said, "Dee, I need to tell you something. I don't want you to jump to conclusions."

"Terry, I know you. What did you do?"

"Nothing. I mean not like you're thinking." She paused then said, "I've sort of been doing things to get Reds and Tyler together."

"You're kidding."

Terry shook her head. "Unfortunately not. Now I am so screwed. She's going to kill me. I know she is, I can feel it," Terry said breathlessly.

"Okay, exactly what did you do?"

"The pizzas, the flat tires…the ants in the picnic basket." She smiled sheepishly.

"You did the picnic basket thing?"

"I'm gonna go home and pack up me and the kids' things. Give me a minimal head start before you tell her. I'd say 10 or 15…months should be enough time."

"Terry, she's not going to kill you." Holly walked into the kitchen. She had gone upstairs to retrieve her holster and weapon, which she now wore. She walked across the room to the pantry, opened the door, and took out a metal baseball bat. Checking the weight, she shook her head, placed the bat back inside then picked up a much heavier wooden bat. She nodded, laid the bat next to the back door, closed the pantry door, and headed out of the kitchen.

Dee bit her lip then said, "Oh, my god. I don't know, maybe 15 months is not long enough." Seeing the look of utter fear cross Terry's face, Dee laughed. "I'm kidding."

Terry rested her forehead on the table. "This is not good."

"It'll be all right, we'll just tell her the truth."

"Hell no we won't! Are you crazy?"

"So we're just going to let her go over there and beat the hell out of an innocent man."

"He looks like he's strong enough, and he's probably pretty agile. I'm sure he can handle himself."

"Terry."

"Damn, Dee, I was only trying to help. I didn't mean anything by it. I just want Reds to be with this guy. I think he would be good for her. I just want her to be happy."

Dee was thoughtful. "Terry, I know you do. I do, too."

"I should have just minded my damn business. I go feeling sorry for people and this is what I get. I knew that that kid would be the death of me," Terry said more to herself.

"Abby? Abby's in on this?"

"Yeah. No, not really…well, kinda."

Dee laughed, "This is great, you teamed up with a 7-year-old to help get a crazy woman who was once your mortal enemy a man."

"Well, it sounds really stupid when you say it." Terry heaved a heavy sigh, and then said, "Dee, you can't tell Reds that Abby helped me. There's no sense in both me and the kid dying."

Dee continued to laugh. "Don't worry about it, it will be okay."

Holly walked into the kitchen wearing a pair of dark blue sweatpants and a black sweatshirt with her hair in a ponytail.

"I need you guys to stay with Abby for a while," Holly said, her voice eerily calm.

"Holly, sit down, I have to talk to you."

"I have to go." Terry stood quickly.

"Terry, sit down," Dee demanded. Terry looked at Dee then Holly before sitting slowly. "Hol, I'm going to tell you something. I don't want you to be upset." Dee took a deep breath. "I did it."

"Did what?"

"Everything, the mail, flat tire, the works."

"What? What the hell is wrong with you?"

"Before you start yelling, listen to me." Dee raised her hands palms out. "I did it because I thought it might get you and Tyler together."

"Dee, have you lost your mind?"

"No."

"Then why would you do that? I told you I wasn't interested in him."

"Yeah, but you don't act like it." She placed a hand over Holly's. "Whenever you see him you look like a love-struck puppy."

"I do not," Holly denied.

"Yes, you do. I was just trying to help you get over the hurdle that you placed in front of yourself."

"I didn't—"

"Yes, you did. Holly, you said yourself that you think you might be ready. Now you have someone that you're really interested in. Take the time to get to know him. If it doesn't work out, then I promise I'll let it go." Holly looked at her like she didn't believe her. Dee held up her hand. "I promise."

"Girl, I swear, if you weren't pregnant."

"Yeah, I know. You'd kick my ass. Promises, promises," Dee said, rising from the table and walking to the refrigerator to forage for food. Dee glanced back meeting Terry's relieved gaze.

"Thanks," Terry mouthed. Dee winked back. She grabbed a bottle of water and an orange from the fridge and sat down again at the table.

"So," Terry said, "Are you and Tyler going out next week?"

"I don't know, he hasn't asked me yet."

"You guys have reservations at La Lan for next Saturday," Terry said, and then she paused, meeting Holly's gaze and quickly added, "Um…Dee told me."

"Uh, yeah, I told her," Dee interjected.

Holly looked at first Terry and then Dee, "Sure you did."

"Anyway," Dee said, "What are you gonna wear? I think you should wear that new green silk top you just got. It'll bring out your eyes."

"No, she should wear red. She'll be hot," Terry said.

"Red is for love. Red is good," Dee agreed.

"I don't like red," Holly said, her statement going unnoticed.

"Oh, yeah, like a sexy siren." Terry nodded. "Or better yet, something slutty. I saw the perfect dress in Nordstrom's the other day."

Holly laughed and then said, "Hmmm, slutty? Uh, no."

"Slutty is in, right, Dee?"

"Oh, um, I don't know, she might give him the wrong impression and scare him away."

"No she won't. That way she can hook him right away and reel him in."

"It's just a date, guys," Holly reminded them.

"And," Terry went on, "If she wears something sluttish…hmm, it might make him hot, too. Do you think they'll make it back here before they do it?" She wiggled her brows when she said "it."

"I don't know," Dee said, laughing. "They might do 'it' on the table in the restaurant."

Holly groaned. "I swear, I don't know why I hang out with you two."

"'Cause you love us," Terry answered quickly.

"'Cause we're fun," Dee added.

"No, seriously," Holly said, sighing and shaking her head

Chapter Eighteen

Holly checked her reflection in the mirror, turning from left to right, and than left again. She adjusted the front of the red v-neck dress she wore and she ran her hands through her hair, fluffing it more. She opened her jewelry box to select a thin, gold chain and small hoop earrings. When she went to lay out her clothes for the evening, she was torn between wearing the red dress Dee and Terry insisted she had to have and a simple white blouse and slacks. Then she threw caution to the wind and selected the red dress. She had to admit she looked fabulous. She even wore her sexy red panties and bra. She laughed to herself: Dee and Terry would be proud.

After Dee had confessed to her scheme to get Holly and Tyler together, Holly, Terry and Dee gathered up the kids and went to the mall in search of the perfect date outfit. Holly couldn't believe that she didn't figure out what was happening sooner. Everything that happened had had classic Terry written all over it. And under different circumstances Holly would have been pissed, but she knew that Terry only meant well. She would have told Terry that, but she knew she'd have a better chance of Dee fasting for a week than getting

Terry to admit what she had done. When the doorbell rang, her stomach did a quick flip-flop. She crossed the room, slipped on three-inch black strappy sandals, and took a deep breath. Then she walked downstairs to answer the door.

Tyler straightened his burgundy, geometric-print tie and brushed down the lapel of his charcoal gray suit before ringing the doorbell. When Holly answered the door, he hesitated and then smiled. If possible, she looked even more radiant. "Good evening, beautiful." He stepped inside the house and gave her two yellow roses tied together with a white ribbon. "I found this on my stoop this afternoon with a note that said that I was supposed to give the roses to you this evening."

Holly took the roses, smelled them and then smiled. "Terry. Sit tight, while I take these into the kitchen and then I'll be ready to leave." While Holly was in the kitchen putting the flowers in a vase, she explained to Tyler Terry's plan to bring them together.

When she walked back into the living room Tyler was grinning at her. "You have some—interesting friends."

"You have no idea," Holly said, picking up a small black purse from the table next to the door and waiting as Tyler opened the door for her.

She raised her eyebrows at him as she walked through. "Your aunt taught you your manners well, I've noticed."

"That's right," Tyler grinned. "She told me to always make sure I opened doors for gorgeous women." He took her arm politely and led her down the sidewalk before opening the car door and helping her in.

As they drove, Holly tried to shake the awkward

feeling left over from her misunderstanding of Tyler. Watching him in the glow of the dashboard lights, she wondered how she could have thought for a second that he was a sexual predator interested in her daughter. He'd been nothing but kind and honest with her since she'd met him, and she felt like she'd betrayed him by even considering what she had. He turned and smiled at her warmly.

"You're quiet tonight. Should we have brought Abby along for conversation?"

"No, she probably would have just chattered our ears off. And I don't know if she would have really been into Le Lan's style of cuisine. Pizza is more her speed." Suddenly, she blurted, "I'm sorry."

"For what?" he asked in surprise.

"I thought...I mean, Terry's plan...I thought it was you trying to arrange the whole thing. I was, um, kind of weirded out there for a little while."

Instead of getting angry, Tyler laughed loudly. "I'm glad you told me. If I had gotten your mail one more time, I told myself I was going to sit you down and have a good, long talk about how you didn't have to play games with me. And then I was going to ask you out."

"You thought it was me?!"

"Why not? I'm irresistible." He flashed her a toothy grin.

She punched him lightly in the shoulder, feeling better. The rest of the ride passed quickly, and it seemed like no time at all before they were getting out of the car in valet parking. Seeing the restaurant, Holly was glad she'd chosen the red dress. Through the moon-shaped window, she could see that Le Lan was full of beautiful, sophisticated couples.

She and Tyler were led back to a small, private table. After she sat down in the chair the maitre d' pulled out for her, she ordered a glass of white wine, and Tyler asked for a bottle of Pinot Grigio. Holly watched him with interest; the man knew his wine, too.

The entrée items on the menu were a mix of French and Vietnamese cuisine. Holly peered over the top of her menu at Tyler. "What looks good to you?"

"Would you like me to order for both of us?"

Normally, Holly would have preferred to order her own meal, and in the past if any of her dates had ever tried to do it for her, she would have laughed in their faces. But this was Tyler. She was curious to see whether she'd like what he picked out.

He was right on the mark. Holly thought she might have to fight him for the last wild mushroom dumpling appetizer, but their dinners arrived just in time.

"How did I do?" Tyler asked, as she took her first bite of pork tenderloin.

She just closed her eyes, shook her head, and took another bite. "Mmmm. Less talk, more eating." But they did talk, and by the time Holly noticed the maitre d' throwing them dirty looks, she realized they'd been there for two hours.

"We'd better go," she whispered, nodding her head toward the man, who was staring in the direction of their table. "They're going to kick us out." She was a little tipsy from the wine, and couldn't remember ever having such a great time.

The two of them giggled like kids as Tyler paid the bill.

When they left the restaurant, Tyler took Holly's hand. "Walk with me?" She smiled at him nodding. He led her half a block down Clark to Chestnut and then they made a right at Chestnut, walking a couple blocks to Michigan Ave. Tyler led her to Ghirardelli Chocolate Shop and found a table in the corner. Tyler went to the counter to place and pick up their order. He ordered the Butterscotch Fudge Sundae, which has butter pecan ice cream, butterscotch sauce, almond nuggets, hot fudge sauce, whipped cream, almonds, and a cherry, for them to share, and two decaf coffees. When Tyler walked back to the table with the tray, Holly's eyes grew large.

"Gee, that's some sundae."

"Yeah, it is. I was thinking that we can maybe bring Abby here sometimes, but I'm thinking with all this sugar we might be peeling her off the ceiling."

Holly laughed. "Yeah, you're right. You know, I like that you think about Abby, and doing things with her. She needs that. Ben does things with her, he's great, but you know…Thanks."

"Abby's a great kid, and I like doing things with her." He looked into Holly's eyes. "I like spending time with her mother as well."

Something inside her twisted at his words. She put her hand over his large, warm one where it rested on the table. "Her mom likes spending time with you, too." Immediately, he turned his hand over and laced his fingers with hers.

Cool it, girl. It's just hand-holding. Don't get so turned on. But that was easier said than done when his rough fingertips were making small circles on the soft, sensitive underside of her wrist.

Holly and Tyler spent another hour just learning about each other: their childhoods, careers, best moments, tragedies, and dreams for the future. Finally, in a pause during the conversation, Tyler lifted Holly's hand from the table and looked at her watch. "We'd better head home, Cinderella. It's almost your curfew." She was amazed to find that it was almost midnight and the employees were mopping floors and ringing out the cash registers.

Conversation wound down during the ride home, but the silence was a comfortable one. When they reached Holly's house, Tyler walked around the vehicle, opened the door for Holly and walked her to the front door. "I had a great time this evening," Holly said.

"I did, too." Tyler closed the small gap between them.

Closing her eyes, Holly tilted her head up as he leaned forward. A surprisingly gentle kiss brushed her lips, and she felt his fingers lightly touch her cheek.

Forcing himself to walk casually from the porch and over to his house, Tyler couldn't believe he'd had the strength to turn away. But he thought this was the best thing. At least for the time being. He didn't just want to have a relationship with Holly, he wanted to share his life with her. One day he wanted Holly, Abby and himself to be a family, and he was going to take things slow and make that happen.

Holly's eyes popped open and she watched speechlessly as Tyler left the porch. She frowned, slightly confused as she watched him walk across the yard. He turned back to her. "How about Monday morning after your run, I make breakfast for you and Abby before you leave for work?"

Holly licked her lips before saying, "That would be wonderful."

He nodded. "'Nite."

"Goodnight."

• • •

All Sunday, when she didn't hear from him, Holly told herself that it had just been so long since she'd gone on a date, that she'd read too much into her and Tyler's night out. The last thing she expected early Monday morning was to find him on her front porch, smiling that devastating smile, with two grocery bags full of food.

"Can I come in?" he asked holding the bags up for her inspection. "I brought food."

She stepped back, and he headed for the kitchen. The man was crazy. Cooking for her and her daughter first thing in the morning when she knew that they both had to work that day.

Pretty soon, the mouthwatering scent of frying bacon filled the house, and Tyler was telling Holly about his latest run-in with his cousin at his aunt's house on Sunday, when Abby came running down the stairs. "Mr. Tyler! What are you doing here?"

Tyler grinned, pointing to the apron he was wearing—a purple one that obviously belonged to Holly. "Your mom forgot how to cook breakfast, so I'm teaching her. Do you like homemade pancakes?"

"That sounds great! But I heard Aunt Terry telling Aunt Dee on the phone that she was hoping Mommy would be cooking you breakfast on Sunday morning. Did Mommy forget how that day too?"

Holly's face reddened and Tyler tried to choke back a chuckle. Their eyes met over the little girl's head, and they both started laughing.

Chapter Nineteen

Pulling his car into the garage, Tyler turned off the ignition and rested his head on the headrest for a moment. It had been a very shitty day. At work, things were not only physically but mentally demanding. Then when he got off he went to see his aunt, only to have Yvette finally hoist her lazy ass out of bed at 6 p.m., come to the kitchen, and stay throughout his entire visit with Aunt Jos. She had sat at the table to his left and interjected something about everything that he'd said. And every time he looked at her she'd give him her sneaky shit-eating grin. She was, in her subtle way, antagonizing him, and it made him want to jump across the table and choke the shit out of her.

Grabbing his gym bag, he went into the house and dropped his bag next to the door leading from the garage into the kitchen. He went into the living room, turned on the stereo and stopped at the front window to watch Holly as she retrieved the mail from the box. Abby came running across the street, and Holly stopped at the end of the walk, looking around waiting for Abby to catch up. She said something to the child, her body language looking as if she were scolding her daughter. Probably reprimanding her for running in the street without looking first, Tyler thought.

She was beautiful in her floral dress with her hair hanging down her back. From this distance, Tyler could see her freckles, made darker from the summer sun. Over the weekend, he'd taken Holly and Abby to the movies. They'd had a great time, laughing and joking. It felt perfect, felt natural. And he could tell that Abby liked him, she asked him a lot of questions about his job and his family. As the evening progressed, he felt like he and Holly were getting closer, then suddenly she seemed to shut down. He could almost see her pull away. He had noticed it happen almost every time they were together. He glanced at his watch, checking the time, and then crossed the room to pick up the phone and dial her number.

"Hello?"

"Hi. How are you?"

"I'm good."

"Have you guys had dinner yet?"

"No. I was going to heat up some meatloaf. If you'd like to—"

"I was thinking that I could take you guys to dinner."

"I—"

"If you like, we could go down to Kitsch'n's. It's a nice place for kids and the food's good."

"Um, sure. That would be fun. Give us half an hour."

"See you then."

After showering, Tyler chose an olive tee and a pair of jeans. Slipping on a pair of brown sandals, he hurried downstairs, grabbing his keys on the way out the door.

Once they were seated, the server immediately brought them their menus, and after bringing them drinks, took their orders. Abby ordered chicken fingers and curly fries, and both Holly and Tyler ordered the Chipotle Bar-B-Que Ribs.

As they waited for their food to arrive, Abby couldn't seem to sit still. Her fidgeting and constant turning around to look at everyone in the restaurant and moving everything on the table was starting to get on Holly's nerves, which were practically shredded after a particularly irritating confrontation with her boss that day. That, combined with her conflicting feelings about Tyler, had her temper close to snapping. When Abby started messing with the napkin dispenser again, Holly didn't mean to take the events of the day out on her daughter, but her tone still came out sharp.

"I told you to knock that off, Abby. Sit still, now."

Abby, gave her a wounded look and mumbled, "Mommy, you're grumpy tonight."

Before she could say anything, Tyler stepped in. "Abby, you know how hard your mom works, right?"

"Yes," Abby said, still in a sulk.

"Well, she has bad days just like you do. You remember how you were telling me about that fight you and Paige had last week?" Holly watched as her daughter nodded. "Remember how your mom didn't get mad at you when you slammed the door and knocked that picture off the wall? And how she asked you what was wrong and talked to you about it?" Abby dropped her head, picking her nails as she nodded again.

"That's your mom's way of respecting and loving

you, and when it looks like she's had a bad day, she deserves that same respect and love from you."

Abby looked up at Holly, her eyes big and serious. "I'm sorry, Mommy. Was your day really bad?"

Holly felt her heart twist a little as she hugged Abby and met Tyler's eyes over her little girl's head. Damn, but this man was getting to her.

• • •

At 1 p.m. all of the patients got a break for an hour. Janet decided to go down to the unit library. She walked purposefully to the library with her eyes straight ahead and a bounce in her step that wasn't there a few weeks ago. She walked down the aisle, first picking up a book on poetry, then selecting two large art books. She carried them, holding them close to her breast. Scanning the bookshelves, she ran her fingers along the books. Then turning down the next isle, she casually glanced over her shoulder before she made her way down the health isle. She quickly scanned the titles. Finding the book she wanted, she picked it up and placed it on top of the other books. She walked to the corner of the library, took a seat with her back against the wall and opened one of the art books. Then she opened the book with the names of medicines and laid it inside the art book. Going down the list, she looked up the many drugs that she was required to take. She had a plan; now all she had to do was set everything in motion. Her plan was to drug one of the staff nurses, dress the victim in her clothes and then change into the nurse's outfit and get the hell out of here. Ben was waiting for her, she knew he was, and time was running short.

She went down the list of medications she was being given. She looked in the medication reference dictionary under A for the first medication, Amytrip-toline. *Let's see, I take 100 milligrams two times a day.* She read that with high doses above 50 milligrams it could cause sedation, nausea and vomiting. She started to giggle because if she gave someone her 100 milligrams of Amytriptoline that would knock them out. Hmm…how am I going to get her to take the pill? Instantly she realized that she could dissolve it in a liquid such as a soft drink. Yes, it could be done. She thought of what other pill she took that she could mix with the Amytriptoline to make a potent potion. She now looked under H for Haldol. She took 50 milligrams twice a day…why was she on this drug anyway… "Hallucinations, combativeness…" And what were the side effects, she looked for them quickly, her eyes scanning the page, her heart beating faster.

A cold sweat broke out on her forehead and behind her neck, yet she felt flushed. She was actually getting excited about what she needed to do. This was the most alive she had felt in a long time. The last time she felt anything at all was when Ben came to see her, and that was a few weeks ago. She squirmed in her seat, trying to contain her excitement. Both her medications were covered with a hard covering so she would have time to pouch one of them. She knew she could get away with it because she had a flap of skin in her left cheek alongside her molar where she could push the pill. Then as soon as she got back to her seat she would spit it out in a piece of her napkin and stick it in her pocket. It would be so easy and none of these fools would be the wiser. Smiling to herself, she closed the dictionary. While putting the book back on the shelf she found herself humming.

Chapter Twenty

At 4 p.m. the first shift of nurses and all the doctors had already been gone for half an hour, and the new shift of nurses was on. They were the same old faces, except she noticed that Melissa M. was still working. She casually crossed the room. "Hi. I see you all over the place here; it seems like you never go home."

Melissa looked up smiling. "Hello, Janet. Sometimes it feels like I'm here every minute. I'm doing 12-hour shifts, rotating days and nights. This week I am on days and next week I will be on nights, so you won't see me until 7 p.m. next week."

"I'm not complaining, you're one of the nicer people on staff here." Then tilting her head she asked, "What made you decide to be a nurse in a place like this?"

"I was tired of all the med-surge nursing and wanted to get into something less bloody," Melissa stated as she made eye contact with Janet. Janet saw warmth and caring in the light brown eyes of the other woman. She also saw something else. Trust.

"Well, there are some bloody moments around here, let me tell you!" Janet laughed to herself.

"Yes, there are a few, but it will be nothing compared to the other type of nursing."

"Well, you have to be careful here." Janet took a conspiratorial look around then whispered, "You have to keep your head up and always watch your back. There is a lot going on here you could miss. You could get hurt like I did."

"Bonnie said that you fell?"

Janet glanced around again. "The staff can't be everywhere, and they can't protect everyone. And sometimes it can be…dangerous to talk too much. You seem like a nice person. Just be careful."

Melissa looked like she wanted to ask more questions, but bit her lip and then nodded. "Thanks, Janet."

Janet smiled at her and knew she had her victim, as long as she played it cool.

Halfway through dinner, at the far south side of the room the top half of a door opened and a nurse called out the patients' names one at a time. They were expected to walk up to the half-door and take their medications in front of the nurse on the other side of the door. There was always another nurse who stood outside the half-door watching to make sure the patient took all of her medications. Mouth checks were done before the patient could leave the area.

Janet watched others go up to get their medications. Most of the time it was a smooth transition, but occasionally a patient would refuse to take their medications and would start to scream and yell that they had rights. Yes, they did have rights, or so she was told, but if they did, damn if anyone seemed to care. And she sure didn't care. All she cared about right now was getting the hell out of there.

They called the patient by room number so Janet knew she would be called shortly. Knowing that her room would be called next she edged her way toward the med room. "Janet Summers." When they called her name, she was right at the door with her left arm extended so the nurse could identify her identification band.

"That's you, Janet. How are you feeling today? I heard you had a nasty bruise on your head. Where'd you get it from?" the med nurse asked.

Janet blinked at the other woman. You want to make small talk now? "I tripped and fell, hitting my head. Can I have my medication now so I can get back to my seat?"

"Here you go, Janet. Are you sure you tripped?"

Janet glared at the woman and downed her pills with a whole cup of water. She placed the Styrofoam cup back on the counter and without even looking at the nurse standing beside her she rushed back to her seat. No one stopped her; they knew she would swallow all of her pills. She always did.

Chapter Twenty-one

Before going to his aunt's house Tyler called to see if Yvette was home. After his last visit when she was there, he thought it would be best to call first and make sure she was out. Part of him felt really immature and petty for doing such a thing, but he knew that if he didn't do this, Yvette would just continue to push him and push him until he reached his limit and he would end up in prison.

Tyler knocked on the front door, and a moment later his aunt appeared.

"Hi, baby."

"Hi, Aunt Jos." He stepped inside the house and gave her a hug. "How are you?"

"I'm fine. Come on in the kitchen, I'll make us a cup of coffee."

Tyler followed his aunt to the kitchen. He looked into the living room and saw boxes stacked in the corner. "You're collecting clothes for the church charity drive?"

"No," she said sighing. "Those boxes belong to Roland."

"Roland?"

"Yvette's new boyfriend. He asked me if he could store those until he gets a new place."

"Aunt Jos, you should have told him no. You know as soon as Yvette gets a chance she's going to have him moved in here.

"Rashard told me the same thing. But Yvette said it was only going to be for a week or two."

"How long has it been?"

"A little more than a week."

Tyler nodded. "If this becomes a problem, you call me."

She nodded. "So, how has my favorite nephew been?"

"I've been good,"

"Home ownership really agrees with you, you look great."

Tyler grinned and said, "I met someone,"

Jos sat up straight and leaned on the table, "You have?"

"Yes, ma'am."

"So tell me about her."

"Her name is Holly. She's a police officer, and she has a 7-year-old daughter, Abby. Holly is beautiful, funny, and smart. And Abby is a great kid."

"Where'd you meet her?"

"She's my neighbor."

Jos rose from the table, went to the counter and got two cups. "Is she divorced?"

"No, she's a widow; her husband was a police officer as well."

"Oh, that's sad." She carried the cups to the table and sat across from Tyler.

"Aunt Jos, I really care about Holly, and I want

you to meet her. I was thinking that next weekend you and Rashard could come over for dinner. I could invite Abby and Holly."

"I don't see why not. That sounds fun."

Tyler tapped the side of the cup, "Aunt Jos, can you do me a favor?"

"Sure."

"Please, don't bring Yvette.

"I know there's a lot of tension between you two—"

"That's putting it mildly."

"But, she is your family."

"I know, Aunt Jos, and family will always love you."

"Yes, family will always love you…but that doesn't mean that you have to like all of them. Okay, I won't bring her. But, Tyler, are you ready for this? I mean are you prepared to take on a readymade family?"

"Aunt Jos, you had one. When you and Uncle Tim got married, Yvette was already living with you."

"Yes and you see how that worked out." Jocelyn had married her second husband, Alvin Winchester, six months before Tyler had moved in with her. Tyler loved his uncle, and he loved to watch him with his Aunt Jos. Seeing them together showed him what a loving relationship was. That was until his uncle ran to the store for cigarettes one afternoon, telling Jos he'd be right back. They didn't see him until seven months later when he'd showed up at their stoop asking Jos to forgive him and asking her to take him back. When she refused, Alvin moved in with a woman ten years his senor who lived less than a mile away. When Tyler had gotten older he had heard rumors that during the seven months that Alvin had disappeared that he'd been staying with the same woman and that his aunt knew where his uncle was staying. That when he walked away she said good riddance to him and never looked back.

"Aunt Jos, I'm not Uncle Alvin. When you took me in, you loved me and raised me as your own. You taught me what love is. I love Abby and I would never turn my back on her." Jos reached across the table, squeezing Tyler's hand.

"Who's Abby?" Yvette said standing in the kitchen door.

Chapter Twenty-two

Since she had not been taking all of her medication, Janet felt as if she was becoming more alert, more herself. She was able to think things through, plan things more precisely. She watched everyone and everything.

Lying in bed Janet thought about the pills that she had tucked in the seam of her mattress. Five little pills, three Amytriptoline and two Haldol are what she had. She didn't need that many really, only a few would do, but she'd started making a game out of seeing if she could manage to hide the pills without getting caught. And she did fine until one day the nurse who checked the patient's mouths to be sure that they swallowed their medication thought she'd seen something in Janet's mouth. When Janet turned to walk away, the nurse had called her back. Janet quickly swallowed the pill, and then turned to the nurse opening her mouth. The nurse peered in Janet's mouth, nodded, and sent Janet on her way.

She initially had ten pills, five of each, but a week ago she decided now would be the time to repay her friend the barbarian bitch. Janet would keep an eye on the barbarian whenever she could, partially she wanted to be sure that freak didn't sneak up on her again, but Janet also wanted to get an idea of the sort of person she was. Janet needed to know these things so she could devise her plan of attack. For the most part the barbarian lived up to the stereotype of her namesakes. She would rape and pillage the village or the hospital as best she could without being caught. She would sneak into other patient's rooms and steal, try to take their food and bully them whenever she felt like it. A few weeks ago, Janet entered the lounge and scanned the area for a place to sit. She spotted a seat by the nurses' station that was separated from the others. When she finally reached her seat and sat down the barbarian approached her.

"Listen, chick, that's my seat! So get out of it now."

Janet looked up at the woman standing over her. "Look, bitch, you haven't been in this seat in the past ten minutes, the amount of time it took me to get here. This is not high school and you don't own anything around here. Go find another seat because I am not getting up," Janet growled.

The barbarian looked at her, stunned. She looked around as if she were not sure what she should do. "Well?" Janet asked. The other woman's eyes shifted briefly then she walked to the other side of the room and sat down between two husky women who shifted nervously when they saw her approaching. She hadn't bothered Janet much after that other than to glare and make nasty remarks.

But Janet hadn't forgotten the attack in the hallway. One of the obvious things that Janet had seen was that the barbarian liked to eat. And she especially liked sweets. One day while they were having dinner Janet chose a cupcake for dessert. She moved from her usual seat to the table closer to the barbarian, not the same table of course, but one table away. Not close enough to be within reach but close enough for the barbarian to see what Janet was doing. Janet laid her napkin on the table and then watching out of the corner of her eye she made sure that the barbarian was observing her. She picked up her cupcake and placed it on the napkin, wrapped the cupcake in the napkin and placed it in her lap.

Janet smiled to herself when she noticed that the barbarian watched her intently for the remainder of their meal like the rabid animal that she was. Then with the cupcake sitting in her lap, Janet pushed a few of the pills inside of it. She took her tray back and left the dining room, then she walked down the hall slowly enough to give the barbarian time to catch up to her.

"Give me that cupcake, girl," the other woman said, grabbing Janet's shoulder and spinning her around. Janet held the napkin to her breast as if she were trying to keep the other woman from taking it. "I said, give it to me," the barbarian demanded, snatching the cupcake and pushing Janet against the wall at the same time. She shoved the cupcake in her mouth paper and all. Janet glared at her, pushed past her and walked down the hall. Janet heard the barbarian laughing as she made her way to her room, but the other woman did not know that Janet was laughing harder. Later that evening the barbarian was taken out of the institution via ambulance. Janet didn't know what happened. She didn't ask. She didn't care. She only knew that that evening in the hallway was the last time she ever saw the barbarian.

Now it was time to lay out the rest of her plan. She

knew that another good time for her to carry things out would be around 11:45 p.m., because the new shift would be coming on and they would be trying to read up on the patients at that time. A distraction would work nicely so that she could sneak out with the nurse's keys. The last two times Melissa worked the evening shift Janet had asked her to come to her room. When Melissa arrived, Janet asked if she could get them a cranberry juice. When Melissa returned with the juices, they sat and talked. It was only for a short time, 10 minutes, or so, but it was enough for Janet. In that short amount of time, Janet felt that she'd won more of Melissa's trust. Janet had told her about being attacked in the hall and who'd attacked her. She said that she didn't trust anyone enough to tell them what had happened. No one except Melissa. Janet had said she was afraid that if she told someone else that she would ultimately get hurt. She also told Melissa she saw the way Lloyd seemed to become more alert when Melissa was close by, and that she thought Melissa should be more careful. What most people didn't seem to notice was that if anyone looked Lloyd in the eye, brushed or touched him in any way, and then looked him in the eye again, it would sometimes set him off. She'd seen it several times and had made the connection.

Her observation of Lloyd's actions was one way she'd won Melissa's trust. Melissa would always talk to Lloyd, and she always made eye contact with him. A few days after Janet's warning Janet saw Melissa making her rounds in the break room. Janet moved closer to where Lloyd was sitting, waiting until precisely the right moment. Melissa had looked at Lloyd, said good morning, looked down, and placed crackers and apple juice on the table in front of him. Just then, Janet walked behind his chair, gently brushing the back of his neck as she did so. When Melissa looked up, she met Lloyd's gaze again and smiled. That was all it took. He jumped up and lunged. Janet practically screamed for help before the man touched Melissa, and from that day on, Melissa seemed to love Janet.

Next week Melissa would be working the night shift. Janet would ask Melissa to come in her room again, and while she was there Janet would ask if she could get two cranberry juices. When Melissa brought them to the room, she would ask Melissa to go back and get some cold bubbly ginger ale to make a cocktail. While Melissa was gone, she could mix the crushed drugs in her cranberry juice. She would act as if she were just opening her juice when Melissa returned, mix up the cocktails and she'd be free.

"Yes. What a grand idea. Soon, Benji, we'll be together soon."

Janet lay awake most of the night thinking about her plan and how she would execute it. Smiling to herself she finally fell asleep some time past midnight.

• • •

Tyler was feeling a little déjà vu. It was another Sunday afternoon, the house was filled with the mouth-watering smell of roasting meat (a delicately-seasoned chicken this time) and the doorbell was ringing, announcing the arrival of visitors.

Rashard stood with Aunt Jos on the front steps, carrying a bakery box with an apple pie in it, and wearing a huge grin. Aunt Jos stepped up and gave Tyler a hug. She immediately asked, "Where's that adorable Abby at?"

"Not here yet, Aunt Jos. She and Holly had to run

some errands, but they'll be by as soon as they're finished. Come on in—I'll take that, Rashard."

"You look right at home in that apron," his cousin teased, punching him on the shoulder lightly as he looked around the living room. It was still light on furnishings, Tyler hadn't found the right sofa and armchair yet, but he'd decorated it using what he had. "Nice place you got here, bro. Yvette would shit a brick if she could see this—you know how jealous that girl gets."

Tyler rolled his eyes. "You managed to leave her at home, for which I'm extremely grateful, so let's not even bring her up. Come on in to the kitchen, and I'll get you guys something to drink."

They'd barely settled around the kitchen table when the front door flew open. "Mr. Tyler, Mr. Tyler!" came Abby's excited voice from the living room. "We saw the coolest puppy today, but I haven't talked Mommy into getting him yet." The little girl flew into the room like a bullet and attached herself to Tyler's leg.

Holly walked in after her, shaking her head. "Sorry to barge in like that. Abby, haven't I told you that the polite thing to do is knock before you blow somebody's door off its hinges?"

"Sorry, Mommy."

Abby hung her head, but smiled when Aunt Jos winked at her. The older woman opened her arms. "Can I have one of those hugs?" Abby looked at Jos, and then at Tyler. He nodded that it was okay, then she went to Jos, who gave Abby a warm hug.

"Abby, Holly, I'd like you to meet my Aunt Jocelyn, and my irritating cousin Rashard."

"Hi, Auntie Jos. Hello, Mr. Rashard," Abby said politely. "It's nice to meet you."

"It's nice to meet such a good friend of Tyler's," Rashard said to Abby. "I've heard a lot about you."

"Nice to meet you, Jocelyn, Rashard," Holly said, shaking both their hands. "We've heard a lot about you." Rashard gave Holly a silly look and she laughed. "All good, of course."

"Well guys, anybody hungry for some roast chicken?" Tyler asked. "Abby, will you set the table for me, honey? You know where the plates and everything are. Holly, can you help me dish everything up?"

Tyler missed the look that Rashard and his Aunt Jos exchanged. "They'd make a good family, wouldn't they?" Rashard whispered to his aunt over the clatter of dishes.

"Yes, they would," she whispered back, smiling. "I'm beginning to think Tyler knows exactly what's best for him after all."

Chapter Twenty-three

Pushing the car remote Janet walked through the rows of cars frantically searching for a light that would let her know which car was Melissa's. She needed to find the car and get out of there in a hurry. Her heart raced as she looked right and left, periodically glancing over her shoulder at the building. Her escape plan had been working like a charm—it was going smoothly until Melissa started getting drowsy. Then she did the unexpected and tried to run from the room. Janet realized what she intended a moment after the woman lunged for the door, and Janet grabbed her, wrestled her to the floor and tried to cover the woman's mouth with her hand. Melissa tried to scream for help but her scream was more like a moan. Janet knew just one scream wouldn't bring the staff running to investigate. There was always screaming, moaning, or wailing in this place. Even in her weakened state, Melissa tried to fight Janet off, pushing at Janet's hand and trying to call for help.

Janet quickly rose up slightly and rammed her left knee into Melissa's stomach. Air rushed from Melissa's lungs leaving her momentarily stunned. Janet scrambled away from the woman and grabbed a pillow from the bed, then she dropped back down on top of Melissa. She struggled with her while she held the pillow over Melissa's face. To Janet it seemed like it took forever for the woman to stop moving. But it couldn't have been very long when Janet moved the pillow and looked down at the blank staring eyes of Melissa M.

Janet knew she couldn't waste time. She quickly stripped Melissa, dressing her in yellow pajamas and then slipping on the nurse's uniform and shoes. The shoes were a little big so she had to tie them extra tight to keep them from flopping when she walked and possibly draw attention. After laying Melissa on the bed she turned her to face the wall, covered her with the blanket and turned off the lights. Peeking into the hall, she looked both ways and then walked from the room leaving the door partially open. She forced herself to stroll down the hall in that casual easygoing way Melissa did. If she ran, she would draw attention to herself. She made her way down the hall to the stairway and unlocked the door, instead of taking the front entrance and walking past the nurse's desk. After walking down what seemed like a million steps she was on the first floor and made her way out of a side door.

She'd found the car parked between a gray Honda Civic and a black Dodge Dakota. A bright red 2004 Ford Windstar. Janet grimaced, that twit would have to have a vehicle that was going to look like a bright red bullet flying down the road. She pressed the button on the remote to unlock the door and slid behind the wheel. She started the car and drove toward what she thought would be the exit of the parking lot and freedom.

After driving for an hour and an half Janet

searched the glove box and found Melissa's registration card with her address. She drove to Melissa's house. The tiny house was tucked in the corner at the end of a narrow one-way street with the surrounding houses all too close together. Janet knew that it wouldn't be safe to hide here. She knew that once the police found Melissa this would be one of the first places they checked when they realized that the van was missing. She just hoped they didn't find her until the morning. That would give Janet time to look around and find some essentials. It was almost 2 a.m. and most of the lights in the houses were off.

Janet slid from behind the wheel watching for movement before she walked toward the house. She tried several keys before she found the right one then slipped inside the house. She quickly crossed the room to draw the shades and then went from room to room checking out each and searching for Melissa's bedroom. She opened the closet door and selected a pair of black slacks and a white button-down blouse, throwing them on the bed. Then she searched the bottom of the closet for shoes. Not finding anything that wouldn't slip off she decided to keep the nursing shoes. She scanned the clothes hanging in the closet and picked out two more pairs of pants and two more tops, throwing them on the bed as well. She searched the room for money and didn't find any. Going into the kitchen, she searched the cabinets and didn't find anything. She turned to lean against the counter and saw a colorful pottery jar on the center of the table with the words "shoe fund" written on the front. She grabbed the jar, pulled off the top and reached inside to pull out eight one-dollar bills. In the bottom of the jar was at least $30 in change. "I can't believe this is all she has."

Sighing, Janet shoved the money inside the jar, taking it with her to the bedroom. Then searching the room she found a green overnight bag and put two of the blouses, and two pairs of pants inside along with the jar of money. She searched the room once more finding an 8- by 10-inch black metal box with a small padlock on it. She dropped the box on the bed, got on her knees and jerked the padlock several times trying to see if the box would open. Then looking at the dresser she rose quickly and rummaged through a container that held little miscellaneous items. She chose a bobby pin and went back to the bed and tried to open the box again.

"Damn it," she whispered, and then rising to her feet, she searched the room further finding an envelope with Christmas scrawled on the front of it. Inside it was $220. She dropped that into the overnight bag as well. Then she went into the bathroom and took some of the toiletries, a spare toothbrush, makeup, and a hairbrush. Back in the bedroom, she chose a nightgown and found two new pairs of panties. She quickly stripped off her clothes looking around the room as she undressed. Dropping the uniform on the floor, she kicked it to the side and went to the closet selecting one of the clean uniforms and putting it into the bag. "This just might come in handy." She paused long enough to notice a picture of Melissa on the dresser. She picked it up. Melissa was standing next to a man. He was a handsome man, tall, brawny. Janet peered closer at the photo. He wore a uniform. A police uniform. She glanced around the room again. He definitely didn't live here, but on second observation she saw that a male stayed there from time to time. She'd seen two toothbrushes in the bathroom but hadn't thought anything of it. Now she saw a man's sweatshirt lying across the back of the chair and a large pair of flip-flops under the bed. She immediately panicked dropping the photo on the bed. She grabbed the metal box shoving it inside the tote, and then snatched up the tote racing from the room. In the living room, she turned off the light and peeked outside before stepping onto the porch, closing the door behind her.

When she reached the van, she tossed in the tote and other things she'd taken. Then she drove several blocks and pulled into the parking lot of an apartment complex. She had to figure out her next move. She couldn't keep the van; the police would be looking for it. She had to find somewhere to stay. Somewhere that was safe. She couldn't rent a room with no ID. Maybe she could stay at a boarding house. She had less than $250; that wasn't going to get her far.

"Okay, Janet, you can figure this out." First, she needed to change her appearance; she didn't want anyone to recognize her. Things were a mess. Why did Melissa have to try to fight, that stupid bitch. All she had to do was let the pills take effect. Janet would have walked out of there, and everything would be fine. Sure, she would be a fugitive, but she would be someone who escaped from the nut house. Now she was a murderer…again. Janet rested her face in her hands. She had to think. Ben would understand this; she knew he would. He hated violence of any sort but he would understand that Melissa was trying to keep her from leaving that horrible place. That she would have tried to keep Janet from coming to him. She needed somewhere to stay until she had a way to reach Ben to let him know where she was.

After sitting in the van and collecting her thoughts,

Janet drove to the Greyhound bus station on 95th & Dan Ryan. She rummaged in the glove box, searching for anything she might need. Nothing. She looked in the storage compartment between the seats and found a few hair clips, half a pack of gum and some change. She took everything, putting it inside the tote and got out of the van. She locked the door preparing to put the keys in her pocket, then she unlocked the door and stuck the keys in the ignition. She hoped someone would steal the van. If the police searched for it, maybe the thief could lead them astray before they realized it wasn't Janet. She entered the terminal and stopped. Dropping the tote, she reached into her pocket and pulled out a hair clip. As she gathered her hair putting a clip in it, she scanned the buses scheduled to depart within the next hour. She walked to the ticket counter with her head held high. When she reached the counter, she purchased a ticket to La Marque, Texas. The clerk had told Janet that she was in luck, that the bus was delayed and that it was presently boarding at Gate 7.

Janet lingered at the ticket counter talking to the clerk hoping that the surveillance camera was getting a good enough view of her. She walked to Gate 7 and promptly struck up a conversation with an elderly couple, George and Audrey Spalding. She'd told them that she was going to Texas to visit her ailing father, and that Audrey, looked like her mother who'd passed away two years ago. They'd invited her to sit with them but she declined saying that she'd had a rough few days with very little sleep and that she'd probably sleep until they reached Memphis. She said that in Memphis, since they had a one-hour layover, she would catch up with them and they could share a meal. She only hoped they didn't look for her before the bus reached

Memphis and that with the Spalding's help the authorities would think she had ridden the bus and gotten off at one of the other stops. When everyone boarded the bus, Janet subtly maneuvered the Spaldings and herself close to the front of the line, all the while talking to the elderly couple as if they were old friends. When the couple decided on a seat, Janet pointed to a seat near the back on the bus and told them that she would see them in a few hours. While the bus was bustling with people getting on and off, Janet slipped, unnoticed by the Spaldings, off the bus.

Walking north from the bus terminal, she immediately jumped on the Chicago public transit bus 95E, heading west. She asked the driver how much. When he told her she dug into the tote bag producing a handful of change and dropping the appropriate amount into the coin slot. Then walking to the center of the bus, she sat down resting her head against the window. The bus went several miles passing an all-night drugstore on the left.

"I want to get off here," Janet yelled to the driver. He continued a half-block to the next bus stop. Gathering her things, Janet got off the bus and headed in the direction of a Walgreens.

Going inside the Walgreens drugstore Janet walked from aisle to aisle, picking up the things she needed: a pair of shears and a box of dark brown hair dye, soap, shampoo and toothpaste. She strolled through the aisles. Maybe she could go to her parents. Ask them to help her. No, that wouldn't work. Her father, he would worry about someone finding out that he had helped his fugitive daughter and how it would hurt his business. And her mother. Well she would help, that is until she found out about Melissa, than the police would be on their doorstep before her mother had a chance to complete her phone call. No, she would not find help there. When she reached the front of the store, she stopped next to a stand and selected a pair of wire-framed reading glasses and then proceeded to the checkout counter. Next to the register was a display of Halloween lapel pins. "What's today's date?" Janet had asked the cashier.

"September 23rd."

Janet smiled. "Thanks." October, that was the month that her parents usually took their annual holiday in Acapulco. She'd be free to hide out for an entire month, well that is after the cops searched for her there. Until it was safe to go there, she still had to find somewhere to stay. She walked out of the store and to the bus stop. She was so tired but she didn't dare sit down. If she did, she could end up raped or killed, or worse, on death row. She noticed more cars on the street now and it looked like there were more people out. She walked to two women standing on the bus stop. "Do you have the time?"

"Five forty-seven," one of the women said.

"Thanks," Janet said and then looked around. "You wouldn't happen to know somewhere I can rent a room…I don't have any ID. My boyfriend kicked me out, and he kept all of my stuff, I could only grab this bag." She patted the tote bag.

"Man, that's messed up."

"Yeah, that's some cold shit. My sister Theresa, her husband tried that shit with her. She came and got me and my brother André and we went and kicked his ass out of the house." The two women laughed.

Janet smiled, *come on damn it, I didn't ask you for your family history, just someplace to stay.*

"You know what? There's this place down about seven blocks on the left. It's kind of dirty and the ho's go there a lot, but they don't ask for ID."

Janet nodded, "Thanks."

"Hey," one of the women called as Janet turned away, "My brother André will kick your old man's ass for fifty bucks." Janet just nodded giving the other woman a fake smile. Then turning away, she quickly walked down the street to the motel.

To her relief Janet was able to get a room without a problem. When she walked into it, she knew why. It was vile. The room smelled like there had been a flood and the carpet was soaked through and had never dried out. There was an odor of mildew and dirty animals. The bedspread looked so dirty that you could probably stand it up in the corner as a screen. The bathtub was so nasty that it looked like something was literally living in the bottom of it.

Janet dropped the tote bag on the bed and sat down next to it. Her hip hit the box that was inside the bag. She removed the box examining it. The box had a 2-inch padlock on it. She jerked the lock, and then shook the box. She could tell there were a few things inside the box by the rattle. Setting the box down, she took the scissors from the Walgreens bag. She tried to open the box with them, but the only thing she managed to do was cut her finger.

She looked around the room for something that she could use to jimmy the lock. She opened the drawers to the dresser and the nightstand. There was nothing. Biting her lip, she went outside and picked up a heavy rock. Back in the room she struck the small padlock with the rock. It took several hits, and she ignored the banging and cursing from the neighboring room about it being too early for that shit, but Janet finally got the box open.

She paused before she removed the contents. There was a pair of gold-hoop earrings, and a gold chain with a cross pendent and a diamond tennis bracelet. Janet took the bracelet from the box examining it. "Cheap," she murmured. If she didn't know anything else, she knew good jewelry, and this was anything but. She estimated the cost to be about two to three hundred dollars. Janet dropped the bracelet back into the box and then she slowly picked up the last item…a 22-caliber handgun. She held the gun firmly in her hand feeling the weight. She knew a few people that she would not mind getting rid of with this baby.

She lay back on the bed. Closing her eyes, she pictured a time years ago, a time when she was free. The time before Ben was taken from her. If she had done things differently, her life would be perfect. She would be married and she and her handsome husband would be doing something fabulous, maybe taking a cruise around the world with both their parents. *If I had had this beauty back then, I could have just walked up to her and rid Ben and myself of that disgusting woman.* As she dreamt of the perfect future, a future with her and her love, Janet drifted off to sleep.

Chapter Twenty-four

Sitting behind the steering wheel of her car, Holly looked around at the cars on the street in front of the brownstone that housed Meyers Investigation. She had talked to some of the people who were investigating the escape of Janet Summers. Apparently Summers had killed a nurse who worked at the institution and using the nurse's keys and clothes she was able to slip out.

The authorities seemed certain that she had gotten on a Greyhound bus headed to Texas. They had interviewed several people, and they all had a different story. Some said that she was on the bus. Some said that they didn't remember seeing her. But one couple specifically said that they remembered seeing her. They said that she seemed like a nice girl and they were going to have dinner with her when they reached their destination. They said they were sure she at least made it as far as Memphis, Tennessee. They both said they remembered seeing her get off the bus in Tennessee, but the husband was sure he saw her hurry off the bus when it stopped, while the wife argued that Summers was the last one to walk off the bus. If they didn't catch her soon, it could possibly mean trouble for Dee and

Ben. Maybe she did leave the state, but Holly didn't know, maybe a normal person would think to get away from here as fast as possible, but Janet Summers was anything but normal. She was a woman who was obsessed. Holly sighed getting out of the car.

She walked up the steps of the brownstone and on inside. "Good morning, Detective Lawson," the receptionist Lasha said.

"Good morning. Is she in?"

"Yes, she is but Mr. Harrison is with her." Holly nodded and kept walking down the hall. She put her hand on the doorknob preparing to open it but decided to knock first.

"Come in," Dee called. Holly stepped into the office seeing Ben sitting in Dee's chair behind her desk while Dee stood on the other side of the desk with her arms folded. "Hey, Hol. Come on in." Dee turned back to her husband as Holly walked into the office closing the door behind her. "I'm sorry, hon, but we can't name our daughter Hester."

"That was my grandmothers' name."

"I know, honey, but—"

"Guys, I have something to tell you." Both Ben and Dee looked at Holly. Seeing the serious and worried look on Holly's face Dee asked, "What is it?"

"Janet Summers…has escaped from the institution."

Dee's hands automatically went to cover her growing belly protectively. Ben immediately stood and walked to her side and pulled her close. "What do you mean that crazy bitch has escaped? What happened?" Ben asked roughly.

Holly hated being the one to break the news to them, so she got it out as quickly as possible, and as calmly as she could manage. "Obviously, I don't have to tell you two that this could mean trouble for you both," she finished, a little shaky herself after relating the details.

As Holly told them the details of Janet's escape Dee made a little moaning noise. Feeling her trembling, Ben cursed under his breath. She spoke for the first time. "What if she—?" She looked down at her round belly then up at Ben who was now lightly rubbing her back trying to sooth her. She turned to Holly. "You said she actually killed one of the people that worked there? Didn't they know what she was capable of?"

"It was their job to know, and they let her out," said Ben, the look on his face making Holly glad that she wasn't in the shoes of that facility director right now.

She tried to calm him a little bit. "Ben, that woman that she killed—Janet worked her over. According to other guards and inmates, she made that woman feel sorry for her, and Janet manipulated that poor woman until she had her right where she wanted her. You know how she was at manipulation. It wasn't anyone's fault but Janet's."

"Bullshit." Ben's jaw was clenched tight, and Dee put her hand on his chest.

"Honey, getting mad and placing blame is not going to help right now." Her slightly panicked gaze went to Holly. "What do we do now? She's going to come here. My God, that's probably the only thing she's thinking—that she's gotta get to Ben. What are we going to do?"

Later that evening Holly picked up Abby at the childcare provider's and headed home. On the way, she stopped at the grocery store, picking up some milk, eggs, bread, and spinach. "Oh, man, spinach again?" Abby whined as they walked to the self-checkout aisle.

"You know what? If you promise to eat all of your spinach without complaining this evening, I'll let you get a candy bar." Abby looked at the candy sitting on the stand next to the conveyer. She bit her lip looking at the bag of spinach and then back at the candy. Then nodding, she chose a Snickers candy bar. When they finished checking out Abby grabbed for the candy. "No, not until after dinner."

"Just a little piece, Mommy? Please?"

"No." Holly took the candy and slipped it in her purse.

Using two potholders Holly took the pot roast from the oven, setting it on the stove. "Abby, I need you to set the table."

"Mommy, this is the best part; Snoopy is about to do his dance." Abby was watching the DVD, *It's the Great Pumpkin Charlie Brown.* She loved the part when Snoopy dances on the piano and would get up and dance along.

"Abby, pause the DVD."

"But, Mommy."

"Abby!" After a moment, Holly heard Abby come up from the family room into the kitchen. She walked to the stove, looked at the roast and frowned. Holly passed her the plates, and she set the table with three plates. After putting the dishes on the table, Abby went to the pantry to get napkins. She folded them, placed them next to the plates and then put the silverware on the napkins.

Tyler knocked at the back door as Holly set dinner

on the table. Abby rushed around her mother opening the door. "Hi," she grinned up at him.

"Hey, Squirt." He gave her a box from the bakery. "I stopped by and picked up dessert on my way home. I hope you like cherry pie."

"Cherry? No apple?" Abby asked looking from the box to Tyler.

"You don't like cherry pie?" She shook her head. "Man what kind of princess are you? I don't think I've heard of a princess anywhere that didn't eat cherry pie. He sighed, glanced at Holly and winked. "Well, I guess the guy at the bakery knows more about princesses than I do, he gave me half a cherry pie and half an apple."

Abby giggled carrying the box to the counter.

"I guess we'll just have to teach Tyler all there is to know about princesses, won't we?" Holly asked her daughter.

"Yep," Abby nodded.

"Go get cleaned up for dinner," Holly said as she put the mashed potatoes and spinach on the table.

Tyler walked over next to Holly while she put dinner rolls in a bowl. "How are you?"

"I'm fine,"

"You sure?"

Holly looked at the entrance to the kitchen to be sure that Abby was gone before she said, "Before Dee and Ben were married, he was seeing this woman. When they broke up she couldn't accept that he'd moved on and she did pretty awful things."

Tyler frowned. "Such as?"

"Such as trying to kill Dee." Holly told Tyler everything about Janet and what she had done.

"Wow, that's extreme."

"Yeah, she killed someone else, and was sent to prison. And almost a year ago she was sent to an institution for the criminally insane…last night she escaped."

"Damn," Tyler said, shoving his hands in his pockets. "How are Ben and Dee taking it?"

"The authorities think that she's on her way to Texas, but I'm really afraid for them. If she decides to come back, I don't think she would hurt Ben, but Dee." Holly shook her head. "I just hope they are careful."

After dinner, Tyler helped Holly clean up. Once they were finished cleaning the kitchen Holly went up to shower and change out of her work clothes, while Tyler helped Abby with her homework. The hot water from the shower made Holly feel better, and helped clear her head. What she would do is keep in close contact with the investigating officer that was working on the Summers case. That way she would at least know if they thought that she was still in the state. She had suggested that Ben hire a security team to guard them, especially Dee. Holly knew that Dee did not like that one bit, but it was better to take every precaution. Before she'd left Dee's office Ben was on the phone with a security firm and the director of the facility where Janet had escaped.

Once she was dressed, Holly went down into the family room in search of Tyler and Abby. She found them in front of the television. The DVD *It's the Great Pumpkin Charlie Brown* was playing and Abby was showing Tyler her Snoopy dance. Smiling, Holly leaned against the doorframe and watched as Tyler and Abby enjoyed themselves.

Chapter Twenty-five

It was 7:15 a.m. and Janet was smiling. She had a lot to smile about; she had been free from that horrid place for almost two weeks and she had somewhere to stay until she was able to reach Ben. She would have never imagined when she sat in the park ten days ago that her luck was about to change.

It was on a Tuesday afternoon, and Janet had left the hotel room and walked across the parking lot to use the phone booth outside of the rental office. She had tried to call Ben several times, but the person who had answered at his office was screening his calls and she would not put Janet's calls through. She would always connect Janet to his personal assistant. Eventually Janet tried calling Ben's cell phone. She was surprised to find that after all these years he still had the same number. She did not leave a message the first time she called. She had tried a few times, and the third time her heart nearly stopped when a female answered Ben's phone. Janet recognized that voice, and she wished that she could reach through the phone and grab the other woman's throat.

Janet immediately felt as if she could not breathe. Leaning against the phone booth, she slammed the phone on the hook. After what seemed like an eternity, she walked down the street from the hotel to the park. She sat on a bench and tried to figure out what to do. She had been at the hotel for only a few days but already she was running out of money. She could not talk to Ben to let him know where she was. She was alone, completely alone. Tears slowly welled in her eyes, and before she knew it, she was sobbing uncontrollably. She wrapped her arms around her waist and rocked herself as she sobbed.

"Miss? Are you okay?" Janet looked up into the face of a Latino woman. She looked to be about 30 with a pretty round face and compassionate brown eyes. "Do you need me to call someone for you?" she asked with a slight accent.

Janet sobbed, "There's no one, I'm all alone," and the flow of tears started anew. The young woman slid next to Janet, putting her arm around her. And she allowed Janet to cry on her shoulder.

Janet learned that the young woman's name was Risa Ulpius. Risa had lived in Chicago for the last five years and before that, she lived in Ohio with her husband Julian, and their two children. Julian's cousin had offered Julian a better-paying job in Chicago and someplace to stay until they saved the money to get their own place. The Ulpius' packed up their children and all of their belongings, and moved to Julian's cousin's five-bedroom house. Along with them, there were four other adults and three children in the house. Risa and Julian lived with his cousin for three months before they were able to get their own apartment. A year ago, Risa got a knock on the door. It was the police, and they were there to tell her that Julian had been robbed, and that the robbers had killed him.

Janet had told her that she had just come from Texas, that she was there for two months, against her husband's wishes, to care for her terminally ill father, and that a week ago he had passed away. After the funeral, she had returned home only to find that her husband had moved everything from their home. He had taken their daughter and everything and left, and that she did not know where he'd gone.

Risa lived in a two-bedroom apartment with her children, nine-year-old Julian and seven-year-old Tony. She offered Janet a spot on her sofa, and Janet gladly accepted. Risa's apartment was not much, but it was clean. Janet would have preferred one of the bedrooms but she had to take what she could get. During the day Risa was a custodian for the Chicago Board of Education. During the evenings she worked for a cleaning service part time.

Risa had arranged for Janet to go to work with her, and on the third day of staying with Risa Janet was off to her first cleaning job…her first job. Ever.

Other than going out to work during the evenings or going to the store late at night Janet seldom left the apartment. She had dyed and cut her hair while she was at the hotel, and she always wore the wire-rimmed glasses that she had bought, but she was amazed that no one recognized her.

• • •

"So," Daley said to Holly, "Do you like this guy."

Holly glanced over at her partner. Mitch Daley had been her partner for the last four years. Mitch was 48 years old. At six foot three and 235 pounds, he was what Holly liked to think a gentle-as-a-teddy-bear older brother would be like. At the age of 30 Mitch gave up his career as a paramedic to join the police force. He was a latecomer and made detective the year before he and Holly became partners. Holly had asked him why he had given up being a paramedic to take a job where half the public hated you. He said that he wanted to help people, but losing a patient en route to the hospital was more than he could handle. After talking to his wife, Krista, and convincing her that this was the right move for him, he joined the force. When he first joined the force, Krista had threatened him, telling Mitch that if he went and got himself killed in the line of duty she would take everything he'd worked so hard for and spend it on a young stud just to piss him off.

"Yeah, I like him, he's a nice guy."

"You never thought about dating another cop?"

"Why, Mitch, are you asking me out?" Holly teased.

"Na, you're cute and all..." he grinned glancing over at Holly and then winked. "But you can be evil. I mean, you're tougher than Krista. And that's saying a lot."

"Hey, I'm not evil," Holly said, pretending that her feelings were hurt.

"Not evil? What do you call arriving at work early every day this week just so you can go into McGuiness' office and rearrange his desk?" Holly knew that McGuiness liked everything on his desk a certain way. If you picked up anything and set it back down in the wrong place, he would casually move it back in the proper location.

"A practical joke," Holly said offering him an innocent smile. He gave her a "like I really believe that" look. Holly sucked her teeth. "All right, that's evil, but sometimes he just drives me crazy."

"I think he has a crush on you."

"What?"

Daley nodded.

"You're nuts."

"Why do you think he's always watching you?"

"Because he wants to catch me goofing off and jump in my shit."

"No, because he likes you," Daley teased as he pulled the car to the curb at the corner of Michigan and East Lake.

Dee and Terry had asked Holly if she could meet them there for lunch. Holly put her hand on the door handle and then turned back to Daley. "Are you messing with me?" He laughed and she shook her head. "I'll be about an hour."

"Take your time. I'm going to go down to Billy Goats Tavern and get me a triple cheeseburger…uh, don't tell Krista. Okay?"

"Your secret's safe with me." She got out of the car, crossed the street and entered Bennigan's. She scanned the crowd until she spotted Terry and Dee sitting at a table. She weaved her way through the crowd. "Hey."

"Happy birthday!" Terry and Dee yelled throwing their arms in the air. Dee pulled back a napkin with a four-inch mini cake under it. In the middle of the cake was a single candle.

Holly laughed shaking her head and sat down. "Thanks guys."

After the waiter delivered their food, Terry asked. "So you got any details you want to share with us?

"Details about what?"

"About Mr. Tyler. We know you guys have been spending a lot of time together, but is he as good in the bedroom as he is out of it?"

Dee laughed and covered her mouth to keep food from falling out. "I can't believe you just asked her that."

"Well, I'm sure you want to know, too."

"Not particularly."

"Oh, please," Terry said turning back to Holly. "So?"

"There's nothing to tell."

Dee's brows rose. "What do you mean nothing?"

"See, I knew you wanted to know," Terry gloated.

Dee rolled her eyes. "You and Tyler haven't—"

"Not yet."

"Is he gay?" Terry asked.

"Uh, No! We just want to take our time, get to really know each other."

Terry grunted. "The time I've had to go without since David and I separated has made me grouchier than a bitch, and she's choosing to abstain."

Holly chuckled. "Going a week without sex makes you grouchy." Terry bit her lip in thought and then nodded. "Besides, I'm still trying to work my way through this dating thing. Sometimes I feel…guilty."

"Guilty about what?" Terry asked leaning in close. Dee pushed her shoulder. "What?" Holly sighed, "I know it's been five years, but sometimes I feel like I'm being unfaithful."

"Honey, you shouldn't feel that way," Dee said placing her hand on Holly's. She continued, "Do you really think Ed would want you to be alone? To raise Abby alone?"

"She's right, Reds," Terry added. "He'd want you to be happy."

"Yeah. I mean, I know what you two are saying is true, I just don't know."

"Humph, look at it this way," Terry said. "Vulture Valerie is just waiting to pick that carcass clean if you don't swoop in first."

Once they finished their lunches, Holly cut the mini cake into three pieces. "So we're coming to your house for your birthday dinner tonight," Dee was saying. "I'll bring the meal, and Terry you can bring David and Keith."

Terry frowned, "Hey, why can't I cook?"

"I don't know, I've been asking myself that question for years."

Terry pushed her shoulder. "I did a good job making that cake." She pointed to the small piece of cake that Holly was putting in her mouth.

Holly set the cake down. "See, this is supposed to be my happy birthday, and you two are planning ways for me to spend it in the emergency room." Dee busted out laughing and for the next ten minutes, they had to listen while Terry told them how she was a good cook and that no one had to go to the hospital from eating her food since the first year of her marriage.

After dinner, everyone sat in Holly's living room while she opened her presents. Terry had apologized for not being able to buy a gift; she'd said that since David had left her she was barely making it. He'd helped her the first month then after that his contributions were few and far between, so she gave Holly a homemade gift certificate to do her laundry for two weeks.

Dee and Ben had given her a gift certificate to a spa. Tyler had given her a plush robe, and he'd taken Abby shopping so she could pick out slippers to give to her mom.

"Thanks for the birthday gifts, guys. I love them all."

"Oh, yeah, there's one more." Terry jumped up and ran to the table next to the front door. She practically bounced into the living room, and grabbing Dee's hand she pulled her to the sofa. Dee sat next to Holly while Terry stood behind the sofa leaning over Holly's shoulder. "It's from me and Dee…Open it! Open it!"

Holly tore off the bright pink wrapping paper and opened a white box to find an equally bright pink vibrator.

Terry leaned down whispering. "I hear that if you don't release yourself your head will blow off." Holly slammed the top of the box shut. Her face turned a vivid shade of red.

Abby, who was sitting on the floor on the other side of the coffee table, rose to her knees. "What is it, Mommy?" She leaned close to her mother. Holly's eyes filled with tears as she held back her laughter. "Nothing, baby. Just mommy stuff."

Dee leaned close to Holly examining the tears running down Holly's cheeks. "I hear it sometimes turns into tears, too."

"Yeah, maybe Tyler can help with that little problem." Terry beamed at Tyler.

Tyler looked from Terry to Dee suddenly realizing what was in the box. He blushed and looked at Holly.

Ben looked at his wife and then at the box Holly held. He laughed. "I can't believe you guys."

"Believe what, Uncle Ben?" Abby asked confused.

"Nothing, honey."

Quickly, Holly stuffed the box down between the sofa cushions, plopped a pillow on top and then sat on the pillow. Dee sucked her teeth shaking her head. "I don't think you're doing it right."

"Girl, shut up," Holly shot back. She quickly glanced at Tyler, saw the amused look on his face and then turned away. She didn't think she'd be able to look him in the face for the rest of the night. "I'm the birthday girl," she began, changing the subject. "So where the hell is my ice cream?"

Later, after an entire quart of mint chocolate ice cream had been polished off, talk turned to the kids and Halloween. Holly was sitting back in her seat, holding her full stomach and groaning, when Tyler spoke up. "I was thinking that Holly and I could have a party for the kids. We could do it here, and Abby and Keith could invite a bunch of their friends. Do you want to help decorate, Terry? And I was thinking Dee could help plan out some games. The kids will have a great time."

As Dee, Terry and even Ben started volunteering ideas, Holly stared at Tyler. Had she heard him right? Holly had mentioned to him that she was thinking about doing something for the kids, and he'd just assumed that they'd plan it together. The man was beginning to take a lot for granted, and she had to put a stop to it.

Chapter Twenty-six

When Holly walked out of the community center where they held the monthly neighborhood association meeting she was pissed. She knew her anger was unjustified and irrational, but as much as her subconscious told her she was taking the argument too far she couldn't stop herself. She got out of her car slamming the door. Tyler got out of the passenger side and quickly walked around the car. "I don't see what the big deal is?"

"The big deal is that you had no right to tell them that we're having a Halloween party for the kids."

"If you don't want to have a Halloween party, that's fine."

"No, I have a problem with your telling those people that *we* are doing anything."

"Why? Am I missing something here? We are seeing each other; we are dating, what's the problem?"

"The problem is that you and I are not a 'we'."

"Damn it, woman, why does everything have to be so hard with you?" Tyler asked as Holly turned and walked away. She walked across the yard to her porch with him following close behind. When she walked onto the porch Tyler grabbed her arm pulling her to a stop.

"The only thing that's hard is your head, and you're not understanding that there is not an us and that there isn't going to be any us."

Terry's car pulled in the driveway behind Holly's, and Abby and Keith jumped out, running to the back-yard to play on the swing set.

"Well excuse the hell out of me. I thought that was what we were working toward!" Tyler threw his hands in the air in frustration. "The problem is you're afraid!"

"Son of a bitch!" Both Tyler and Holly glanced over seeing Terry struggling as she pulled a large green garbage bag from the trunk of her car. The bag tore and laundry spilled out. Tyler turned back to Holly as a stream of profanity drifted from Terry's direction.

"I'm not afraid of anything. You're crazy. What the hell do I have to be afraid of?"

"You're afraid of being in a relationship. You're afraid of being hurt, of being left alone again. You're so afraid that you're willing to let life pass you by."

"That's ridiculous."

"You're afraid of what we could have and your feelings for me."

"You know what, people have called me a lot of things, but no one has ever called me afraid." Terry dragged a second bag to the porch, leaving the torn bag and clothes on the ground behind her car. When she reached the bottom step Tyler walked down and carried the bag on to the porch and set it inside the front door. "Terry, describe me in one word."

Terry looked up at Tyler saying, "Thanks." Then

she looked at Holly and frowned, wiping perspiration from her brow. "Surly."

Holly nodded in satisfaction. "Thank you."

"Woman, you're making this way too hard."

"Life's hard, deal with it," Holly said following Terry into the house and slamming the door.

Tyler stood on the porch for a moment and then walked down the steps. A few minutes later Terry walked out of the house carrying a new garbage bag.

"What crawled up her ass?" she asked walking down the steps and across the yard. She bent to pick up the clothing from the front yard before looking up at Tyler, raising her eyebrows.

Tyler kicked the front steps in frustration. He didn't really want to get into it with her, but Holly and Terry were friends. Maybe she'd have some ideas for him.

"Every time I think I'm getting somewhere with that stubborn woman, she slams the door in my face. Not usually literally, though." He glanced up at the front door. "What is it with her? Can't she see how good we are together?"

"Hmm." Terry rubbed her forehead. Her butting in had already almost gotten her in deep trouble. But the sight of this man in so much misery over her pigheaded friend swayed her. Besides, someone had to do something. She sighed dramatically.

"You know her husband died, I assume."

"Yeah," Tyler said, his hazel eyes sad. "It's something we've got in common. I lost my wife, too."

"Well, I'm sure you know that she's afraid to throw her heart out there again," Terry said. "What she and Edmond had…they were truly happy. I'm not usually into sentimental crap, but they were so in love that everyone around them could see it. Hell, they could feel it. They had this perfect little life going on. I mean, the perfect marriage, the perfect family...you name it, it was theirs." She paused for a second. "Don't you ever feel kind of guilty—kind of like you're cheating on your wife by seeing a new woman?"

"No," said Tyler truthfully. "I mean, I did at first. I would date different women, but I never really opened my heart to anyone, not until I met Holly. Felicia, my wife, would have wanted me to move on and try to find happiness again. She was such a giving woman, she would have hated for me to spend the rest of my life alone and miserable."

"I'm sure Edmond would have felt the same way," Terry sighed again. "Just give it time, Tyler. Holly will eventually figure that out. Just be patient and be there for her."

Terry walked into the house with a purpose. She knew Holly needed some straight talk and she was just the bitch to give it to her. She'd never pulled any punches in the past, so why start now.

"Where you at, Reds?"

"In the kitchen." Holly's voice sounded dull and lifeless. This was getting ridiculous—it was time for the girl to move on. Terry squared her shoulders and entered the kitchen. Heading to the fridge, she pulled out a can of soda.

"Help yourself," Holly said wryly.

Ignoring the sarcasm, Terry turned to face her. "How much longer are you going to play the idiot?" she asked bluntly.

Immediately, Holly's temper returned. "What the hell are you talking about?"

"I'm talking about that man you keep reeling in and then kicking in the ass. You think Tyler's going to sit around and take that for much longer?"

Holly's green eyes flashed. "I don't see how that's any of your business."

"Sure it is. I'm single now. I'm on the market. You've got one nice fish dangling on the hook that you don't even want, so why don't you throw him back so the rest of us can have a chance at him?"

Holly's jaw hardened. "Go for it. Like I'm even interested."

Terry rolled her eyes. "Oh, yeah. Convince me. Every time Tyler's around, I can practically see little cartoon hearts and birdies circling your head—but you catch yourself thinking lovey thoughts and you just shoot those birdies right out of the sky. Do you really think Edmond would want you raising your daughter alone when there's this sweet, good-looking, responsible, caring man waiting to jump in?"

"I will repeat," Holly growled through gritted teeth. "Not…your…business."

Terry's voice softened. And she took a step closer to Holly. "Yeah, girl, but I'm making it my business. Chew my ass out if you want to, yell at me, and call me names even, but somebody's got to make you see that you're throwing a chance away." Terry paused and then said, "How many people do you think are lucky enough to find love even once in their life, and you've got the opportunity to do it twice. Some of us just *think* we've got it…" Terry's voice broke, and she turned away.

Setting the soda on the table she said, "I'm finished with your laundry. I'll be back for Keith later."

After Terry had gone, Holly stared through the doorway for a long time.

• • •

If Tyler had gone for a walk instead of pacing, he would have ended up in South Bend before he'd realized how far he'd gone. First, he'd told himself to just lay off—Holly obviously wasn't ready to move on, so it was time for him to quit fixating on her. But then, he'd think about her eyes, her hair, her prickly personality, the easy way she had with the people she loved, her protective streak…and he would start pacing all over again. He never thought it would happen after the pain of losing Felicia, but he was doing it again. He was falling in love.

• • •

"Hey." Holly greeted Dee and Ben when she opened the front door.

"Hey," Dee said, giving Holly a quick hug as she entered the house. "We want to show you something."

"Okay." Holly looked from Dee to Ben as she waited.

"We're waiting for Terry, I told her to meet us here." Dee took the bag that Ben held.

"What is it?" Holly asked, looking first at Dee then Ben. Ben grinned sheepishly at her. "I'm not going to like this am I?"

He shook his head. "Probably not."

"Oh, Jesus, Dee!" Holly yelled.

"We brought steaks; I'll go get them started," Dee said, giving Holly a quick peck on the cheek and heading toward the kitchen.

Holly turned to Ben. "I see you as a brother; you gotta help me out here. Please."

Ben laughed. "I'll see what I can do."

Two hours later the three women and Ben sat in the living room watching a very up-close and personal birthing tape. Ben and Dee sat cuddling on the sofa; Terry sat on the floor looking as if she were struggling to stay awake. Holly sat in the armchair wishing that she had not changed from her work clothes; if she had her note pad and pen in her pocket, she could use the pen to put her eyes out, or better yet, if she had her gun, she could shoot the television set.

When the DVD stopped, Holly jumped up, raced across the room and popped the DVD from the player. "Wasn't that beautiful?" Dee said tearfully.

"Sure was," Terry said dryly. "I don't know about you guys, but I just love to look at some chick's bloody snatch an hour after I eat a medium-rare steak."

"Terry," Dee said nudging Terry's shoulder with her knee, "We're in mixed company."

"Well, if Ben hasn't heard that word before, I don't think he should be getting anyone knocked up." Ben burst out laughing.

"Terry," Dee said again.

"I'm just saying."

"I know what you're saying," Dee said standing. Holly dropped the movie case on the table. "So what did you think? Did it help you get past the fear of being in the birthing room with me?"

Holly wanted to tell her that it made her want nothing more than to take Abby and leave the state, but she was way too tired to have that discussion now.

She massaged her brow. "I don't know, let's talk about it tomorrow."

"But?"

"Sweetheart," Ben said. Stepping behind Dee and wrapping his arms around her, he nuzzled her cheek. "She's tired. I'm sure it's been a long day. Let's give Holly some time."

Dee nodded, picking up the video box and handing it to Holly. "Why don't you keep this so you can watch it again, I'm sure it will help."

Holly nodded tightly. "Sure."

Dee and Terry went into the kitchen to clean up everything left from dinner, while Holly straightened the living room. Ben went down to the family room to spend some time with Abby, David and Keith, and to keep the kids out of their mothers' hair while they finished their tasks. Coming from the kitchen, Terry said, "The coffee maker is set up, I used the Hazelnut."

"Thanks," Holly said walking everyone to the door. After everyone left, Holly made sure that Abby actually got into the bathtub instead of just sticking her feet in. Then after supervising Abby's tooth-brushing she braided her hair and tucked her in to bed before heading to her room. She took a quick shower and then put on a pair of old light blue cotton pajamas. They were two sizes too big and ratty enough to go to the dump but they were comfortable. She went into the bathroom to wash her face and brush her teeth. Then she sat on her bed and brushed her hair before going downstairs to lock up the house.

Standing in the kitchen, in the same spot where Terry had ambushed her earlier, Holly ran her hands through her hair, and grunted in frustration. Damn it, this is why I didn't want to get involved with anybody again. It's so freaking complicated.

In her heart, she knew that Terry was right. Edmond wouldn't have wanted her to be alone for the rest of her life. He'd have wanted her to find someone else. But she couldn't help it. It felt like she'd be throwing away everything wonderful she and Edmond had created together.

Everyone assumed that it was so hard for her, being alone. But the reality was, it was a lot easier to just rely on herself to take care of Abby, to be both a mom and a dad. Because as soon as she let somebody else into that circle, it opened up the possibility for more pain. Tyler had already eased his way into her life and if she let him in the rest of the way…well, life wasn't a sure thing, and she didn't know if she was strong enough to go through something like that again.

• • •

Tyler had looked out his living room window for the fifth time in the last half-hour. Besides Holly's car, he saw Dee and her husband Ben's car, and Terry's car was on the street in front of the house. The last time he'd looked he saw both cars leaving, and it took him an additional fifteen minutes to get up his nerve to go and talk to Holly.

He walked onto his front porch closing the door behind him. Then he sat on the steps examining his hands. Okay, what are you going to say? *I'm sorry I said that you were afraid of me, even though I know you are. And before you throw me out, let me say that I think I'm in love with you.* "Yeah, like that will work," he said to himself. "That will go over real big with her." Tyler looked to his right, seeing the living room light in

Holly's house go off. He took a deep breath and walked from the porch, cutting across the yard and taking the steps two at a time. As he gently knocked on the door butterflies moved through his stomach.

Holly was halfway up the stairs when she heard the light tap on the window. She turned, descending the steps to peek out the window. She saw Tyler standing on the other side of the door with his head down and his hands shoved in his pockets. She opened the door looking up at him. "Hey."

"Hey," he said, meeting her gaze. "Um…"

"It's late, whatever you need will have to wait," Holly said, quickly jerking her pajama top into place.

"I was wondering if we could talk."

"I'm really not up to it."

"I need to talk to you; just give me five minutes." She remained silent, not opening the door any more than an inch. "Please?"

After a moment she nodded then opened the door and let him in. After closing the door, she stepped back folding her arms. "What is it?"

"I'm sorry; I didn't mean what I said."

"Don't apologize, you did mean it.

"Yes. I mean, I did, but not in the way that you think. I meant that I know you're afraid. I see that look in your eyes often, and I recognize it. I saw it for several years after Felicia died. I saw it every time I looked into the mirror." He took a step toward her. "Baby, I know you're afraid…because I was afraid too. I was afraid to give my heart to someone only to have them leave me in the most unimaginable way. A way that is permanent. And regardless of what anyone says or does, they can't change it and they can't take that pain away. I was afraid of feeling that pain again, of feeling as if I want to stay in bed every morning and not face the day, and want to die every night. I was afraid, until I met you. I'm not afraid of that pain anymore. I'm not afraid to give my heart and my love to you. I'm only afraid that you could never feel the things for me that I feel for you."

The room fell silent. The only thing Tyler heard was his heartbeat thundering in his ears. He nodded, satisfied that he had said what he'd come to say, and moved to the door.

"Hey," Holly called. When he turned she rushed into his arms, grabbing the front of his shirt and pulling his head toward her. He brought his hands up, burying them in her hair, and turning he backed her to the wall. Kissing, they backed up until his bottom hit the back of the sofa. He maneuvered her around the furniture never releasing her. Holly didn't notice when Tyler moved the pillows to the floor, and she didn't realize that he'd removed her top. He lowered her and eased her to the floor.

Holly held him close as his tongue traveled from her lips to her neck. He sucked her neck gently and then slowly moved from her neck to her breast. Slowly his tongue circled her hardened nipple and then he drew it into his mouth. Holly suppressed a moan as her body shuddered with pleasure. His palm slid to her stomach then down to her pajama bottoms. He didn't slide the cotton over her hips, instead he eased his hand inside. Holly opened her legs for him as his fingers penetrated deep inside her fiery channel. She gasped as her body tightened around his fingers and she bucked her hips to meet his hand.

Tyler quickly removed her bottoms and then just as quickly discarded his clothes. He rose above her;

there was a heartbeat while he was poised there before he cursed.

Sitting up, Tyler quickly grabbed his pants pulling out his wallet. He fumbled with it, dropping the contents on the floor as he pulled a small plastic packet out of one of the compartments. Using his teeth, he tore it open. Holly laughed at his eagerness, reaching for his hand. "Here, let me." With her eyes still on him, she ran her fingers along his engorged erection from the base to the tip. His eyes fluttered closed and he moaned. She began to smooth the condom down, and then he leaned forward capturing her lips as his body sank into hers.

Holly moaned in delight when he entered her. Bringing her right leg up she wrapped it around his waist as he began to move, each stroke taking him deeper. She rose to meet him as she moved to match his rhythm.

Tyler moaned, good heaven he could not remember ever being inside a woman and it feeling so good, so perfect. He clenched his teeth and used all of his control to move slowly and build the heat between them until she cried out in ecstasy. "That's it, baby," he whispered, "That's it, come for me…oh god yes." Tyler groaned and then threw his head back as pleasure washed over him.

Holly felt like her body was wound tighter and tighter before the most intense and earth-shattering climax she had ever had claimed her. She could swear the house moved and she was sure she saw stars.

Tyler held her tightly, his face buried in her neck. "Wow," Holly whispered.

"Yeah,"

"Shhh. You'll wake Abby." Holly placed her fingers to his lips.

Tyler laughed. "Me?"

Tyler squeezed her close, and they sat in a comfortable silence for what seemed like an hour. Finally, when Holly had begun to think he'd fallen asleep, he whispered, "What changed your mind?"

"I don't know," she began quietly. "I was just thinking about you…and about my marriage. I'd almost convinced myself that the best thing to do would just be to keep my distance. Part of me thought that giving in would be betraying Edmond, and another part of me just wanted to stay sealed off so it couldn't get hurt again." She turned her face into his chest, and mumbled, "You were right. I was just afraid. I still am."

Tyler's arms tightened around her for a moment. "Nobody knows what's going to happen in the future. That's why I think it's just pointless to waste even a minute of our lives. And I can't say that I'll be there for you forever, because some things just aren't in my control, but you can bet that I'll never leave you voluntarily."

"Then we'll just take it one day at a time," Holly said, rolling over to her side.

Holly pulled the cover up around her shoulder. She wiggled her bottom close to Tyler who was spooning her from behind. He gently tightened his grip around her waist. She smiled in a sleepy haze, and then her eyes popped open. She looked at the wall clock, it read 5:50 a.m. "Oh shit." She jumped up, quickly putting on her pajamas. "Oh shit, you gotta get up.

"Hmm?"

"You gotta get up and out of here before Abby wakes up."

Tyler rolled onto his back rubbing his face. "Uh?"

"I don't want Abby to find you here like this." Tyler watched her for a moment and then rose and slid his pants on. Holly rolled up the blanket that he must have gotten sometime during the night and threw it in the bottom of the coat closet.

"Mommy?" Abby called.

"I'm coming. I'll be there in a minute!" Holly grabbed Tyler's shirt and shoes, shoving them into his arms and pushed him toward the door.

He grinned whispering, "You're cute when you get flustered." She opened the door pushing him onto the porch, and when he leaned forward kissing her she almost melted.

"Mommy?" Abby called again bringing Holly back to realization.

"Wait a minute!"

"I'll miss you today," Tyler teased, knowing that Holly was trying to get him out of the house as soon as she could.

"Yeah, yeah. Me, too," she said closing the door in his face and running across the room and up the stairs.

"Mommy, who were you talking to?"

Chapter Twenty-seven

"Why does Dracula have no friends?" Abby asked grinning at her mother.

"I don't know. Why doesn't Dracula have any friends?"

"Because he's a pain in the neck!" Abby laughed hysterically, and Holly chuckled. She was having a wonderful day. An arrest warrant was issued for one Steven Rivers. Not for the murder of Jessica, not yet. Holly and Mitch were still gathering information for that case. The warrant was for the child abuse and assault of his daughter. Mrs. Atkins decided that she wasn't going to let some criminal stop her from doing what was right, she had told the D.A. And to Holly's pleasure and surprise, McGuiness called her in to his office to tell her the news personally, and he handed her the warrant so that she and Daley could go pick up Rivers.

She had arrived home early enough to prepare dinner for Abby, Tyler and herself, help Abby with her homework, and now spend some much needed quality time with her daughter.

"Now, it's your turn, Mommy."

Holly tilted her head to the side. "Okay. Knock, knock."

"Who's there?"

"Avon."

"Avon who?"

"Avon to drink your blood," Holly said.

"Uh?"

"You know, like a vampire, *A-von* to drink your blood," she said trying to imitate a vampire.

"Oh…that must be an old-people joke," Abby said, her eyes large. Holly grabbed Abby, wrestling her to the floor as Holly tickled her.

After having a dinner of baked salmon, broccoli and wild rice, Tyler and Holly sat at her kitchen table discussing the events of the day.

"We still have to prove that he killed his wife, and so far what we have looks good."

"That's great, baby," Tyler said as Holly rose from her chair.

"Would you like a cup of tea?" she asked walking to the sink and filling the teakettle.

"Where's Abby?" Tyler asked standing and walking behind Holly. He placed his hands on her shoulders.

"She's at Paige's. Abby said that they wanted to open a lemonade stand. I tried to tell her that it was a little late in the year. But you know Abby."

"Lemonade stand, huh?" Tyler said massaging her shoulders. Holly leaned back against him as he let his hands travel down her shoulders to cup her breasts. "So, how long do you think the planning of this lemonade stand could take?"

"I don't know, could take an hour, maybe more." Holly turned her head and captured his lip between her teeth. Tyler eased his right hand under her blouse, letting the tip of his finger brush the bud of her nipple as he slipped his left hand inside the waistband of her slacks. Holly moaned rotating her hips against his as his fingers crept along the top of her panties.

The front door banged open and voices traveled from the living room to the kitchen.

"I just don't know what you were thinking," they heard Dee yell.

"I said I was sorry," Terry answered back. Tyler released Holly and moved to stand next to the table. "I didn't mean it, it just happened."

"Well, we won't have to worry about it happening again, 'cause you can't go with me anymore."

"Come on, Dee?"

"No."

"What's going on, guys?" Holly asked as she turned to face them.

"Terry asked me if she could go to work with me."

"I need a job and I thought I could help."

"And, dummy me, I said yes. Well, we go to the restaurant where this guy is meeting his mistress and take a seat on the other side. I ask Terry if she could take notes as I dictate them to her and I start doing my thing, you know." Terry rolled her eyes, folding her arms. "The next thing I know, this one," Dee jerked her head in Terry's direction as she sat at the table, "Is jumping from her seat and marching across the restaurant. She starts yelling at my subject about how he should be ashamed of himself for cheating on his loving wife, and how he's leaving his sons broken hearted for some pregnant bimbo. The guy turns to his mistress and asks her, 'Are you pregnant?' And, she yells, 'You have kids?' And my case is all but shot to hell."

"I'm—sorry," Terry moaned loudly as Dee started

ranting again. Terry looked from Holly to Tyler and back at Holly. "Dee. Dee. Dee!" She nudged her cousin.

"What?" Dee yelled, and Terry nodded in Holly's direction. Holly brushed her hair from her flushed face and turned back to the sink. "Oops, sorry," Dee said, rising from the chair. "We didn't mean to interrupt. Just pretend we weren't here."

When Terry walked past Tyler, she thumped him on the chest. "Make sure you use protection while you're knocking the boots. We don't want you getting our girl in the family way."

"Terry," Dee said, "I thought you were going to work on the language."

"Well, if he doesn't—"

"I know, if he doesn't know those words, he shouldn't be knocking the boots."

"No, I was going to say if he doesn't know those words, our girl is going to rock his world before she's done with him." They both broke out in a roar of laughter as they went out the front door.

"I swear I don't know why I hang out with those two."

"Because you love them," Tyler said moving across the room toward her.

She chuckled. "Like nobody's business."

• • •

"Dee, you guys don't need to do this. If I want to go out, I'll call you and drop Abby off."

"This isn't just about you going on a date, I know Tyler likes spending time with Abby, but you guys could use some time alone. Plus, this will give you a break, some time to yourself," Dee said as she packed the clothes that Holly passed to her in a small purple carry-on bag. "And it's about us spending time with Abby. She will spend the next four days with us. Ben, Abby and I will have a great time. And we'll have time to spoil her a little more."

"Can she possibly become any more spoiled?" Holly asked playfully.

"Duh, yes." Dee snorted and then she laughed when Holly rolled her eyes. "Anyway, Ben and I have everything all figured out. He will drop her off, and I'll pick her up. You will have a four-day weekend, and on Tuesday, you can pick Abby up from daycare. Besides, Ben already told Abby that he would have a limo take her to school, the driver wearing the uniform, opening the door for her, the whole bit."

Holly laughed. "Like I said, you guys spoil her so."

"We're her godparents. We love her, and its fun. Of course we're going to spoil her."

• • •

Janet felt like she had been waiting for hours. She looked at the clock on the dashboard of Risa's 1986 dark blue Ford Festiva. It was 8:10 a.m. She moved the seat back a little, trying to stretch her legs in what she'd come to think of as one of the smallest cars ever made. But it ran well, and Risa didn't have a problem letting Janet use it once Janet told Risa that she had a tip where her husband was hiding with her daughter. Risa did not ask any questions, she just gave Janet the keys and ushered her out the door telling her to be safe and find her child. After that day, as long as Risa didn't need the car she would allow Janet to borrow it.

A grey limousine came to a creeping halt at the curb in front of the Harrison International building.

Janet bit her nail as she leaned forward trying to see in the window of the car. The windows were tinted so dark she couldn't see inside. The driver got out of the car and walked to the back passenger door opening it. Janet's heart leaped in her chest as she watched Ben step out of the car. Tears immediately welled in her eyes blurring her vision, and she struggled to open the door with a trembling hand. She finally got the door open and dodged across the street, weaving through several cars that were beeping their horns. She ran breathlessly across the sidewalk and into the massive revolving door. When she reached the lobby there were so many people that she couldn't see Ben.

"Janet?"

She spun around trying to find the source; she knew that voice, that beautiful silky voice. Ben. He was near and he was calling to her. She looked around frantically...Then he was there. He looked down at her, his green eyes shining with love and concern. "Janet, where have you been? Everyone has been looking for you." He stepped toward her taking her in his arms. "Sweetheart, I'm so glad you're safe, I've missed you so."

Janet smiled and let out a contented moan. Her eyes fluttered open and she looked around the confines of the small car, sighing. She was waiting to get a glimpse of Ben. If he was alone, if it did not look like the police were watching him, she would approach him. He would be happy to see her and he would take her somewhere safe. Then after he made slow sweet love to her he would arrange for them to slip away and go where no one would find them.

Starting the car, Janet pulled away from the curb. This was her third time around the block. She had

parked in a no parking zone since there was no parking
on the street except metered parking during business
hours. And of course, as luck would have it, there were
no available meters. She had circled the block after
waiting half an hour because she did not want anyone
to notice her car parked in the same location for too
long. The second time a police cruiser slowed next to
the car, and she became nervous and pulled off. The
third time she'd just become frustrated and decided to
give up for now. After going a few blocks, she circled
back around and stopped in front of the office building
once again. She breathed a weighty sigh just as a dark
blue limo pulled to the curb directly in front of Harrison International. The back passenger door opened,
and Janet's heart nearly stopped. It was him. Her Benji.
Tears welled in her eyes, and she brought a hand to
her mouth suppressing a sob. Her pulse raced, and she
let out an almost hysterical laugh. Then she froze. She
watched as Ben held the door open for someone else. A
child. Janet leaned forward slightly, trying to get a closer look at the child, but all she could see was a mass of
sandy hair pulled back in a loose ponytail. He looked
down at the child, laughing at something the child had
said, and with his finger, he lightly touched the tip of
her nose before taking her hand and leading her inside
the office building.

Janet began to rock slowly. "No, this can't be." Her
sobs started quietly, tears burning her eyes like acid.
Then her sobs became a more intense, low wail. She held
her waist tightly as she rocked back and forward. The
pain was so intense that she felt as though her insides
were on fire. She jumped when someone tapped on the
window to her left. She froze. "Miss?" she heard a female
voice call. She slowly turned her head to look up at the

older woman peering in the window with a concerned look on her face. The look Janet gave her made the other woman recoil as if Janet were a venomous snake who was about to strike. The woman shook her head slightly, then quickly moved away from the car.

Janet glared back at the limo still parked across the street. That's why he couldn't come to me. That's why he stayed with her, because he has a child. Oh god, this can't be happening. He can't have a child, not with her. Janet leaned forward draping her arms around the steering wheel and resting her head on her arms. Why didn't he tell me? Why have me break free of one prison only to have me condemned to a hell of knowing that she's given him something that I was not free to give him?

Ben walked back out of the building, his little girl's hand lovingly held in his. He opened the door and waited patiently for her to climb inside the car, then gracefully slid in next to her. The limo pulled from the curb and Janet quickly pulled from the curb to follow. A short while later they stopped in front of a public school. The limo driver and Ben got out of the car simultaneously. The driver walked to the passenger side opening the back door moving in the direction of the front passenger door as he did so. Ben walked around the car to the passenger side as the child climbed from the car. Squatting, he said something to her. She smiled at him giving him a hug. The child had a milky fawn complexion, and was so stunning that Janet stared at her momentarily mesmerized. But what Janet noticed most was the color of the child's eyes. They were a brilliant, beautiful green. And at that moment Janet's life changed forever. This was indeed Ben's child. The child she and Ben should have had together.

Chapter Twenty-eight

After getting dressed, Tyler went down to the living room to finish setting up everything for his and Holly's special evening. Digging inside a shopping bag, he removed a white linen tablecloth and napkins, several scented candles, a bag of bath salts, and a small bag of rose petals. He set the table, complete with tapered candles and a bouquet of red roses at the center. On each shelf of the bookcase, he placed two candles, one at each end, and lit them. Then after lighting the tapered candles, he walked to the dining room entryway and turned to observe the room. He reached for the light switch, flipping it off, and he smiled, pleased with the outcome. He went into the living room and changed the CDs in the CD player, putting in the Isley Brothers, Robin Thicke and Walter Beasely and setting the player to standby.

He went upstairs into the bathroom and placed several scented candles around the bathtub and on the countertop, leaving the bath salts and rose petals on the counter as well. He went into his bedroom. Getting a mini CD player and taking it into the bathroom, he set it on the counter. He ran downstairs, getting another CD with the Isley Brother's Baby Makin' Music.

He set the player to play the song Blast Off when he pushed the button. After making sure everything was perfect, he went back down to the kitchen to check on his dinner.

● ● ●

Holly dressed in a lightweight pink sweater and tan slacks. Tyler had told her that he had something special planned for the evening. She had asked him what it was, saying that she needed to know what to wear, but he had just told her to be her stunning self and she would be fine. It was Saturday, the second day of her four-day weekend as Holly the woman. Not Holly the cop, or Holly the mommy, just Holly. Last night she and Tyler had gone out to a movie and dinner, returning before 10 so that Tyler would have time to change and head off to work. Holly called Dee to speak to Abby and say goodnight. Then she took a nice long bath and went to bed early, reading for an hour or so before falling asleep.

She walked downstairs, grabbed her keys from the table and went out the front door. When she walked onto Tyler's porch Valerie Logan was just about to knock on the door. Valerie turned to her. "Hi, Holly."

"Hey, Valerie."

"I'm looking for Tyler," Valerie said looking at the door. "I see his truck but he's not answering the door."

"I'm sure he's home…"

"Well," Valerie hesitated for a moment before saying, "Can you just give him this?" She handed Holly a plate of cookies. "Tell him I said thanks for last night."

Holly looked at the plate and then gave Valerie a puzzled look. "Last night?"

Valerie smiled shyly. "Um, yeah."

"You know what? Why don't you give these to him yourself?" Holly shoved the plate into Valerie's hands before turning and leaving the porch. She heard Tyler call her name as she crossed the yard, walked into the house and slammed the front door.

Holly walked into the kitchen throwing her keys on the table. Then digging in the back of the freezer she took out a quart of double chocolate ice cream. She took a spoon from the drawer and went up to her bedroom. Flopping down on the bed, she kicked off her shoes, popped the top off the ice cream and dug in. When the phone rang, she glared at it and then turned away and shoved another spoonful of ice cream in her mouth. After five rings, the answering machine picked up the call. The caller didn't leave a message, but Holly knew who it was. After a few minutes, the phone rang again.

"Holly…can you pick up the phone, please?"

"No!" she said angrily at the phone.

"Holly, please talk to me, tell me what's wrong.

"Oh, you know what's wrong all right, mister!" she spoke to the phone again.

"Listen, baby, I don't know what happened, but whatever is wrong is a misunderstand—" the answering machine cut the message. A moment later, the phone rang again. "Holly this isn't how adults handle things. Stop being childish and answer the damn phone."

Holly snatched the phone from the base. "Who the hell are you calling childish!"

He laughed. "I knew that would get you."

She paused. "Go to hell!" She slammed the phone down and unplugged it.

Tyler looked at the phone as if it were something

he had never seen before. "Damn it, woman." He hung up and dialed her number again. It rang ten times before he hung up. *Forget it.* He went upstairs, taking off his jacket as he entered the bedroom and dropping it onto the bed. He removed his tie, throwing it on top of the jacket. "To hell with it. I'm not going to let her do this to me."

A minute later he went downstairs and turned on the stereo, changing the music to something upbeat and increasing the volume. He went into the dining room. He blew out all of the candles and stacked all of the china and flatware to one side. After he'd finished in the dining room he went into the kitchen. He reached into the cabinet for the plastic wrap and covered the shrimp cocktail. *I'm not going to let her drive me crazy. It's not worth it.* "This is bullshit. If she can just turn off her feelings like that, then she's not who I think she is." He angrily tore off another piece of plastic wrap, then reached for the blackened chicken. Sighing, he balled up the plastic tossing it on the counter. "It doesn't matter to her that I wanted to make things perfect for her. That I wanted to show her how special she is to me. It doesn't matter that I wanted to show her how much I love her." Tyler paused. He leaned against the sink dropping his head. *I am not going to let it hurt me…I am not going to.* He didn't know what had happened. Last night everything had been okay. And this morning when he talked to her everything seemed to be fine. "I love that woman, damn it…I love her." Pushing himself off the sink Tyler walked out the back door and to the end of his yard. He reached into his pocket, pulled out his keys and unlocked the padlock that secured a twenty-foot ladder between the fence and the garage.

Hoisting the ladder, he carried it from his yard out

into the alley and into Holly's yard. Fighting with the ladder, he stood it against the house and positioned it in front of the bathroom window. He only hoped that Holly was like a lot of other people and forgot to lock the bathroom window. He did not want to break in. But he would.

Holly sat slouched on the bed with her back resting against the headboard. She stabbed the spoon into the ice cream as she grumbled. "That son of a bitch." *I knew that I shouldn't have trusted him.* As she thought, she realized that she could have been wrong. But why would Valerie need to thank Tyler for the night before. He had told her that he had to work. If he worked, how did he see Valerie? "Freaking jerk."

"Why the hell did you hang up on me?" Came a voice from the doorway.

Holly screamed, dropped the ice cream and was off the bed attacking the figure in the doorway before she realized who it was. She'd hit Tyler before he had time to realize what she'd intended to do. Before he could block it, she had kicked him square in the chest, sending him practically sailing across the hallway. The impact with the wall knocked the wind out of him, and he slid down the wall.

"Oh, no." Holly quickly rushed to his side squatting next to him. "Are you all right?"

"Damn, woman, are you that angry with me."

"What are you doing here?" She pushed his shoulder and then stood, folding her arms. "And how the hell did you get in?"

"Why did you hang up on me?"

"Why don't you ask Valerie?"

"What does she have to do with this?"

"Why were you with Valerie Logan last night?"

"I wasn't with her last night."

"Then why did she ask me to 'thank you' for last night."

Tyler sighed. "She called me and told me that she was having problems with her ex-husband and that he was at her home and wouldn't leave. I called this guy I know who's," he paused for a moment, "Persuasive, and asked him to go over to her house and ask her ex to kindly leave."

"Why didn't she call the police?"

"She didn't want a squad car coming to her house. And, I don't know, she just called me." He grinned at her, then grimaced as the pain she had inflicted smarted. "You're a cop; you should really lock that bathroom window."

"Oh, shut up," she said, squatting again and helping him to his feet. He really didn't need to but he leaned on her slightly as she helped him into her bedroom. Holly helped him sit on the side of the bed and then she attempted to unbutton his shirt.

He brought his hand up stopping her. "We need to talk."

She met his gaze and then cast her eyes downward. "I know, I was wrong."

Tyler cupped her chin tenderly, bringing her eyes up to meet his. "Hey, I don't like what just happened. I mean you not talking to me when you were angry."

"I'm sorry."

He placed his fingers to her lips. "Let me finish. I would never hurt you." And then after a pause he said, "I love you…I wouldn't play games with your emotions. But I ask the same from you. If you're angry with me, come to me and tell me. Don't just turn your back on me, talk to me. Okay?"

Tears slowly found their way down her cheeks. She knelt in front of him taking his hands in hers. When she spoke her voice sounded small and frightened. "I'm sorry. I really am. It's just that when I thought that you were with Valerie, I became so angry. I can't...I... can't lose someone that I love again." Using her free hand, she wiped the tears from her cheek.

Tyler leaned forward and kissed her gently. When he pulled back, in his eyes she saw everything that she needed to know. "I love you, baby, and I'm not going anywhere unless you want me to go."

Holly got up to sit on the side of the bed, and looked into his eyes. "I love you too." She moved close and kissed him slowly. His tongue traced her lips and sent shivers through her. She moaned and pulled him down as she lay back on the bed. She reached for the buttons on his shirt again. "Ow."

"Oh, I'm sorry. Is it bad? Do you need to go to the hospital?"

"No I'll be all right, but I feel sorry for any fool who would ever decide to break in—"

At that moment, Terry burst in the room, and froze when she saw Holly and Tyler lying on the bed. "Hey, Reds, I thought you were gone out. Uh, carry on," Terry said waving her hand toward the bed. "I'm just looking for Abby's skates?" Holly remained silent, pointing toward the closet. Terry walked across the room, opening the door as she spoke. "Dee and I are taking the kids skating, and Abby says she can't go skating without them, and I don't want to listen to her and Keith whining." She squatted down, crawling in the back of the closet as she continued to talk. "You know what? They are going to start doing ice skating at the rink. I talked to the manager and she said that it would be starting in November. I was thinking that—"

"Is she always like this?" Tyler asked as he watched Terry pulling the skates from the closet.

"Unfortunately," Holly said.

"So," Terry was saying, as she draped the laces of the tied-together skates over her shoulder and crossed the room to the door. "I'll get out of your way." She walked through the doorway, and then turning back to Holly and Tyler, she said, "You guys know that it's more fun doing that naked." Tyler laughed.

"I sort of remember that," Holly said.

Terry nodded "Oh. Just thought I'd mention it."

How's your chest?" Holly asked running her finger along the front of Tyler's shirt.

"Oh, it's killing me. I can hardly stand the pain," he said faking a groan.

"Poor baby. What if I kiss it and make it better?"

"I don't know," he sighed. "I guess we'll have to try it and see."

She unbuttoned his shirt, kissing his chest then slowly slid her tongue across the tight muscles of his chest to his left nipple. Her warm tongue swirled around his nipple and then she gently pulled it into her mouth bringing an instant moan from him. Looking up she smiled at him as he watched her in fascination. He traced the tip of his finger across her lip and she grabbed it, pulling it into her mouth and gently sucking it as he slowly pulled it out. Her teeth gently nipped his stomach and then she unbuttoned his pants.

His cell phone rang and he ignored it, focusing

only on Holly. "Shit. If I have a heart attack, please don't call the ambulance," Tyler joked as he looked down at her.

His cell rang for the third time.

"I think you should get that."

"No," Tyler said reaching for her as she sat up and reached in his pocket for the phone. She handed it to him. "What?" he barked.

"Can I speak to Tyler?"

"Who is this?"

"My name is Crystal. I'm calling about Rashard."

Tyler quickly sat up. "What about Rashard?"

"He's been arrested."

Chapter Twenty-nine

On the way to the police station Tyler remained silent. Holly rode next to him realizing that he needed this time to think. She reached for his hand squeezing it, and he glanced over at her thankful that she was there with him. Tyler could not imagine what Rashard could do to get himself arrested. He was a good guy, hard working, honest, easygoing.

When Tyler and Holly walked into the station house, Tyler spotted his aunt sitting in one of the chairs that lined the wall. She was next to a young woman who looked just as concerned and afraid as his aunt did. Holly told him that she would go into the back and see what she could find out. As Tyler approached the woman, Jocelyn stood. "Tyler."

He hugged his aunt. When she pulled back, she turned to the woman next to her. "Crystal, this is my nephew, Tyler. Tyler, this is Rashad's friend, Crystal Raymond."

Tyler nodded shaking the woman's hand and then turned back to his aunt. "Aunt Jos, what happened?"

Jos shook her head. "I don't want to talk about it right now; I just want to get my baby out of this place."

Tyler sat down on one side of Jocelyn while Crystal sat on the other. Tyler looked over at his aunt; she looked so tired and old to him at this moment. He took her hand and kissed it. She looked at him with tears welling in her eyes.

"Hey," Holly said walking toward them. Tyler, Jocelyn and Crystal all stood.

"How's my baby?"

Holly nodded. "He's okay. He has never been in any trouble before and he has a few other things in his favor. I'm told he will probably be released on his own recognizance."

"Were you able to see him?" Jos wanted to know. "Is he all right?"

"I saw him. He's okay."

"Did he tell you what happened?" Tyler asked.

Holly looked at Jos, and then at Tyler. "Um, yeah."

"And?"

Holly didn't answer. She just looked at Jocelyn. "Jos?"

"Tyler, I want you to stay calm."

"Aunt Jos, tell me what happened?"

"Tyler."

"Aunt Jos, please tell me what happened."

She sighed. "I went out to run some errands this morning, and when I got home Yvette and that Roland was in my bedroom." She paused. "When I went to see what they were doing Yvette was sitting on my bed and he was going through my jewelry box. I asked them what they were doing, and Yvette said that they were just looking around. I took my jewelry box from him and told him that I wanted him to leave my house immediately. He got real angry, and started threatening me and calling me names,"

"Oh, I'm gonna kill him." Tyler clenched his fists.

"Tyler, calm down." Holly placed a hand on his arm.

"Then he pushed me," Jos said quietly.

The muscles in his jaw flexed. "First I'm going to beat the hell out of him and then I'm going to kill him."

"No, I don't want you to do anything. Let the police handle this. That's why Rashard is here now." Tyler closed his eyes, rubbing them with the heels of his hands. "I didn't hear Rashard come in," Jos continued. "When Rashard walked into my bedroom and saw Roland practically standing over me cursing me, Rashard hit him. And he kept hitting him. Crystal and I tried to pull him off Roland, but he was so angry. That was when Yvette called the police and told them that someone was beating up her boyfriend."

"What? She called the police on her cousin, not caring that her asshole boyfriend was threatening you? That bitch." Tyler's jaw tightened. "Okay, where are they?"

Holly, seeing how close he was to the breaking point, put her hand on Tyler's arm. His muscles were tense with anger barely held in check. "Tyler, think about this. Going over there tonight is not going to do anyone any kind of good. We'll tackle it in the morning. Your aunt needs you calm right now."

Tyler took a few deep breaths and was silent for a moment, but he finally nodded. "You're right. I'll handle this tomorrow." He looked up at her, and his eyes were hard. "But I will handle this. That asshole's going to answer to me."

Tyler was quiet on the ride over to his aunt's the next morning. Abby was still at Dee and Ben's, and Holly had insisted that he pick her up on the way. Tyler seemed calmer today, but there was cool determination in his eyes that made her glad she'd come along. She wouldn't let him get himself thrown in jail too over this piece-of-crap Roland.

She was half-surprised when Tyler pointed out his car in her Aunt's driveway. "I can't believe he has the nerve to be here today. I would have thought he'd have been long gone by now."

"That's fine," Tyler said quietly. "I'd have been disappointed if I hadn't gotten the chance to talk to him."

"Tyler…."

"I know, Holly. Just help me keep my cool…if you can."

The two of them walked into the house and found Yvette and Roland both lying on the couch, watching TV. Tyler didn't raise his voice, but his tone had both of them looking up fast. "Roland, get your sorry ass out of my aunt's house."

Roland glared back. "I didn't do nuthin', and I ain't goin' nowhere unless your aunt tells me to. What business is it of yours anyway?"

Tyler didn't answer. He headed into the kitchen, where his aunt was frying bacon. "Aunt Jos, why's he still here?"

She turned to him, and her eyes were tired. "They were both here this morning when I got up. I didn't have it in me to get into a shouting match first thing in the morning."

"So you're cooking them breakfast," he asked flatly.

"Tyler—."

"Do you want them in this house?" he interrupted.

"Of course not Roland, but Yvette..."

"I understand."

Tyler went back into the living room. "Looks like you won't be staying, asshole. My aunt wants you out." Tyler walked to the corner, picked up one of the boxes and walked to the front door. Juggling the box, he opened the door, walked onto the front porch and threw the box in the yard.

Yvette and Roland immediately jumped up. "Man, what the fuck is wrong with you?"

"You're what's wrong with me." Yvette opened her mouth. Tyler didn't even look at her. "Shut up, Yvette." Surprised, she closed her mouth. "Unless you want to have your ass beat again," he looked pointedly at Roland's black eye and busted lip, "I suggest you go." Roland took a step close to Tyler. He was shorter than Tyler and Tyler outweighed him by at least thirty pounds. Tyler grinned nastily. "Oh, please, give me a reason."

Roland looked Tyler from head to toe, but took a step back. "You can kick me out now, but you can't keep me out. Yvette wants me here."

"That's right, baby," Yvette purred, glaring at Tyler. "This is my house too, and I have a say in who stays."

Before Tyler could answer, Holly stepped to his side. Pushing her coat back, so Roland could see her sidearm, she pulled out her badge and flashed it. "I don't think we've been introduced. I'm Detective Holly Lawson. And I know who you are. You're Roland Jackson. Matter of fact," she added casually, "Word is that you're wanted for questioning on an attempted murder case in Bolingbrook. If you're staying here, I'll be sure to provide your new address to the Bolingbrook PD."

Roland immediately paled. "No problem, uh, Officer. Actually, my mom wants me to come stay with her for a while—she's getting old now, and you know, uh…."

"Roland!" Yvette screeched. "What the hell? No, I want you to stay here!"

"Where does your mom live, Roland?" Holly asked sweetly. "Around here?"

"Uh, no," he stammered, not looking at Yvette. "Ah, down south. Georgia."

"No, he's not going anywhere," Yvette declared. She looked at her aunt who was standing in the hallway that leads from the kitchen. "If he leaves, I leave."

Jos shook her head and sighed. "If that's the way it has to be." She turned and walked back to the kitchen.

Roland stepped next to the stack of boxes in the corner "My stuff, I just need to put it in the car."

Yvette turned and headed toward the kitchen, but Tyler blocked her path. "Where the hell do you think you're going?"

"I'm going to talk to Aunt Jos,"

"No!" Rashard, who was coming in the front door, followed by Crystal, said. "You're going to pack your shit and you're getting out of my mother's house."

"But—" Yvette murmured.

An hour later Yvette was putting the last of the bags that she had room for into Roland's car and they were driving off.

Tyler sighed and turned to Holly. "Baby, thanks for being here with me. But you know, I was really looking forward to at least breaking his nose or something."

"Maybe next time." Holly patted his arm in sympathy.

Chapter Thirty

The season was moving from summer to fall. Holly, Abby, and Tyler were settling into a comfortable pattern. On the mornings that Holly and Abby went out for their run, Tyler would rise early, do his workout in his home gym, and then have breakfast ready when Holly and Abby arrived at his house. On the other days Tyler would go to the gym where he had a membership then he'd go home to shower and go over to Holly's where she and Abby would prepare breakfast for the three of them.

"T, can I get these?" Abby asked Tyler as she held up a bag of Garden Salsa Sun chips. Tyler did not look up, he just nodded as he dropped a jar of salsa and tortilla chips in the shopping cart. For the last three days, Holly and Abby had eaten their meals at Tyler's house. Holly had been putting in extra hours at work and she hadn't had time to go grocery shopping. Tyler told her that he would wait for Terry to drop Abby off, and he and Abby could do the grocery shopping together.

"I don't think that's a good idea," Holly had said to him when he'd suggested that he take Abby and do the grocery shopping.

"Why not? I do my grocery shopping."

"No, I don't mean the shopping part. I mean the taking Abby shopping part.

"You take her with you all of the time don't you?"

"Yeah, but I'm used to it. She usually finds something in every aisle that she wants and you have to keep her from getting too much junk."

"I can do that. I just need to keep her busy, I'll send her to pick up a few things, and she'll be so busy helping out that she won't focus on the snack foods."

Holly just laughed saying, "If you say so."

Now, standing in the supermarket, Tyler checked off the items on his list. He would have Abby run and get a few things to keep her occupied. "Hey, Squirt, I need a medium size box of rice," Tyler said as they turned down the next aisle.

"Okay…T, what's your favorite soda?"

"Hmm, I don't think I have a favorite," Tyler answered while he compared the contents of two different cans of soup.

"Can you grab two cans of gravy? One chicken and one beef," Tyler said studying the shopping list. Abby nodded and dropped the box of rice in the cart before disappearing again.

A moment later she was back with two cans of gravy. "T, do you like chewy or crunchy chocolate chip cookies?"

"Chewy."

They went down the cereal aisle, and Tyler checked the shopping list as he pushed the cart. He nearly ran someone over. "I'm sorry." Tyler looked up and into the face of his cousin Yvette.

Yvette was as surprised to see Tyler as he was to see her. "Hey, Tyler."

"Yvette." Tyler took Abby's hand and pushed the cart around Yvette.

"You don't have time for your cousin?" Yvette said when Tyler walked past her. "You still think you're all that don't you? But you're still that same little dirty kid whose junkie parents didn't want him." Tyler kept walking. "Hey, little girl. You better hope Tyler's a better father to you than his daddy was to him!"

Tyler's jaw clenched. He walked to the end of the aisle with Abby and squatted down next to her. "Hey, Squirt, wait here for a minute, will you?" Abby nodded as Tyler rose and walked back to Yvette. Yvette's posture went rigid, and her eyes darted from side to side.

"You know, the only reason that I haven't slapped the hell out of you before now is because I am a real man. Unlike that sorry son of a bitch you've been laid up with who robs and terrorizes old ladies. You are the one who is still that same bitter little girl who was devastated by her parents abandoning her. But now she needs to grow up and realize that no one owes her anything and that if she's ever going to have anything in life, she has to earn it." She opened her mouth and Tyler raised his hand. "You know what, I don't care what you say to me anymore, you're nothing to me and you can't hurt me." He looked over his shoulder at Abby, then turning back to Yvette he took a step closer to her. "You see that little girl over there, she means the world to me, and if you EVER say anything to hurt her. I swear I am going to kick your ass. Do you understand me?"

She swallowed hard and then nodded. Tyler took a step back, seeing a man come up on her right. "You aw'right?" He asked Yvette. She nodded again.

Tyler glared at the other man, giving him a once-over that said 'you're not worth acknowledging,' and then turning, he walked back toward Abby. "Hey, Tyler?" Yvette called, "Tyler?" He glared over his shoulder. "Do you think you can lend me a couple dollars?"

Shaking his head Tyler took Abby's hand and led her to the cash register to check out.

When Tyler and Abby returned home from the grocery store, they put the bags on the table and started taking everything out. Tyler started putting the groceries away while Abby sat at the table watching him. Looking down at the food stacked on the table he frowned. Funny, he didn't remember there being so much junk food on the list. There were two bags of chips, a large pack of cookies, a two-liter bottle of cola and a few other things. He picked up a six-pack of Snickers and looked at Abby.

"You said that you liked them."

"Does your mom let you buy stuff like this when you two go grocery shopping?"

"No, Mommy doesn't like to buy good stuff,"

Tyler rubbed his brow. "Your mother is going to be so mad."

"Hey," Holly called from the living room.

Tyler looked at all the junk food on the table. "Crap." He scooped most of it up and stepped to the sink opening the door underneath and shoving everything inside. Abby was behind him and passed him the cookies and two-liter soda. He put them in and quickly closed the door just as Holly walked into the kitchen.

When Holly walked into the kitchen, she saw Tyler and Abby standing with their backs to the sink smiling at her. Holly stopped looking at the suspicious looks on their faces. She laughed walking all the way into the kitchen. "How'd it go at the market?"

"It was fine; we got everything that was on the list, plus a few extra things," Tyler said.

"Hi, Momma." Abby smiled up at her mother.

Holly laughed shaking her head. "Hey, baby. Did you do your homework?" Abby ran to her mother giving her a quick peck on the cheek and then went off to do her homework.

Holly crossed the room and stepped into Tyler's arms. "Hi."

"Hey, beautiful," he leaned forward kissing the corner of her mouth, "I've missed you."

Holly grabbed his bottom lip between her teeth, teasing it lightly before releasing it. "Oh yeah?"

"Mmm." He moved his lips covering hers, and slid his hand down slightly, squeezing her bottom. She parted her lips, and he deepened the kiss, sliding his tongue inside her mouth. She kissed him back with a hunger she didn't know she had.

Pulling back, Holly said, "Abby might come down." She bit her lip looking up at him. "We'll finish this later." He growled at her and she laughed.

"Oh yeah, guess who I saw at the grocery store?" Tyler said as he moved to the table picking up some of the packages and putting them in the cabinets. Holly took the eggs from the table and opened the carton, putting the eggs in the refrigerator door.

"Who?"

"Yvette."

"How'd that go?" Holly asked crossing the room and dropping the egg carton in the recycle bin. Tyler shook his head slightly and hunched his shoulders.

"Abby and I ate dinner before we went shopping. We had lasagna. I put a plate in the microwave for you." He crossed the kitchen to the doorway. "I have a few things in the truck that I need to take in the house. Be right back."

"Hey," Holly called from where she stood next to the sink; she had opened the cabinet doors. "I'm thinking you might want to keep yours and Abby's stash at your house."

Chapter Thirty-one

It was 6:35 in the morning, and Janet was sitting at a corner table of Bella Internet Café working on her second cup of coffee. She scanned her surroundings and with shaky hands, she picked up her cup and sipped the cooling drink. A man about 35 walked past the table looking down at her. She pulled the brim of her hat down and brushed the dark hair of her wig over her shoulder. She felt like crap. She had a headache, an upset stomach and her head was hot and it itched like hell because of the damn wig she wore half of the time when she went out in public.

So far, things at Risa's place were going okay. No one seemed to notice her in the office buildings where they cleaned, and the environment that she was living in… Well, to Janet it was like living on a different planet altogether. They did not have the luxuries that she took for granted when she was free, no housekeeper, or nanny to take care of the children. No unlimited cash flow. Hell, Risa didn't even have a computer. But the good thing was that no one bothered her, no one looked at her. No one ever talked to her and that was just the way she wanted it.

Aside from her living arrangements, things had

totally taken a turn for the worse. She had been free for almost a month. By now, she and Ben should have been in each other's arms, or better yet, on a plane together headed to a faraway island oasis. No, this was not good, not good at all. Now she knew why he hadn't left that woman, why he'd stayed away from his true love all this time. Because of the child. His child. No…not only his child, their child.

Janet watched as a group of seven nurses walked into the coffee shop. As she watched them, she smiled. Things were not the way they should be, but she was going to change that. She was going to make things right. She headed up to the counter to get a refill on her coffee. Pulling out her purse, she grabbed a five-dollar bill. Casually, she dropped it on the ground. Leaning down close to the nurse in front of her, she picked up the bill and unfastened the nurse's ID, which was clipped to the lab coat slung over her arm.

"Excuse me, ma'am," she said, pocketing the ID and holding out the bill. "You dropped this."

The woman smiled at her. "Thank you, that's so nice of you!"

"Just doing my good deed for the day." Janet smiled.

"Let me pay for your refill. It's not too often that people go out of their way to be nice these days," the woman said, handing over the money to the cashier.

Janet accepted the cup, and with a friendly wave to the appreciative nurse, she left the coffee shop.

Three hours later Janet walked to her parents' door, felt for the hidden key, and let herself inside the house. The house was quiet and cool. When Janet had woke up that morning she felt great, better than she had felt in years. Today was the day that she would be reunited with Ben and her stolen child. She told Risa that she had to leave and gave her three hundred dollars of the money she had earned. She packed up all of her things and called a cab, having the driver drop her off three blocks from her parents' house.

Taking her tote with her Janet went up to take a shower. After the shower, she dressed in the nurse's uniform and put on her glasses. She walked to the bed and picked up the nurses' ID that she had stolen while she was at the coffee shop that morning. Peering at the photo, she looked at herself in the mirror. The hair was all wrong, but she could be mistaken for the nurse in the photo. Janet dug inside her tote bag and carried the scissors to the bathroom with her. She cut two more inches off her hair and smiled. "Perfect," she told herself. "Good morning, I'm Nurse Devers, and I'm here to go over the student records for the school board." As she left the bathroom, she said. "Now let's hope they left the keys for the cars in the same place."

Janet went downstairs and checked her father's office. He usually kept the keys for the vehicles in the top drawer of his desk. She opened the drawer, and bingo. She let herself into her parent's four-car garage and slid behind the wheel of a silver 3-Series BMW. When she stuck the key in the ignition and turned it the car started. *Oh yes*, she thought, tapping the leather-bound steering wheel with her balled fist, *Janet Summers, this is YOUR day.*

Irene Devers, RN, parked in the spot reserved for the school nurse at Westwood Heights elementary. She marched purposefully up to the school office and looked the receptionist in the eye.

"Good morning," she said. "I'm Nurse Devers with the County Board of Health and the Chicago Board of Education. I'm here to go over your student medical records."

"Good morning, Ms. Devers...Ms. Naderi, our school nurse isn't due in today. She goes to Linden Park elementary on Tuesdays and Fridays."

"Janet looked inside the portfolio she had taken from her father's office. She flipped through a few sheets of paper and then looked back at the receptionist. "Well, I'm sure she knew that I was coming, she must have forgotten." She sighed. "I suppose I can go through the files alone, although it would be quicker if she were to assist in identifying any new admissions."

"I don't know if I can let you in the health suite without her permission."

Janet raised her voice slightly. "This is not the only audit that I have to do this week. I have a tight schedule and I cannot just change it just because someone else cannot keep track of his or her appointments. Look Ms—" she looked at the nameplate on the woman's desk, and then deliberately softened her tone, "Wulf, I know this isn't your fault, and I'm not trying to give you a hard time. It's just not possible for me to postpone this."

The young woman paused and then said, "Wait here, please." A moment later, she disappeared into the nearest office. Emerging a couple of minutes later, she said, "Nurse Devers, I'm sorry for the mix-up. Let me get the key to the health suite and I'll let you in."

Once in the health suite Janet thanked the other woman for her help and waited for her to leave the office and close the door behind her. She walked to the file cabinet and opened the drawers. She searched the files for the name Harrison. There were five, three were boys. She scanned the two files of girls with the last names of Harrison. The first was Candice; the file said that she was in kindergarten. Janet was not sure but she thought that the child had looked a little older. She opened the file checking it. Parents Clara and Walt.

She shook her head dropping the file and opening the next one. Angela Harrison was closer to the right age. Janet's heart raced as she opened the file. Parents Angelina and Bill. "No!" she threw the file across the room. Slamming the file cabinet drawer, she placed her hands on her hips. "Yes, of course." That selfish bitch would want to give the child her surname instead of Ben's. Opening the file drawer that contained the M's. She searched for the file that said Meyers. Only one. She pulled it out. Keith Meyers, Parents Terry and David.

This cannot be happening. "Mother Fu—" The knock on the door drew Janet's attention. Janet crossed the room and opened the door. "Yes?"

Ms. Wulf smiled at her. "I just wanted to let you know that there's coffee in the office if you'd like some."

Before Janet could speak, she saw two girls walking down the hall. "Good morning, Ms. Wulf."

"Good morning, Abby. Good morning, Briana." Janet could not believe it. She thought that she would have to spend some time trying to find their daughter, and at this point she had doubted if she would, but here she was coming right to her. *Yes, Janet this is your day. Abby, our daughter's name is Abby.*

"Thank you, Ms. Wolf," Janet said closing the door and leaning against it. She giggled as her excitement built. She opened the door to peer out and saw the two girls leave the office and head down the hall. Janet stepped from the office and followed the girls to a second-floor classroom. Then she quickly made her way back to the health suite. "Okay, Janet, everything is going good. Now you need to figure out how to get her alone and out of the building."

Abby carried her tray to the table as she talked to Briana and Paige. Once she sat down, she shook her milk, opened it and took a drink. "Abby?" She looked up at a woman in a nurse's uniform. The nurse squatted as she spoke to Abby. "I'm Ms. Devers. I'm filling in for the school nurse today, and I need you to come to the nurses' office when you've finished your lunch. It's very important, okay?" Abby nodded. "Don't forget."

Abby nodded again. "Yes, ma'am."

Forty-five minutes later, a relieved Janet was threading through the traffic with Abby beside her. She had told Abby that there was an accident and that her mommy had been hurt. She could not believe how easy the child had bought the story. When she had heard that her mommy was hurt she did not ask any questions, she just obediently followed Janet out to her car after Janet had told her that she would take her to her mommy. "Don't worry, Abby, it's nothing serious, your mommy will be fine." She glanced over at the child. "But I need to make a small detour on the way…Um, you wouldn't happen to have a cell phone?"

"No, ma'am," Abby answered, a dazed look on her face. On the verge of tears, she stared bleakly out of the window.

At 1:45 p.m. Janet pulled into her parents' driveway. She used the remote to open the garage door and drove inside. Abby looked up at her, tears flowing freely down her cheeks. "I just need to pick up some documents and I'll take you to your mommy." Janet got out of the car, going to Abby's door and opening it. "Come inside with me, it'll only take a moment." Abby brushed her tears away and slid out of the car, following the nurse inside the house.

Janet lowered the garage door and quietly locked the deadbolt to the door leading to the garage, and slipped the key into her pocket.

"Why are we here? Where's my mommy? I want to see my mommy," Abby said, her words spilling out nonstop.

Janet put her arm around the child's shoulder, and said, "Abby, I need to tell you something."

Pulling away, Abby looked up at her. A look of doubt crossed her face. "Who are you?" she demanded. Then after a pause, "You're not a nurse! What's going on?" She dashed to the front door, but found it locked. "Open the door, I want to go home. I want my mommy!"

"Abby, relax—please. Sit down for a minute. I can explain everything. First off, you're safe with me; I just had to do things in a slightly…unorthodox way. Do you know what that means?"

Abby remained rooted in her place next to the front door. "I know what you get for kidnapping," Abby shot back. "Let me go NOW!"

Janet stood and walked toward her. "Tell you what, honey, I'm going to get you a nice warm glass of milk and some cookies. Then I'm going to turn on the TV and you can watch it while I change out of my uniform. After that, we're going to have a nice chat, you and me, and everything will be fine. You'll see. Trust me."

She disappeared into the kitchen, returning a few minutes later with the milk and cookies. Then, with a smile and a reassuring nod, she switched on the TV, and offered the remote to Abby. Abby looked at the remote and then at Janet. Janet sighed, setting the remote on the table and heading upstairs.

Abby gave her 30 seconds, and then made a grab for the closest phone. She was halfway through dialing her mother's cell, when she realized that there was no dial tone. She whimpered. "Um, the phone has been temporality disconnected," Janet's voice called from upstairs. "Sorry, Abby, I forgot to tell you. How about you just relax awhile, and I'll explain everything. Okay?" Abby dropped the phone.

She began to look around for something light enough to throw, but heavy enough to smash a window.

"Oh, yeah, and before you try breaking the windows. Reinforced double glaze, not so easy to break," she called cheerfully from the shower.

Abby spun around looking at all of the windows. Tears welled in her eyes and streamed down her cheeks. Wrapping her arms around her waist, she sank to the floor next to the window and cried for her mommy.

A short while later, feeling refreshed and clean, Janet came downstairs. She stopped in the doorway seeing Abby sitting on the floor rocking to and fro. She glanced at the plate of cookies and the glass of milk sitting on the table. Sighing, she walked to the sofa. "Abby, come sit next to me." She patted the spot beside her. Abby looked up at her with large frightened eyes, shaking her head.

"Okay-y-y," said Janet, a note of irritation creeping into her voice. "First things first. As you guessed, I'm not Nurse Devers. I'm Janet, and I know your daddy very well. In fact, we are special friends. Really special," she added emphatically.

A frown spread across Abby's brow.

"Forget the nurse thing for a moment," Janet continued. "Now, your mom is fine. There was no accident and nothing happened, she couldn't be better. Got that? No problem, no worries, good as gold." This statement seemed to have little effect on the child, to Janet's amazement.

"What do you mean, 'You know my daddy?'" Abby asked.

Puzzled, Janet replied, "Your daddy and I, we had something very special—and we still do." Complete fear rose in Abby as she listened to Janet explain. "Your daddy and I are going to get married. We are going to move away to a tropical island and live happily ever after. Your daddy, me and, of course, you. I'm going to be your new mommy." Abby briskly shook her head. "Yes. And, I promise I'll be a wonderful mommy. You'll see. And we'll have the perfect family."

• • •

At 3:15, Saundra got out of the van and walked to the passenger side. She glanced at her watch again. Abby should have been outside by now. She glanced back at the van and then at the school again. Then turning to the van, she unloaded the kids and marched to the building. "I'm looking for Abigail James."

The receptionist looked up at her. "All of the children should be gone. "

"Abby didn't come out yet. Can you check to see if

she's helping her teacher or had to stay for detention?"

After calling the classroom, Ms. Wulf turned back to Saundra, her eyes large and frightened. "Abby went to the nurse's office after lunch and didn't return to class."

Chapter Thirty-two

The school was abuzz with cops. The teachers that were still in the building and other staff members were being interviewed in classrooms, while the areas around the nurse's parking spot, the main office, and the health suite were being swept by Crime Scene officers. The moment Holly walked into the building it was evident that all hell was about to break loose. She stormed down the hall with her fists clenched, her nostrils flaring and a take-no-prisoners glare in her eyes. When she entered the office, she immediately wanted to know how a total stranger managed to walk out of the school with her child. Then she asked to see the stupid bitch that didn't check on Abby after she hadn't returned from the health suite. Captain McGuiness asked the principal if he could use her office. He immediately ordered Holly to follow him into the office and told her to close the door.

"Lawson you need to calm down." Holly paced the room. "You getting these people riled up isn't going to help find your daughter." He paused. "I'm not going to tell you that I know how you feel, because I don't. But I've been doing this long enough to know that you're striking out because you're afraid for your child. Calm down so we can do our jobs. We'll find her. Whatever we have to do, we'll find her."

McGuiness and Holly emerged from the principal's office as McGuiness' phone rang. "McGuiness." He nodded and then snapped his phone shut. "They brought Rivers down from upstate; he asked to speak to you personally." Holly nodded and they left the school headed to the station.

Against his better judgment, McGuiness allowed Holly to go into the interrogation room with Daley while he questioned Rivers. When Holly walked into the questioning room, she nodded at Daley and closed the door behind her. "Detective Lawson, what a pleasure. Don't you look lovely?" Rivers said cheerfully.

"Rivers, what do you want?" Holly demanded as soon as she had closed the door.

"No hello, no hug and kiss for your old friend Stevie?" Rivers' asked. Holly struggled to keep her temper in check as she looked at the man sitting at the end of the table. He shrugged his shoulders. "Always the one to keep things all business…" He sat back folding his arms and grinned. "I hear that your kid is missing."

"Where'd you get a notion like that?" Holly said, sitting on the far end of the table and folding her arms.

"A little bird told me." He met Holly's gaze.

"Like I asked before. What do you want?"

"I think I might have something you want." Using the pinky finger of his left hand he dug in his ear, checked the wax under his nail and brushed it on his pants. "Something very valuable…to you." Holly's heart thundered in her ears. Just the thought of this pig having anything to do with Abby made her want to be violently ill, moreover it made her want to rip out his throat.

Holly walked to the other side of the room, facing the wall; she took a deep breath, then she turned back around facing the room. Daley grabbed one of the chairs turning it backwards and sitting down on Rivers' right side. She asked him questions with the hope that they would find out if he really had something to do with Abby's disappearance, or if he was just jerking their chains.

After ten minutes, both Holly and Daley came to the same conclusion. Rivers didn't know anything. Holly turned toward the door and said. "We're done here." Daley nodded rising to his feet and following Holly to the door.

"I think we might be able to make a trade. I give you what you want, and you and your bosses," Rivers said jerking his head in the direction of the one-sided mirror on the opposite wall, "Let me post bail."

Daley grunted. "Rivers cut the bullshit..."

"Abby sure is a pretty girl. I don't think that you should be letting her read those Goosebumps books, might give her nightmares." Holly froze with her hand on the doorknob. She turned to look at Rivers. "She has your eyes." Rivers was saying, a sly grin on his face.

Holly looked at Daley. He met her gaze, and then briefly glanced up at the mounted camera and back at her again. Holly looked up at the camera; the red light indicating that the camera was recording was not blinking. Daley walked to the door, opened it and stepped outside.

Daley opened the door to the next room, stepping inside. He paused, surprised to see McGuiness in the room. "I think we could all use a cup of coffee," Mc-

Guiness said to the other cops in the room. They all agreed and filed out of the room, closing the door behind them. "Anybody know anything about fixing that dammed camera?" McGuiness asked.

Holly walked to the table, sitting on the edge, and then using her hands she pushed herself to the center and swung around to face Rivers sitting with her legs folded. She leaned forward a bit. "I'd like to know if you really know something about my daughter's disappearance. Or are you just blowing smoke up my ass?"

He chuckled. "Oh, baby, I'd love to blow more than smoke up that ass of yours."

With lightning quick speed, Holly kicked Rivers, catching him in the upper part of his chest and sending him tumbling backwards. She was off the table grabbing the other chair, spinning it around, slamming it down and straddling it before Rivers could catch his breath. He struggled, pushing at the chair that lay across his torso, and then looking up at the rage- and hate-filled face of the woman glaring down at him, he froze. A bead of sweat ran from his temple to the back of his head.

"Listen up, maggot," Holly said calmly, so calmly that Rivers felt a chill run up his spine. "Your life doesn't mean shit to me. And neither does this job if I don't have my little girl. I lost my husband because of some bottom-feeding shit bag like you and I'm not about to lose my baby. Now." She reached behind her back under her jacket and produced a 38 special. Seeing the handgun, Rivers' eyes grew large and he sucked in a deep breath. "I don't have the patience or the time to fuck with you. I'm going to give you to the count of ten to tell me where she is, or the ME is going to have to use a turkey baster to sop up what's left of what little brains you have." With her elbow resting on the back of the chair, she pointed the gun toward the ceiling. "1, 2, 3…"

"Detective, can't we talk—?"

She pointed the gun down, aiming it directly between Rivers' eyes. "6, 7…"

Five minutes later Holly was walking out of the interrogation room closing the door behind her. "He doesn't know shit," she told McGuiness, Daley and the other cops who were waiting in the hall. "One of the guys up at the pen is the father of one of Abby's school-mates and that stupid ass told Rivers a few things about Abby. He thought he could use it to get out on bail and disappear.

McGuiness heaved a heavy sigh brushing his hair back. He looked at the other officers gathered around. "Give us a minute." He waited until they were alone and turned to Holly.

"Look, Lawson, I know everyone thinks I'm an asshole, but maybe I'm not as big of an asshole as you think I am. I know this ain't easy for you. But here's what I want you to do. Go home. Call your friends and family, sit by the phone. Okay? We got your home phone tapped, as well as your cell, just be there and wait for the call. It'll be either the perp with a ransom demand, or it'll be me telling you everything's fine and we got her waiting for you to pick up. Okay? Now GO!"

"But Cap—" Holly started to say.

His cell phone rang and he pulled it out of his pocket. "GO, Lawson—now that's an order! Let us do what we're trained for, and you go home and stay by the phone."

"Yes, sir," Holly replied. The captain was already talking into his cell phone before she walked away.

• • •

During the last few minutes of a training drill, Tyler felt his cell phone vibrate in his pocket. *Damn it*, he thought, *If Roland's back, I really am going to kill him.* But when he flipped open the phone, he didn't recognize the number.

Before he could get out so much as a "Hello," Terry's voice was yelling in his ear.

"Slow down. What's wrong? Is it Holly?" he asked, fear raising the hair on the back of his neck.

"It's Abby!" he finally heard her say. "She's gone. Get over here—Holly needs you right now." The line went dead.

Tyler was momentarily stunned. He snapped his cell phone shut. What did Terry mean she was gone? Where the hell did she go?

"Steve," he shouted to one of the other trainers. "Take over. I've got an emergency." The man asked what was wrong, but Tyler didn't hear him. He was already in a dead run for his truck.

Chapter Thirty-three

"Janet!" the voices were saying, several voices that sounded like they were coming from different directions. "What are you doing here? Whatever did you do to your hair? Wake up, Janet!"

After she'd tried to calm the child to no avail, Janet found that she could only sit and watch as the child cried herself to sleep on the sofa. Trying to reason with the child was tiring and Janet sat back closing her eyes for a moment and drifted off to sleep. Now she struggled through the layers of consciousness. Shaking her head she found the voices suddenly come together as one—the voice of her mother. She felt her shoulders being shaken.

"Janet, wake up—please!" No wonder it sounded like her mother. On the other end of the voice was Hilary!

"Mother! What are you doing here? Why aren't you in…Acapulco?"

"What are you doing out of—" She paused not able to say the word "prison." "How did you get out of the hospital? What did you do to your hair? And who's that"—she lowered her voice—"that little girl asleep on the sofa?"

Janet looked terrible, like she'd just scrambled out of a train wreck. Her hair was cropped and dyed a deep brown that made her pale skin look almost translucent. Her eyes were sunken in their sockets, black circles surrounding them, and there was a wild look on her face.

"My God, Janet," demanded her mother, "What have you done?" Hilary walked around Janet, moving toward the child.

Janet jumped up and ran around her mother, cutting off her path. "No, don't touch her." Hilary brought her hand up to her mouth covering a sob. Janet looked over her shoulder then back at mother. "Isn't she beautiful, Mother?"

"Janet, please tell me that you didn't take someone's child!"

"No, mother, I would never do something like that. This is my child, mine and Ben's."

Hilary's gaze left the small form on the sofa and rested on her daughter's face. She couldn't believe what was happening. She looked at the woman standing before her and didn't see her daughter. This wasn't the Janet she'd raised. This was a stranger. A complete and total stranger. And the worst part of it all was that this stranger was insane, and dangerous.

Coming out of her trance, Hilary realized that Janet was talking.

"Mother, we're not going to be here for long. In a few days Ben will meet me, and we'll take our little girl and go away."

Hilary shook her head. "Janet, your father postponed our trip for a month because of some big deal he's working on. He'll be home late tonight. Before he gets home, you must go back to the hospital. And that poor girl must be returned to her parents."

"That's not going to happen, Mother," said Janet, before she stormed out of the room.

Abby stirred in her sleep. Then her eyes opened, and she flinched seeing Hilary bending over her. Quickly Hilary put a finger to her lips, indicating "Ssh-hh." She sat on the sofa next to the child. Abby moved away, tucking her body into the corner of the sofa.

"I know you're afraid," Hilary whispered. "You know what? I'm afraid, too." Hilary looked toward the doorway. "My name is Hilary Summers, and I want to help you get home to your mommy and daddy. What's your name?"

Abby didn't answer, just looked up with fearful eyes.

Hilary nodded. "That's okay, I understand. I've got to get you out of here, but I know she won't let me take you home, so we need to have your parents come and get you. Do you understand?"

Abby nodded, tears welling in her eyes. Hilary moved close, pulling the child toward her in an embrace. "Shh, everything's going to be all right." She began to rock the child, and then in a soothing tone she said, "Listen to me." She looked down and met Abby's tearful gaze. "I promise that I'm going to make sure you get home to your parents."

"Mother?" Janet said her voice cold and emotionless.

Hilary looked up and saw Janet standing in the doorway, leaning casually against the doorframe. Her posture wasn't threatening in any way. But her eyes, her eyes were so hateful and cruel that Hilary had to force herself not to cower.

"Mother, what are you saying to her?"

"I was merely comforting the child, Janet."

Chapter Thirty-four

In the family room Ben was reading to Keith, hoping that it would help him fall asleep. When Keith had found out what had happened to Abby he was so upset that he became ill. Terry rocked him for an hour, consoling him. She assured him that Holly and the police were doing everything they could to find Abby and bring her home. Ben had told Terry and Dee that he would keep an eye on Keith and David while they stayed with Holly.

Holly, Dee and Terry were all huddled close together on the sofa, sometimes crying, talking softly to each other or just sitting quietly. "I don't know if I can do this," Holly's voice cracked as she spoke.

Dee brushed the hair from Holly's face. "Do what, honey?"

"If…if we don't find Abby, I don't know if I can handle it."

"Don't talk like that." Dee squeezed Holly's hand.

"I just can't do it." Holly's lip trembled and new tears ran down her cheeks.

"Dee's right, don't talk like that," Terry said, tears streaming down her own face. "Abby's going to be home soon, and you'll be so happy that you'll let her do whatever she wants. You'll even let her skate down the hall." They all laughed for a brief moment.

"Thanks for being here with me, guys," Holly whispered.

"Where else would we be?" Dee asked.

"We're family," Terry said, "And we love you."

Holly reached out pulling both Terry and Dee into an embrace. "I love you, too."

A knock on the door brought Ben racing to the living room. Terry rose from the sofa to answer the door. "Hey," she said to Tyler as she opened the door.

"Hi," he nodded a greeting to Terry. When he walked into the house Holly was already standing. She rushed across the room and into his arms.

• • •

"Janet, Ben is not going to just let you take his child from her mother, don't be absurd. You need to take her home."

"Uncle Ben?" Abby whispered.

Both Janet and Hilary looked at her. Hilary looked at Janet's startled reaction, then back at Abby. "Tell me, child," Hilary asked. "What is your daddy's name?"

"Edmond, Edmond James. Uncle Ben is married to Aunt Dee." Abby leaned closer to Hilary saying, "She says she knows my daddy, but my daddy is in heaven."

Janet looked at the child. Confused by this unexpected bit of knowledge, Janet jerked as if hit, then shook her head abruptly like she was trying to clear it of something. "No, that's not… No. It can't be…" her voice trailed off.

"And what is your mommy's name?" Hilary inquired.

"Holly," Abby said, and then she leaned close to Hilary again, whispering, "My mommy's a police officer." As she spoke, she did not take her eyes off Janet.

Janet felt like her legs were about to give out. She walked to the armchair, and then looked at the child sitting on the sofa next to her mother. This couldn't be. She'd seen Ben with the child, and there was so much love in the way he looked at her and the way he treated her. Janet thought for sure that the child was his. Janet leaned forward covering her face with her hands.

"Janet, did you hear what she said? Her mother is a police officer. What in god's name were you thinking?"

"Shut up, Mother," Janet yelled.

"You need to take this child home, back to her mother."

"I said shut up, Mother!!" Janet took a deep breath then looking up she peered closer at Abby. "What's your relationship to Ben?" she asked. Abby looked tearfully at her. "Answer me!!" Abby flinched moving behind Hilary,

"Janet, you're scaring her."

"I don't care; I want to know what her connection to Ben is."

Hilary turned to Abby, "Honey, can you tell me how Ben is related to you. Is your mother his sister?"

Abby shook her head. "He married Aunt Dee. Aunt Dee and Mommy grew up together."

Janet thought back to the first time she'd seen Dee, it was at a nightclub and Ben was there with her and some other people. The redhead. "Your mother, she has red hair?" Abby nodded. "This is just perfect." Janet sat back massaging her eyes.

• • •

"Ssh, baby, it's okay," Tyler whispered meaningless words as the woman who meant the world to him sobbed in his arms. He looked up at Ben. "What happened? What's going on?"

Ben quietly told him all they knew. "This woman just walked out of the school with Abby," he said, roughly scrubbing his hands over his face.

Tyler felt hopeless rage well up inside him. Whoever had taken Abby—if they harmed a hair on her head, if they touched her... He calmed himself down when he realized how hard he was squeezing Holly.

Holly needed him; she needed him to keep his head. She'd been there for him, and it was time to return the favor. He couldn't think about her green-eyed imp of a daughter whom he'd fallen in love with too, or he'd go crazy.

He pulled back from Holly and tilted her tear-stained face up to his. "Stop it, Holly. Crying isn't going to help Abby," he said roughly and kissed her. "We'll find her and make the son of a bitch who took her incredibly sorry. We'll find her." He pulled her close again.

Chapter Thirty-five

"I have to go to the bathroom," said Abby.

Hilary rose, taking Abby's hand. "I'll take her."

"No. I'll take her. You stay here. She reached for Abby's hand, tugging her toward the entryway. Then turning to glare at her mother, Janet said, "You…don't move." Janet led Abby to a laundry room. "There's a bathroom in here you can use. I'll be waiting right here, call me when you're finished."

When Abby went into the room Janet locked the door and walked quickly back to the living room, but there was no sign of her mother. "Mother!" she called out. "Mother, where are you?"

She strode from room to room searching, and then heard a noise coming from the direction of the garage and saw keys dangling in the lock. Stepping through the internal door, she heard her mother's quiet voice and flipped on the light switch. "Mother!" she screamed. "I told you NO!!" Janet grabbed the nearest garden tool leaning against the garage wall, and raising it high she swung. The sickening sound of metal meeting flesh echoed in the garage. As Hilary fell, her cell phone clattered to the floor. Janet swooped on it, listened, and heard the voice of a 911 operator asking for clarification.

"Operator," she said. "I do apologize. Just a false alarm. My mother is suffering from dementia. We try to keep her away from the phone, but occasionally something like this happens. So sorry to trouble you." Without waiting for a response, she pressed the end-call button.

Swinging around, she prepared to lock Hilary up somewhere. But the woman hadn't moved. Nor would she ever move again. As Janet looked down, she saw a puddle of blood pouring from the back of her mother's head. On the floor beside the body was an ax. The heavy steel head had literally split the woman's skull.

"Now look what you've made me do, you old fool!" Janet hissed, kicking her mother's lifeless body.

"I'm coming. I'm coming, hold your horses," Janet shouted as Abby banged on the laundry room door. "Little brat," she muttered to herself, and then stopped outside of the door. "Abby, listen to me," she called through the door. "I've got to get a couple things organized before I can let you out. Then we'll go see your Uncle Ben, and he can take you home to your mommy. You'd like that wouldn't you?"

"Yes," came Abby's muffled voice through the door. But Janet didn't hear her. She'd already gone.

Half an hour later Janet was driving her mother's Mercedes into the hills to the west of the city. As late afternoon turned into early evening, Janet stopped at a deserted spot with a drop into thick woods below. She wearily massaged her eyes and then checked that the coast was clear. Satisfied that nobody else was around she pulled the lever to open the trunk and climbed from the car. Going to the trunk, she hefted the carpet-wrapped body of her mother out and over the safety barrier. Then she dragged it to the cliff edge, rolled it over, and watched it disappear into the canopy of trees far below.

She paused to say a prayer. Then she returned to the car, made a U-turn, and headed back to town. Janet felt lighter. She couldn't explain it, but suddenly everything made sense to her. Ben did not know how to contact her. That was why he hadn't come for her. And taking Abby…that was a mistake. She knew Ben loved children and he would not leave knowing the child was missing. Janet tapped the steering wheel as she drove. She would call him, tell him that she had Abby and that she would return her to her mother, and then they could leave. No, she couldn't do that; Ben would be furious with her, he may never forgive her. No, she would not tell him that she had Abby, not on the phone. She would set up a meeting, make him think that she was someone else, and then she would tell him face to face. When he found out what she had done, he would be angry but he would forgive her once he saw her and held her in his arms. Her Benji always forgave her.

She reached for the radio and out of respect for the dead, tuned in to a gospel music station.

Before releasing Abby from the laundry room Janet ran upstairs to shower and change again. She wanted to look beautiful for Ben, and the nurse's uniform just wouldn't do. After taking a quick shower, she went into her old bedroom, opened the closet door and went through the clothes hanging inside. She picked up a few tailored suits, throwing them over her shoulder. She chose a green sequined dress. "Ben used to love me in this." Quickly stripping she slipped the dress on and looked at her reflection in the mirror. The dress literally hung on her like a rag. Sighing, she stripped again and slipped on a simple black dress. It was a little loose but looked better than she'd hoped. She brushed her hair, and then going to her parents' bedroom she sat at her mother's makeup table expertly applying her makeup. She rummaged in the jewelry box, choosing a pearl necklace and tiny pearl earrings. Now she needed to call Ben and set up a meeting. She bit her lip thinking of how she could do this. She couldn't call from her mother's cell phone; the name might show up on the caller ID. She nodded to herself, her lips moving as she formed her final plan. She looked at the clock on the nightstand. It was 4:10 p.m. She had enough time to drive down to the business district. She could go to one of the convenience stores in the area and call Ben from a phone booth. She would tell him that she had Abby, and that he should meet her at Harrison International to pick up the child. That would give her enough time to go to Harrison, find a hiding place until the place was closed, and wait for Ben

As evening set in, Holly nervously paced her living room, while Dee and Terry tried to reassure her and calm her down—though they knew if they were in the same shoes, they wouldn't be handling things quite as well.

Ben and Tyler were talking quietly in the corner of the room when Ben's cell phone rang. He checked the number, but it was unfamiliar to him. He pushed the reject-call button and slid the phone back into his pocket.

It rang a second time, and he saw that it was the previous caller again. He stood and walked to Dee saying softly, "Sweetheart, I'll be right back." She looked at his phone, and then nodded. Walking down the hall to the kitchen he hit the call button answering the phone.

"Harrison." He paused. "Hello?" Nothing. He moved the phone from his ear, preparing to close it.

"Mr. Harrison?'

"Yes."

"Are you alone?"

"What?"

"Are you alone? I have something you want."

"Who is this?"

"It doesn't matter who this is."

"Well, it matters to me," said Ben impatiently. With an angry shake of the head, he snapped the phone closed, and put it back in his pocket then turned on the water at the sink. Within seconds, the phone rang again. He turned off the water and reached for his phone.

"Who the hell is this?"

"Mr. Harrison, don't hang up—I have the child."

"What the hell are you talking about?"

"The child Abby. I have her and I'll only return her to you."

"Look, you sick bastard—"

"Uncle Ben?"

Ben's heart nearly stopped. "Abby?"

"Uncle Ben, please come and get me. I want my mommy."

"I know, honey. I'm coming to get you right away, I promise."

"Mr. Harrison." The voice was on the line again.

"What do you want?"

"I don't want anything. I only want to give her back to her mother." Ben waited. "The people who took her don't know that I've moved her, and that I want to return her."

"Take her to the nearest police station, tell me where you are and I'll get there as quick as I can."

"No. I don't want the police involved. I can't go to jail. I don't trust the police. I don't trust anyone. The girl obviously trusts you, so I'll give her to you. But you have to come and get her now! If they find out I'm gone, they'll come looking for me, and I don't know what will happen to either of us."

Once again, Ben heard Abby crying in the background. The voice repeated, "I need you to come right away." He looked toward the kitchen door and then turned back to the sink.

"Okay. Where are you?"

"I'll meet you at Harrison International exactly thirty minutes from now. I'll be waiting in your office."

"That isn't possible, the offices are closed."

"I have a way."

"I want to speak to Abby again."

"Uncle Ben."

"Abby, honey, I'm coming to get you." Then he heard the connection break before he had a chance to say anything else. He clicked off his phone as he moved toward the back door, and was startled to see Tyler standing a few feet away.

Chapter Thirty-seven

Ben took another step forward and reached for the knob on the back door. "Whoa, fella, where the hell do you think you're going?" Tyler asked, stepping in Ben's path.

"I'm going to get Abby."

"No, you're going to tell her mother and the cops where you're meeting these people, so they can go in there and rescue her."

Ben shook his head determinedly. "That's not going to happen. I have to meet this person in less than thirty minutes, and that may not be enough time for the cops to get there first. The last thing I need is flashing lights and sirens at the critical moment."

"Then they'll come up with something. They do this sort of thing all of the time. Don't be foolish," Tyler tried to reason with him.

"Tyler, use your head. I don't know who this person is, but they seem to know me. If they see anyone coming into the building other than me, if they see any sort of movement that vaguely resembles the law, we may never see Abby again. Or worse, they might harm her. I can't take that chance. I won't. I've wasted enough time as it is. I have to go."

"What are we gonna tell the women?"

"We?"

"Yeah, we. I love Abby as much as you do, maybe more. I'm going with you."

Ben ran his hand through his hair. "Didn't you hear what I just said about spooking them?"

Tyler shook his head. "Benji, my friend, you just ain't listenin.' I said I'm going with you."

Ben rolled his eyes. "Come on, then. But leave the women out of this. They want me to come alone—nobody else. It's far too risky to involve the women."

• • •

"Where's Ben?" Dee said looking toward the kitchen.

"He's probably talking to Tyler, I saw him headed in that direction," Terry said watching Holly pace the room. "Reds, did you eat anything today?" Holly didn't answer. "Reds? Holly?"

"Yeah?" Holly answered.

"Have you eaten anything?"

"I'm not hungry."

"You need something."

"No." Holly shook her head.

Terry rose from the sofa and walked to Holly's side. "I'll get you some grape juice and crackers."

Holly looked at her and smiled. "Thanks." Terry brushed a few strands of Holly's hair behind her ear, and nodded.

"Tyler and Ben aren't in the kitchen." Terry announced as she returned from the kitchen carrying a glass of juice and a few crackers wrapped in a napkin. "They didn't say anything about going out?"

"No, Ben had to take a phone call and never came back."

"They're gone," Terry said.

"Ben wouldn't just leave," Dee said.

Holly glanced up sharply. "What do you mean gone?"

"I mean gone, as in they were in the kitchen, and now they're not," Terry said. Holly glanced out of the window to see that Ben's car was missing from the drive.

"Something's not right," Dee said.

Holly nodded. "She's right. Ben wouldn't just leave, not at a time like this. Did he say who he was taking a call from?" she asked Dee.

"No, he just excused himself."

"Shit," Holly said. "Just what we didn't need."

"I can't imagine where they would have gone," Dee said, sounding alarmed.

"Mommy?" Keith said, tugging his mother's blouse.

"Not now, Keith," Terry said then voiced her thought, "Maybe the kidnapers called him?"

"No, they couldn't have; they would have had to make ransom demands, and he would have to have time to get money," Holly reasoned.

"Mommy?"

"Not now Keith. Maybe they told him that if he told anyone they would hurt Abby?"

Dee shook her head. "No. even if he didn't tell anyone else, he would have told me."

"Mommy?"

"Keith!" Terry yelled. His lip trembled. "Damn it Keith, don't start that crying."

"But, I know where Uncle Ben went."

• • •

As they sped toward the business district Tyler and Ben tried to devise a plan to sneak into Harrison International and get out safely with Abby. They decided that it would be best if Ben appeared to be alone, so as not to scare off the kidnapper.

The plan was for Ben to let Tyler out of the car a block away. Tyler would bring the only weapons they had, two baseball bats they had found in Holly's kitchen pantry. Tyler would then cut across the side of the parking lot and ease his way to the front door. When Ben went inside he would leave the main door open and wait for Tyler. This way they wouldn't be seen on the street together.

Ben parked directly in front of the building and sat watching for Tyler's signal. Tyler was going to press the night light on his watch two times to let Ben know he was in place. After seeing Tyler's watch blink twice, Ben got out of the car and walked to the front door. Once inside Ben waited for Tyler to slip in behind him. He asked. "What now?"

"Is there a private elevator?"

"No," Ben said.

"What floor are we going to?"

"The sixteenth." Making as little sound as possible, they walked briskly down the hall toward the elevators. There were two on each side.

"I have an idea," Tyler said. They pushed the elevator buttons bringing each to the first floor. "Here's what we'll do: In case they're watching the elevator lights, let's push half a dozen random buttons on each elevator. I'll ride the first elevator up, get off on the floor below your office. You take the fourth elevator up, and get off at the sixteenth. That way I can take the stairs and come up behind them. I don't know, maybe I can sneak in from behind, and we'll be able to get them one by one."

Ben shook his head. "I don't know, that's pretty thin." He checked his watch; it was a few minutes after the time he was suppose to arrive.

"But we don't have time to come up with anything better," Tyler whispered.

Ben nodded. "Okay, it sounded like a plan."

It would have sounded like a better plan if they had had time to stop and pick up some decent weapons, Tyler thought as he stepped onto the elevator.

"Ready?" Ben asked.

"Nope," Tyler said. "But let's do it."

Chapter Thirty-eight

After leaving Keith with Paige's mother, the three women piled into Holly's car. Dee and Terry held on for dear life as Holly whipped around every car that dared to get within 25 feet of them.

Keith had only been able to tell them that he heard Ben say something about meeting someone in his office and getting Abby back. They had tried to coax more information from him, but that was all he seemed to know. Though Keith wasn't sure, since Tyler had disappeared too, it seemed a safe bet that he had gone with Ben.

Dee sat with one hand on the grip bar and the other holding her rounded belly. "I swear, if Ben dies, I'm going to kill him."

"Calm down, Dee," Terry said. "They're not stupid enough to walk into an ambush. Right, Holly?"

Holly remained silent. She was forming a plan as she drove. She would leave Dee and Terry in the car and sneak into the building, hoping that since the men were crazy enough to go there without the police that they might be foolish enough to leave the door unlocked.

She'd go in, take control of the situation and get

Abby back. The reasonable part of her told her to call for backup, but she didn't want to risk a Code Three—backup arriving with lights and sirens. Besides the emotional part of her just wanted her baby back. She spoke abruptly to Dee and Terry.

"Dee, I want you and Terry to wait in the car while I go in and check things out."

"No way," Dee answered.

"Oh, hell no," Terry said.

"C'mon—this could be dangerous, and I don't want you two to get hurt."

"And what about your getting hurt?" Dee asked.

"I'm a cop; I know what I'm doing."

"Well, I'm not waiting in the car," Terry argued.

"Me neither," Dee agreed.

"Don't argue with me."

"There is no argument," Terry said. Then she added, "Look, if we don't go in with you, you know we'll only wait until you've gone inside and then follow you. Right?"

Holly glanced over at Dee, who was nodding, and then back at Terry, who looked at her with a "don't mess with me" expression. Holly gritted her teeth whispering, "Shit." Then she said, "Okay. But you have to do exactly as I say."

"Absolutely," Dee said innocently.

• • •

Tyler stepped from the elevator on the fifteenth floor. The floor was semi-dark with a few lights that gave a dim glow. He paused momentarily and looked around for any signs of a predator hiding. Satisfied that he was alone, he ran to the other side of the building to reach the stairwell, and then taking the steps two at a time he ran up to the sixteenth floor.

When the elevator doors slid open, Ben took a deep breath before he stepped from the elevator. Balancing the bat on his left shoulder he walked as quietly as he could toward his office. As he rounded the corner to the reception area he stopped, feeling completely vulnerable. The light in his office was on. As he neared the door his heart thundered, his temples throbbed, and his palms were sweating. He wiped his left palm on his pants. Then placing a hand on the door he slowly pushed it open and peered into to the office.

Abby was sitting there alone, her hands tied behind her. As soon as she saw her uncle, she let out a big sob. Lowering the bat, he quickly raced across the room, scooped the child up and held her tightly. "Abby, baby, are you all right?" he whispered stepping back as he examined her. He immediately began to untie the rope that held her arms.

She nodded that she was okay, tears filling her eyes and her lip trembling as she spoke. "Uncle Ben, I want my mommy."

"I know, baby," he whispered, holding her tight as he scanned the office and eased toward the door.

"Hello, Benji," a woman said stepping into the doorway just as he reached it. Ben looked down at her. Though she had dyed her blond hair brown, and was much thinner than when he'd last seen her, Ben knew her immediately.

"Janet?"

"I've missed you," she said taking a step toward him. He turned slightly moving Abby away from her and taking a step back.

"Janet, I'm going to take Abby and leave now. She's scared and she needs her mother." Janet watched him with a dazed look on her face. "You understand that don't you?"

"I know they kept you from me, kept you from coming for me. They hid me in that awful place so you couldn't find me. I remember the last words that you said to me. You said that there was nowhere that I could go that you wouldn't find me."

She took a step forward reaching for him. Her hand moved slowly, slightly trembling. She couldn't believe he was there standing in front of her. Could this be real? Was he real? Or was it an apparition that would disappear the instant she moved too close? She took another step closer, and again he moved from her reach. She froze, a pained look on her face. She swallowed hard, struggling to control her voice. "They've turned you against me, haven't they? The doctors and the police and that whore, she's the main one. She set out to take you from me and she turned you and everyone else against me."

Ben watched her closely. His heart raced as he felt a sudden surge of fear. "No, Janet, no one has turned me against you. How can anyone possibly do that?"

"Yes, they have—I can see it in your eyes."

"No, Janet. I'm just concerned for you…concerned for Abby. I need to take her home to her mother."

"No," Janet said shaking her head.

"Janet," Ben repeated taking a step closer to her. "I need to take Abby to her mother. She needs her mother. I can take her home and then I'll meet you." That was when he noticed the gun she was holding. At the same time, he glimpsed Tyler edging along the corridor.

As Tyler crept down the hall, he heard voices. He slowed his pace trying to make out the number of voices he heard. He heard Ben, then Abby's muted voice and then a third, more shrill voice. A woman. He scanned a large reception area quickly, not seeing anyone, then crossed the hall to a much smaller reception area that was outside Ben's office. He moved close to the wall easing toward the office.

"No, they won't let you. They will try to keep us apart again. My mother, she tried to keep us apart, too," Janet whispered. "She kept trying to convince me that you weren't right for me. That there was someone out there who I would merry…someone other than you. That's when I realized that she was just like the others, that she wanted to keep you away, too. I had to stop her."

She suddenly paused. She didn't know if it was the way Ben's eyes shifted quickly or the look on the child's face, but she knew someone was in the outer office. She stepped to her right with her back against the wall in time to see a man easing down the hall with a baseball bat held firmly in his hands. "If you take one more step, I swear I'll kill the both of them."

"Janet?" Ben said from her left.

"Shut up!" she yelled, trying to watch both men simultaneously. "You," she said thrusting her head in Tyler's direction. "Walk toward me slowly." She jerked the gun at Ben. "Move over to the desk." Ben eased back, while Janet moved to the other side of the office and Tyler eased through the door. "I told you to come alone," Janet said, her teeth clenched. "You said you would come alone. You're just like the rest of them."

With his eyes fixed on Janet's face, Ben gently passed Abby to Tyler. "Janet, listen to me." He took a guarded step forward. "I didn't know that it was you on the phone. That's why I brought Tyler with me. If I had known it was you—"

"Stop lying. You're always lying to me. You lied to me when you said that you would come to me. You lied when you said that you loved me, and you're lying now!"

"Mommy!" Abby's shrill cry filled the room.

Janet swung around toward the door, aiming her gun directly at Dee. Ben yelled as he lunged forward, and a single shot rang through the room.

Holding Abby tight, Tyler hit the floor, covering her body with his as he moved the both of them behind Ben's desk.

As Ben slid to the floor, Janet screamed his name.

"Freeze!" Holly ordered, her gun aimed at Janet. Janet swung around and quickly raised the gun just as Holly let off a single round.

When Dee saw Ben fall, she screamed his name rushing to his side and dropped to her knees. The round that Holly fired hit Janet in the shoulder, spinning her to the left. She screamed in agony and rage raising her gun again and aiming directly at Dee's head seconds before Holly let off another round that hit Janet directly in the chest.

Holly was still holding her gun in shaking hands, trained on Janet's still form, when a familiar voice broke through her concentration. "Holly, it's okay. We're here." Her partner's hand was on her shoulder, and there were at least ten other cops in the room. Paramedics were already checking Ben's vital signs. And Terry was holding Dee's hand and massaging her back.

Daley took her gun gently from her hands, and then she was in Tyler's arms. His hands were running frantically up and down her back.

"Are you okay? God, did she hit you?"

"No, I'm fine—Abby?" Holly pulled away from him, searching for her daughter.

"Right here, Mommy." Abby was already clinging to her waist. She lifted her baby girl up, holding her tightly, and Tyler wrapped his arms around them both.

Chapter Thirty-nine

Holly had learned from Daley that Keith had told Valerie Logan where Holly and the others had gone. Valerie became concerned and called the police. He also said that Janet Summers' father had called saying that he believed his wife was in danger. That he'd just returned home from a business trip to find her car in the garage and one of the cars they seldom used missing. And there was a large amount of blood on the garage floor.

They had just given their statements to the officers who followed them to the hospital. Holly and Terry paced outside the maternity ward. Tyler and Abby each sat in chairs that lined one side of the wall. The doctor walked out of the room. "How is she?" Holly asked.

She's going to have the babies…soon. She's becoming hysterical, asking for her husband. We cannot calm her down, and that might be a problem, we need one of you in there to help calm her down.

Terry and Holly looked at one another, Terry squeezed Holly's hand. "You go, I need to go and check on Ben. When I find out how he is, I'll come back." Holly nodded. She walked over to Tyler and Abby.

Tyler gently stroked her cheek. "I can care for

Abby while you see to Dee." She reached for his hand pressing her lips against his palm.

"You'll be okay?" Holly asked Abby. Abby slid closer to Tyler, laying her head against his shoulder and nodding to her mother.

Tyler put his arm around the child. "You go. We'll be fine."

When Holly reached the outside of the birthing room, she heard Dee yelling that she wanted her husband. Taking a deep breath, Holly entered the room. When she approached the bed, she took Dee's hand.

"Holly, where's Ben?

"He's in surgery."

"Is he okay? What's going on?"

"I don't know, but I'll find out. Right now we need to take care of you and the babies."

"They can't come yet, it's not time."

"These little guys want to meet the world," the doctor said after examining Dee.

"Holly?" Dee whispered squeezing Holly's hand, "Did you get her?"

"Yeah, I got that crazy bitch." Dee bit her lip, suppressing the pain as another contraction hit her. Holly frowned. *God what am I doing here? I almost passed out the last time I had to give blood.* She took a deep breath and whispered, "I can do this. I can."

"Holly, what's happening?" Dee asked, a look of total fear on her face. "What are they doing?"

"Honey, just calm down." Taking Dee's hand, Holly squeezed it tight. "Everything's going to be okay."

"I need to know what's happening. You have to look, tell me what's going on."

Holly gave her a look that said, "You think I'm going to look? Uh, yeah right."

"Please, Hol."

"What's going on down there, Doc?" Holly demanded not taking her eyes from Dee's.

"We see the crown," she heard someone say. Holly wasn't sure but she could swear she heard tearing of skin and she just knew she smelled blood. She heard a faint gushing sound and she tried to focus on Dee's face and block out everything else. Dee asked what sounded like a million questions that all seemed to run together.

"Miss?" Holly looked to her right seeing a nurse. Maybe there were two nurses, if there were, they had to be twins because they looked just alike and they were moving in and out of one another. "Do you need to sit down? Can I get you a drink of water?" Holly shook her head, or at least she thought she shook her head because the room was spinning.

She looked at Dee and everything suddenly seemed out of focus. Holding up her hand, Holly whispered, "Um, I think I'll take that water now." Just before the room went black.

Holly woke with a start. "Abby!"

"Shh, she's right here," Tyler said, brushing Holly's hair from her face.

"Hi, Mommy."

"Hey, baby." Holly sat up slowly and reached for Abby pulling her in her lap. "What happened? Dee?"

"She's fine. Terry's in with her now." Tyler nodded.

"Have you heard anything about Ben?"

"His mother and sister are with him. I'm told he's

going to recover." Holly nodded, tears of relief streaming down her cheeks.

"Are you sad, Mommy?" Abby asked brushing her mother's tears.

"No, baby, I'm glad everything worked out and that I have you back safe and sound."

"And we don't ever want to lose you," Tyler said kissing Abby's hand. "You know what, Squirt? I was thinking…would it be okay with you if you, your mom, and I got married."

Abby squealed, "With a real wedding?"

"Yep, with a real wedding."

"Well…only if you take me to the park sometimes," Abby teased.

"I think that can be arranged." Tyler laughed, and then looking at Holly, he asked. "What do you think?"

She smiled. "I think a real wedding sounds wonderful." She leaned forward, her lips meeting his as Abby giggled.

Chapter Forty

"Thanks for letting me have Keith's birthday party here," Terry said to Holly.

"No problem," Holly said. Terry was standing at the counter next to Holly. Dee walked into the kitchen carrying a baby. Ben followed with the other baby. "Hey, lady, you're late," Holly said crossing the room and kissing first baby Kyle and then baby Ben.

"We had a delay," Dee said glancing over her shoulder at Ben.

"It couldn't be helped. I was changing Kyle's diaper, and the next thing I knew urine and poop were everywhere," Ben said bouncing baby Ben in his arms. "Terry, I saw David outside. It was nice of you to invite him to the party."

"Yeah, well I thought we might as well get past this thing. Since Señorita…"

"Shareese," Ben and Tyler both said.

"Yeah, whatever," Terry said waving her hand. "Is having the kids' brother or sister, and as much as I don't like it, I can't change it. So I figured I'd be a mature woman about it." She paused. "But about 20 minutes ago I thought what the hell."

"Terry!" David bellowed from the front of the

house. Terry's eyes shifted as she turned back to the counter rearranging the hotdog buns on a white serving platter. "What did you do to my tires?"

"I have no idea what you're talking about?" She said, her voice calm and even.

David turned to Holly, "I want her arrested."

"For what?"

"She flattened two of my tires."

"Is that true, Terry?"

"Would I do something like that?"

He glared at Terry, "See, she admits it."

"No, she didn't."

"You heard what she just said? 'Would I do something like that?'" he said mocking Terry. "She as much as admitted it."

"But she didn't admit it, did she? Did you see her near your car? Did you see her do something to your car?"

"No."

"Do you have a witness that saw her touch your car at any time?"

"No, but—"

"I can't arrest someone because you have an *idea* that they did something. You know that as well as anyone."

"Fine. Whatever." He pointed at Terry. "You just wait."

"Wait for what, David? For you to pick up your sons and spend a little bit of time with them? Or should I wait for you to send me the part of the mortgage that you promised you would pay? Humph, I guess paying for that young twat cost you a lot more than you thought it would, huh. Seeing how that's the only way you can get it."

He clenched his fist and gritted his teeth. "You bitch."

"Whoa," Holly said, quickly stepping between David and Terry. "Don't be calling her no bitch."

"You used to call her a bitch all the time."

"That's my family. I can insult her if I want to. You can't."

"Yeah, family can do that," Terry interjected, leaning over Holly's shoulder.

"Just who do you think you are?" Dee asked pointing her finger in his face, as she cradled the baby in her arms.

"Man, are they always like this?" Tyler asked as he stepped next to Ben.

"Yep, but I'm sure it'll get better."

"How long do you think it will take?"

Ben shrugged his shoulders. "Don't know, it's been more than seven years, and I'm still waiting."

Tyler laughed at that. "Do you think we should call them off?"

Ben cocked his head to the side thoughtfully. "Na, let's see if he cracks first."

"And another thing—" Holly was saying, her hands on her hips.

If you enjoyed reading *Forgotten Promises*,
you'll also like *My Angel*
and *My Everything*.

My Everything:

At the age of 20, Benjamin Harrison's father dies, leaving him to provide for his mother and sister. Years later, his sister is in need of a bone marrow transplant, and Ben seeks the help of Meyer's Investigations to find an unknown sibling to save her. His immediate attraction to the sexy female P.I. sets things in motion, and their relationship blossoms.

Adventursome private investigator Deanna Meyers senses her attraction toward Ben, but she is reluctant to date him after seeing what her best friends go through with their own interracial relationships.

Ben's ex-girlfriend Janet and Dee's cousin Terry have one thing in common. They both want Dee out of the picture. But only one will go to any lengths to make that happen. Even kill.

My Angel:

Simone Porter, an inner city youth-center director, has lived her whole life being dominated by her over-controlling mother, yet she retains her romantic nature and idealistic views about life and love. Matthew Turner, however, has been hurt by a materialistic wife, who used his kindness and affection and threw it away for another man. Now his heart is hardened and he feels he will never love again the way he once loved his wife.

Brought together by an almost deadly "accident," Simone and Matthew develop a bond that becomes the basis for a fantastic friendship. Despite the extreme disapproval of Simone's mother and Matt's father, they become best friends. But is friendship alone enough to heal Matt's broken heart? And is Simone capable of going against her mother's wishes and standing for up for what she wants?

As they juggle work, family conflicts, and their own conflicting feelings, the passion and attraction between them becomes too great to ignore. However, Simone is torn between Alan, the man her mom wants for her, and Matt, the man her heart wants for her. Matt must decide between the ex-wife that used to be his everything, and Simone, his "Angel." However, in this battle between true love and family influence, Simone and Matt learn that it is sometimes harder than it should be for best friends to become lovers. And Matt's relationship with his ex-wife proves to be more dangerous to them than anyone could have imagined...

Here's how you can order books directly from Denise Skelton:

Denise Skelton
P.O. Box 60
Lutherville, MD 21094
U.S.A.

Please add $2.50 for shipping and handling for the first book and $.75 for each additional book. Maryland residents, add appropriate sales tax. No cash, stamps, or CODs. Canadian orders require $5.00 for shipping and handling and must be paid in U.S. dollars. Prices and availability are subject to change. Payment must accompany all orders.

Name: _____

Address: _____

City:_____ State: _____

Zip: _____

E-mail: _____
I have enclosed $_____ in payment for the checked books(s).

❏ *Forgotten Promises*

❏ *My Angel*

❏ *My Everything*

For more information, check out www.deniseskelton.com.